TIME FOR US

A SUN RIVER NOVEL

L.M. HALLORAN

COPYRIGHT

Copyright © 2024 by L.M. Halloran

All rights reserved.

This is a work of fiction. Names, characters, places, and incidents are either the product of the author's imagination or are used fictitiously, and any resemblance to actual persons, living or dead, events, or locales is entirely coincidental.

No part of this book may be reproduced in any form or by any electronic or mechanical means, including information storage and retrieval systems, without written permission from the author, except for the use of brief quotations in a book review.

ISBN 979-8864004470

Cover photography from Shutterstock.com

Editing by Emily Lawrence, *Lawrence Editing*

lmhalloran.com

for Andrea

*She said the world was ending
and nothing would be the same
and I replied,*

*Dear Heart, remember
old forests embrace fire
because they want to live again.*

L.M.

1

Celeste

A SPOON of sugary cereal is halfway to my mouth when my twelve-year-old son asks, "How stupid is this shit?"

I don't spit out the cereal. That would be wasteful, and I need the sugar to function. Besides, I don't have a leg to stand on—I have a potty mouth and he knows it. It still makes me wince, his perfectly shaped little mouth saying a "bad" word.

I make a mental note to do some research about the origins of *shit* so I can properly defend its mundaneness on the off chance my boy decides to lob it at, say, a teacher, or coach, or the school librarian.

He won't, though. He's too smart for that.

"Mom? Are you listening?"

"Sure. Yep. Definitely."

Damien's mouth twists in annoyance. "You're such a squirrel."

I shrug. "Say it again?"

"You know that old place near the lake? The cabins and stuff?"

A Fruit Loop almost goes down the wrong pipe. "Sure. It's where you did your fourth grade campout."

And where I spent summers as a kid, back when summer camps were a thing and parents were less concerned about drug use, underaged sex, and doing background checks on chaperones.

I smile wistfully, thinking of the fun Damien's dad and I had up there as kids, and again as camp counselors our junior and senior years of high school. The memories are saturated with gold—that patina of perfection nostalgia provides. I've cultivated that nostalgia, shaped it and thickened it so well it drowns out everything else.

"You're thinking about Dad."

"Always."

Once the word is out, I wish I could bite it back. Lately, Damien has been pushing back when his father comes up—he doesn't want to hear about Jeremy anymore.

Not gonna lie, it fucking hurts.

I can't blame him, though, and not just because I've had a lot of therapy. He never met his father, has never been on the receiving end of one of his signature hugs, or seen the twinkling eyes that he inherited, or heard Jeremy's deep, infectious laugh. His father died on the other side of the world before Damien was born.

"—as I was saying, someone bought it."

"Huh?"

His chair screeches as he shoves it back and stands. "It's freaking impossible to talk to you."

Ah, puberty. One of the joys of parenting.

"Damien—"

He's already gone, too-long legs eating up the floor of our spacious loft in downtown Sun River. His bedroom door slams.

I stare at my soggy cereal until I hear him leave his room and head for the front door.

"See you after practice."

I half-stand from my chair. "You don't need a ride to school?"

"I told you last night—Caleb's mom is picking me up."

Shame pinches my heart. "Okay! I love you. Have an awesome day at school."

"Love you too, Mom," he grumbles.

The front door closes.

Damien has every right to be annoyed with me. I haven't been myself lately.

If I'm honest, it's been a slow decline, beginning a year ago when my best friend Zoey married her soulmate, Ethan. I'm over-the-moon happy for her. For them.

And sad, too.

People talk about wrinkles a lot. There's a billion-dollar industry founded on preventing the signs of aging. But no one talks about the other signs, the other wrinkles. The ones no one can see. Time leaves marks inside us, too, on our hearts. And my ticker is geriatric.

Dropping my spoon into my half-eaten bowl of cereal, I

scoop up my phone and open an app. And there, at the top, is the local news article my son was referring to.

Beloved Landmark Sold to Adler Properties. Development Talks Underway.

My tired heart lurches, my fingers tightening on the phone. I read the first sentence as dread waterfalls from my head to my tingling toes.

Lucas Adler, founder and CEO of Adler Properties, is a Sun River native from Lincoln High Class of—

I lower my phone fast, clicking the screen off. My heart pounds against the skin of my throat. The thick coat of fuzzy gold nostalgia I paint over the past shivers and thins in places, revealing darker threads beneath.

His name is turpentine on my happy past.

Lucas Adler.

Suddenly, I need to move, to get the hell out of my apartment. Rushing into my bathroom, I brush my teeth and splash cold water on my face, following that with a layer of SPF. Less than a minute later, I'm out the door with my backpack in tow, walking briskly down the sidewalk.

The weather is gorgeous, a perfect late-May day in Idaho. Elevation ensures that the breeze on my flushed face is cold, but the air itself holds space for spring warmth.

"I can't believe you want to stay here."

"I can't believe you're leaving!"

Shaking my head against the brush strokes of the past, I walk faster. Everyone I pass says hello—we're that kind of town—but for the first time in years, my smile feels fake, my normally cheery waves unnatural.

Thankfully, Main Street Flowers is a five-minute walk from my loft. As I approach the open front door and see buckets of flowers in the process of being dragged outside, my anxiety melts away.

"Hey, Mom!" I call, swinging into the shop and tossing my backpack behind the counter. I breathe deeply, filling my lungs with the dewy-fresh scent of flowers and greens.

A silvery blond head pops out from behind a table displaying colorful, spring-inspired bouquets. "Hey there, sweets," she replies, smiling warmly.

"Where's Pop?"

"Morning confessional, where else?"

I grimace. "Gross. I'll never understand why you call it that. Just say he's in the bathroom." Mom laughs as I head for the displays still waiting to go outside. "What are you guys up to this fine Tuesday morning?"

"Golfing," she answers with an eye roll. "He's been begging for weeks. I finally caved."

I snort. "Good luck."

My dad has a long history of boasting about his golfing skills, when in reality his swing misses the ball more times than not. When he does make contact, the golf ball is more likely to land in a sand trap or hit a tree than find grass.

In the four months I've been back working full-time at the shop, my parents have been exploring what retirement feels like. Not that they have plans for it. But it's nice to see them relax a bit. In their mid-sixties, they've been running Main Street Flowers for thirty-two years, just the two of them with seasonal part-time support.

Visitors over the next few hours are steady, mostly locals who stop to enjoy the smells and chat. No one buys anything. Luckily, we don't rely on foot traffic to stay afloat. We have a healthy weekly subscription flower program and rolling contracts with many local businesses.

Then again, having reviewed my parents' books last week, *afloat* isn't an accurate description of the shop's financials. More like *on life support*. It's my fault, too. When they wanted me to quit my job at the nursery, my condition for doing so was a salary match. I'm wrecking their bottom line.

I haven't decided what to do about it, but every day I get a little closer to asking for my old job back.

My thoughts scatter as a high-pitched voice fills my ears. "Guess who's at Annie's this morning?" asks Darla Templeton.

There's a telltale gleam in her eye. She's what my friend, Zoey, would call a Lilac Lady: a busybody retiree whose main hobby is lobbing gossip bombs.

My stomach drops. "Who?"

I already know the answer. I can see it in the way she maintains laser focus on my face as she gauges my reaction. Years of practice keep my features in a mask of mild curiosity.

Darla's Pomeranian, Hercules, yaps at the ankles of a woman hurrying down the sidewalk. Darla tugs his leash, but her eyes never veer from my face.

"Lucas Adler."

I nod and smile, ignoring a spike of anxiety at the sound of his name. "I saw the article this morning. He's developing the old campgrounds, right?"

Darla's throat bobs. I imagine she's salivating behind her mauve lipstick. "Have you talked to him? I bet you're excited to see him again. The three of you were thick as thieves in school, weren't you?"

The three of us.

Me. Jeremy. And Lucas.

"We were, yes," I say, but my voice edges toward brittleness. Darla's eyes narrow.

"Celeste!"

I spin gratefully toward the familiar voice. Zoey hustles down the sidewalk toward me, hauling a tote full of groceries and holding two takeout coffee cups. I've never been so glad to see someone in my life.

"Hey, Zoey!" I wave, then turn to Darla with a big smile. "Enjoy the rest of your day. Bye, Hercules."

Darla sniffs at the dismissal but musters a smile before dragging Hercules away.

Zoey reaches me and hands me a latte. Pushing dark hair away from her eyes, she frowns at Darla's retreating figure. "What did she want?"

"The usual. Torture with a side of slander."

"Figures."

I take a sip of latte. "Thank you so much."

Zoey leans over and takes a deep breath near a bucket of peonies. "How's the morning going, besides Darla?" When she straightens, she doesn't quite meet my eye.

Shit.

"So you saw the article?" I guess.

Zoey nods and finally looks at me. The worry in her gaze is alarming. For a second, I think she knows—then I remember she can't know. We were friendly but not friends in high school, and no one knows except Lucas and me why he's the last person on Earth I want to see.

"I know you have a lot of great memories up at the camp. How are you feeling about the plans to convert it into a resort?"

I almost spit out my drink. "Resort?" I echo. At her questioning blink, I admit, "I only read the first sentence."

"Ah. Yeah, they want to turn it into one of those fancy retreat-type places. Rebuild all the cabins. Turn the Lodge and Art Barn into a restaurant and spa."

I swallow hard.

From a business standpoint, it makes perfect sense, and I can easily envision it being a success. Sleepy Sun River, Idaho, has been a favorite escape for the elite and eccentric since the 1930s. Hemingway was a frequent guest, as well as A-List Hollywood types. Not much has changed since then. Our international film festival brings famous faces in droves every spring, and the mountain generates massive tourism every winter. While condo complexes abound, especially outside town, there aren't many luxury resorts in the area.

He's going to make a killing.

"Did you stay in touch with Lucas?" asks Zoey, snapping me out of my reverie.

I shake my head. "I haven't spoken to him in years, not since…"

Jeremy's funeral.

I can't say it out loud, and luckily Zoey doesn't need me to. She doesn't know everything, but she knows enough—how Lucas, Jeremy, and I were inseparable.

Before everything changed.

2

Lucas

I'VE CLEARLY LOST my mind because I swore I'd never come back here. Back to Sun River. To the past.

But here I am, seated at the counter in Annie's Pie Shoppe. Like a living time capsule, everything is exactly the same. Even the dent on the wall by the kitchen window from a baseball I'd dared Jeremy to throw to me. I'd been in the kitchen, as usual, cleaning after my shift. Jeremy and Celeste had stopped by—also as usual—to hang with me until I was done.

"Have you seen her yet?" asks Joan, her gravelly voice triggering powerful sensory memory. She's been a fixture at Annie's since I was a toddler.

I look up from the scramble I'm pushing around my plate. I don't pretend to misunderstand. There's only one person in this town, besides my mother, I give a shit about. *Or used to.* And I already told Joan I was heading to my mom's after here.

"No," I answer, sliding my plate toward her, hoping to distract her.

Joan's heavily lined eyes narrow, ignoring my attempt. "Don't make it awkward, hon. She's over at Main Street Flowers. Say hello."

"I will," I lie, then pull out my wallet and drop several bills on the counter. "Thanks, Joan. Great as always."

She snorts. "You barely ate."

I pat my stomach. "Had a bite before I came."

"Uh-huh."

Sliding off the stool, I throw her the grin I've been using with effect since puberty. But she only grunts.

"Try that on someone who didn't change your diapers."

I laugh. It feels surprisingly good. "I've missed you, Joan."

She squints at me. "You staying in town?"

"Just tonight. I have a trailer coming up tomorrow so I can oversee the groundbreaking at the site."

For the first time, Joan looks uncertain. "And you're sure you want to do this, Lucas?"

She's not the first person to ask me that, but the others were only concerned with the financial risk of the venture, or flabbergasted by my decision to oversee the entire development personally. Having worked hard to build a strong, talented team around me, I haven't taken a hands-on role in years.

But this one is different.

"I'm sure." I try the grin again.

She rolls her eyes and waves me off. "Get lost."

I head outside, then pause on the sidewalk, my gaze veering to the next block. Main Street Flowers is obvious from the bins of colorful blooms stacked outside. I don't have the guts to walk over there. Awkward doesn't scratch the surface of my baggage with Celeste Miller.

No, I remind myself. Celeste *Torres*. She has my best friend's last name.

I imagine seeing her, wondering how she's changed in twelve years. She doesn't use social media, so I have no idea what she even looks like these days. And the bulk of what I remember belongs to the past.

Skinned knees and sharp elbows. Blond hair that turned nearly white in the summer, skin that darkened to bronze. Bright blue eyes, an improbable near-turquoise. Sweaty hands and sweet breath. Whispers and secrets and a confession that destroyed us.

My heart pounding, I turn away.

3

Celeste

AT ELEVEN, my relief comes in the form of our part-time employee. Jen, a college sophomore at Boise State, has been working summers at the shop since she was a freshman in high school. Spring session recently ended, and even if we can't really afford her, I've been glad to have her back.

She clocks in, then comes out to join me on the sidewalk. "How's the day?" she asks, smiling as she draws her hair into a quick ponytail.

I pull my gaze from Annie's Pie Shoppe. He isn't there anymore. Obviously. But knowing he's here, somewhere in Sun River, has made me twitchy. I've been distracted all morning.

"Decent," I tell Jen. "A few orders have come in, and the Simmons did their pickup."

"Sounds good."

Silence reigns for all of ten seconds. "Celeste?

Everything okay? Did I do something wrong closing yesterday?"

"No, Jen. Not at all." I'm usually a chatterbox, but today I don't have the mental bandwidth for anything but basic conversation. "I'm just, um, a bit tired. Do you mind if I head out? I told Mom and Dad I'd feed Lulu lunch. Then I'll finish up with the invoicing at home. You can call me if you need me and I'll come right back."

Jen's eyes are questioning behind her glasses, but she nods. "Sure thing."

I thank her, then grab my backpack. Instead of facing Main Street—and the amorphous, tingly threat of Lucas—I slip out the back.

The house I grew up in is three blocks east of the shop. The neighborhood is old and charming, two- and three-bedroom bungalows built in the 1920s mixing with newer builds. One of my parents' favorite pastimes is talking about how wild the real estate market is, how if they sold their lot to a developer they'd be instant millionaires.

They'll never sell it, or the flower shop, though sometimes I wish they'd unload both. They've worked so hard for so long, I want them to enjoy their golden years without worrying about money. But they've shut down my argument enough times that I've stopped asking.

The little white gate creaks as I open it, and I purposefully don't look at the house to the right.

But the memories come, anyway.

IN THE SUMMER before fifth grade, the most exciting event by far to happen in my small world was a new family moving in next door. My parents had heard from someone who heard from someone else that the family had a young daughter around my age. I was over the moon.

My desperate desire for a sibling was replaced by the prospect of a new friend. This—*this* was what I truly wanted. A partner to walk to the bus stop with, to share secret wishes with, to wander and listen to music with. Who didn't care that my hair was wild and almost always knotted because I never brushed it. Who wouldn't tease me or make fun of my obsession with lime-green Converse, or my tendency to come to school with muddy or paint-splattered clothes.

The day the moving truck pulled onto the street, I could barely contain my excitement. My nose plastered to the glass of our living room window, I watched for hours as furniture and boxes were unloaded and hauled into the house. The house was a new one, recently finished, and about twice the size of ours. The construction had been super annoying and loud, but if my new best friend moved in? Worth it.

Finally, *finally*, a big, shiny sedan pulled into the driveway. A man and woman stepped out. They were so lovely, like models I'd only seen in magazines. The man was taller than my dad, with brown hair slicked back and dark sunglasses. He wore a smart polo shirt and khaki pants. The woman who rounded the car to his side was likewise polished and perfect. Dressed in crisp white pants and a navy blouse, even from yards away I could see the sparkle of diamonds in her ears. Her hair was in a stylish bob, dark blond and glossy, and sunglasses covered half her face. Despite my limited view, I knew she was the most beautiful woman I'd ever seen.

When the back door of the car opened, I didn't at first notice, so taken was I with the adults.

Then a loud, piercing voice shouted, "Mom! Michelle won't stop pinching me!"

I frowned at the sight of the speaker. A boy. Blond like his mother, his shoulder-length hair obscured his face as he raced to the front of the car. I studied his lanky frame, the jeans that were too short. He looked about my age, but boys' ages were always hard to guess. Most of the ones in my class looked a lot younger than the girls.

I assumed Michelle was his sister. My best friend. I waited for her to appear. From my vantage point, a tree blocked the most important portion of the car. All I could see was the woman walking around the other side.

Where are you, Michelle?

At long last, the woman reappeared. I blinked, not understanding. She led a small girl with dark hair by the hand. She couldn't be more than five years old.

"No," I whispered, my gaze veering back to the boy.

Soft footsteps moved up behind me. "What on earth is so captivating out there?" asked my mom.

I looked at her, wide-eyed with panic. "You said it was a girl my age!"

My mom's eyebrows lifted in surprise and she looked

out the window. "Oh, that must be the Adlers. We'll have to bring them some wine later. And look, Celeste, that boy seems about your age. You should run out and say hello!"

With all the angst in my ten-year-old body, I glared at her. "Are you kidding me? No way!" I snapped, then ran away from the window, pounded down the hallway to my room, and slammed the door behind me.

Parents.

So completely clueless.

LULU, a four-year-old mutt, is happy to see me when I unlock the door and bathes my hands with her tongue. I give her some love, then lead her to the backyard to take care of business. Knowing she likes to sniff every spot at least six times before choosing which to bless with her pee, I plop onto a padded chaise and lean back. The morning's chill lingers, but sunlight tingles warmly against my face.

That summer day the Adlers moved in next door is etched in vivid detail in my mind. The cloudy condensation of my breath on the window. The height of excitement and the crushing depth of disappointment.

I didn't go with my parents that evening to bring the customary welcome-to-the-neighborhood bottle of wine. In fact, in the following weeks before school started, I closeted myself in my bedroom with my easel and the two new canvases I got for my birthday, translating my feelings into paintings.

Years later, I read somewhere that art was a two-sided blade. As we cut space in the world for art, the art cut us back. And that's when I understood, finally, that from the moment I first saw him, Lucas Adler was like art. Cutting through the world. Through me.

"Peapod."

I yelp and jerk upright, my gaze swinging to a particular section of the fence, knowing who will be standing there before I see him. Only one person has ever called me that, and he used to live next door.

For a few, breathless moments, I stare at the man whose arms are braced on the divide. Memory creates double vision—skinny arms in the same position, a shock of golden hair above pale blue eyes, a wicked grin aimed at me—superimposing the boy I knew atop the stranger before me.

This man barely resembles his younger self. For one, his arms now are easily three times the size of mine. He's always been tall, but now he's reached the promise in his broad shoulders, which stretch the fabric of his black T-shirt.

I wait for him to dissolve, to go back to that rusty old box in my mind. He doesn't. Nor does he smile.

"What are you doing here?" I ask, and my voice, unlike his, is angry. I'm rattled. I can't see his eyes behind his sunglasses, but from his clenched jaw, I surmise they've turned frosty.

"I'm not allowed to visit my mom?"

I feel exposed, suddenly, even fully clothed, with dirty

Converse on my feet and my hair in a messy bun. I'm exactly the same. He is not.

I look away, silent. My tongue is sandpaper.

The fence groans—the sound itself a Pandora's box of memory—as Lucas swings himself up and over. From the corner of my eye, I watch him pick his way through the plant-and-flower circus that is my parents' backyard. Only when his shadow falls over my legs do I lift my gaze. My heart flutters like a trapped bird.

"Are we going to hate each other forever?" he asks softly.

My voice finally comes, hoarse and low, from an aching place inside me. "I don't hate you, Lucas. I've never hated you."

He pulls off his sunglasses. I play with a small hole in the thigh of my jeans, avoiding his eyes.

At length, he says, "Sorry I startled you. I know you hate surprises."

I mutter, "Only when you orchestrate them."

He laughs—not the unrestricted, joyous sound I remember, but dark and ironic. "Remember the first day of freshman year?"

I groan. "How could I forget the first of so many traumatic locker incidents? You guys were such assholes."

He chuckles with real humor. I want to smile but don't. Or can't. The air between us feels thick and warped. I wonder if he feels it, too—the way the breeze seems to bend around us, leaving us still and hot.

"So classic." He pauses. "I still think we should have

done water balloons instead of balloon animals. We were up half the night making those damn giraffes and bunnies."

My lips curve a little to one side. It's all I can manage past my madly thumping heart and tight lungs. The moment itself—of opening my locker for the first time on my first day of high school—roars forward and flattens me.

I was so nervous and had barely slept the night before. All I'd wanted in the world was to pass through the ocean of high school without making waves. I'd spent middle school feeling like a pariah. Having skipped third grade, I was a full year younger than everyone else and there'd been no shortage of mockery.

But Jeremy and Lucas hadn't cared that I was younger, that I didn't act or dress like other girls in our class. They'd never cared about what anyone else thought. And they'd loved torturing me almost as much as I'd loved being tortured by them.

The memory chips further at my composure. Jeremy apologizing over and over for the balloons. Lucas merely rolling his eyes at my outrage. The contrast of the two of them. Dark and light—devil and angel.

Only the angel had turned out to be the devilish one.

4

Celeste

DRAGGING BREATH INTO MY LUNGS, I force words past my dry throat. "I was sorry to hear about your dad."

His shadow shifts on my legs as he tucks his hands into the pockets of his jeans. No more too-short pants. Now they fit him just right.

"Thanks. You know he died five years ago, right?"

I look up, taking in his stony expression. "Yes, but we haven't spoken in over a decade. Which begs the question —why are you talking to me now?"

Lucas sighs and plops onto the end of the chaise. For a brief, electric second, my foot touches his thigh. I scoot back, pulling my knees to my chest. Lulu lopes over to investigate the newcomer, her tail wagging as she sniffs his shoes. He gives her a quick rub before she hears something rustle near the back fence and takes off.

I watch her flight, my skin prickling under the weight of Lucas's gaze searching my face. Eventually, he sighs.

"I should have known you wouldn't make this easy on me, Peapod."

The old nickname makes my eyes sting and my heart swell. Irritated by my reaction and overwhelmed by his nearness, I say nothing, instead staring blankly across the backyard. But no matter where I look, all I see is him. His broad, muscled back rising and falling. The shoulders that absorbed my tears on more than one occasion. The arms that sheltered me, held me, and ultimately turned my world inside out.

When he touches my foot, I jerk and nearly kick him. "Are you okay?" he asks softly.

My eyes snap to his. The contact is a punch to my gut, turning my voice acidic. "What do you care?"

Our last conversation rises between us, yelled through driving rain, dripping with a darkness far more consuming than that of the night sky. A darkness of onyx and crimson—my sobs and his helpless fury.

"You could have stopped him! He would have done anything for you!"

"You're blaming me for his death? You think I want to be a pregnant widow at twenty-one? Fuck you, Lucas. You weren't here. You disappeared off to your fancy college and forgot about us. I tried to talk him out of it—for months—but when Jeremy set his mind to something—"

"You know what? Stop. I don't care. I never want to see you or this place again. As far as I'm concerned, you're both dead."

"You're never going to forgive me, are you?" he asks now.

Blinking my way out of the past, I meet his gaze. What I see in his eyes makes my stomach churn, makes the backyard blur.

"Why now?" I whisper, and what I'm really asking is why he came back.

"I don't know." He shakes his head, gaze falling. "It's been a weird couple of years. Lots of… change. Six months ago, I saw the old camp property come up for sale. I didn't think—I just bought it. Then, of course, I had to figure out what I was going to do with it."

"Besides burn it to the ground?" I mutter, then wish I could take the words back.

"Yeah. Besides that."

Another memory whispers for attention, but I slap it away. "So instead of making it a place the community can enjoy again, you're turning it into a resort only accessible to the super wealthy. Great choice."

He sighs. "I don't expect you to understand."

I stiffen. "That's right. The poor girl doesn't understand economics."

"Celeste—"

I leap off the chaise and point at the fence. "Just go, Lucas. Let's go back to pretending the other person doesn't exist. It was better that way."

He stands, shoulders tight and gaze averted. This close, the difference in our heights is pronounced. My eyes snag on the base of his throat and the pulse thrumming beneath tanned skin. Suddenly, I can't get enough air. I try to step backward, but my calves are against the chaise.

I blurt, "Have you always been so freaking giant?"

His gaze snaps to me, glimmering with challenge. "Have you always been so short?"

The bristles on his jaw catch the sunlight as he tilts his head. Waiting to see if I'll play. The old, competitive edge in me ignites. My eyes narrow.

"Still can't grow a beard, can you?"

"Still can't grow balls, can you?"

My mouth drops. "What the fuck, Lucas!"

He smirks. "Zero points out of ten, Peapod. You still suck at this game."

I glare back, zeroing in on the dark blond hair curling against his ears and neck. "All your money and you can't afford a haircut?"

His smile widens. "Good one. How many combs broke trying to get through that rat's nest on your head?"

My teeth grind. "How many people know you cry every time you watch *Neverending Story* and that you watch it at least once a year?"

Something shifts in his eyes. He takes a step forward. "Maybe I don't watch it anymore."

"You do." My chin lifts. "How many?"

"Just one."

The solemn look in his eyes tells me it's the truth. *How many more secrets do only I know?* The question dances through my mind, pools on my tongue. I force it down with a heavy swallow and look away.

From the bordering backyard, we hear his mother's voice.

"Lucas? Where are you, dear?"

The molasses-thick space between us grows rigid. I imagine it the color of mud, shot through with defiant streaks of gold. Once upon a time, we were something to each other, but that precious ore is now smothered in shit-brown.

Lucas clears his throat. "That's my cue. Better go before your dad comes after me with the hose." It's an old joke—my dad would never. He hesitates. "Do you still paint, Peapod?"

"No."

He studies my face so long my cheeks heat. I look down, away from the sympathy in his eyes.

"That's a shame," he says softly.

I shrug. "Take care, Lucas. See you in another decade?"

"Maybe, maybe not."

"Cryptic as always," I retort.

His lips curve as he turns away. I don't watch him go, instead forcing my feet into motion. Picking my way to the side of the house, I zero in on the faded coil of our ancient hose.

The backyard needs watering, and I need badly to do something with my hands.

After nearly drowning every plant my parents own, I

feed Lulu and head home. Invoicing for the shop only takes twenty minutes. I finish a load of laundry and prep dinner for Damien and me. When that's done and I still feel insane, I compulsively clean the apartment, emptying trash, changing bedsheets, and sweeping and mopping the floors.

Anything to not think about Lucas. About his voice, his physical presence, his eyes, all familiar and not. And about that brief banter, trading insults as easy as passing a frisbee. In the moment, I'd been electrified, swept up in the old game. Now all I felt was guilt and shame.

Jeremy never understood why I tolerated Lucas's teasing. Why I dished it out in return. But Jeremy was different from us. He didn't have an angst-filled bone in his body. While he participated in the long-running prank war between us, he never delighted in the results.

But he worshipped Lucas and loved me. So he stayed in our little trio, and everything was fine until the summer before our senior year.

"I just don't get why you let him talk to you like that. Why you think it's so funny."

"Because it is *funny. He doesn't mean any of it. Neither of us does. It's how we, I dunno, blow off steam. We've always been that way."*

Jeremy hesitates, then asks in a different, lower tone, "Does he still hop over the fence every night?"

Shocked, I look across the front seat of the car. The tension in his shoulders and jaw makes my stomach twist. This—exactly this —is why I wanted to say no when Jeremy asked me out.

"No," I finally answer. "He doesn't."

The words are true—Lucas stopped visiting me a few weeks ago—but so is the disappointment I keep from my voice.

Jeremy's shoulders relax and he grabs my hand, squeezing it tightly. "Okay." He throws me a wide smile that, as always, brings an answering smile to my lips and wipes away my melancholy.

While the dynamic of our trio is irreversibly changed with Jeremy and I getting together, I can't bring myself to regret it. I even think I'm starting to fall in love. Or maybe I've always been a little in love with him. He's the best, kindest person I've ever known, and he makes me happy.

Kissing him is pretty great, too.

"Mom?"

Damien's voice startles me and I slam my head on the underside of the kitchen table. "Ow! Dammit!"

He drops his keys on the entryway table and bends down, blinking big brown eyes just like his dad's. I stay on all fours, rubbing the sore spot on the back of my head.

"What are you doing?"

"Just cleaning." I grab my soiled, wet rag, carefully back out past the chairs, and stand. Tilting my chin, I smile and reach up to ruffle his hair. "When did you get so huge?"

Lucas's face flashes in my mind, but I ignore it.

Damien grins, batting my hand away. "Around the same time you shrank."

I laugh even as a spike of pain lances through my heart.

Old pain with a new edge. The old—Jeremy isn't here to see his son becoming a man. And the new—my friendship with Lucas is still a part of me, and therefore, whether I like it or not, he'll always be a part of his godson's life.

5

Lucas

"EARTH TO LUCAS..."

I snap out of a thought I'd rather not admit, even to myself—involving long legs and Converse-encased feet—and focus on the road and the conversation happening via Bluetooth.

"I'm here."

My partner, Jasper, is silent for a moment. "How's your mom?"

I roll my eyes, knowing that he doesn't actually care. I'm pretty sure Jasper's a sociopath and only mimics normal human conversations. Still, he's trying.

"She's fine, thanks for asking."

"Are you sure you don't want me to—"

"I can handle it," I snap, then add quickly, "What were you asking me?"

His tone shifts to professional. "I asked how the

meeting with the mayor and town planning committee went."

I reflect on my conversation this morning. "The start was rough, but I showed them the projections and can say they're now cautiously optimistic."

He chuckles. "Hard to say no to a prospective boost to local economy."

But will there be one?

I don't ask the question that's been worming its way through my head the last few days, even prior to Celeste's aggravating comment yesterday about the resort's exclusivity. It bothers me. And making money has never bothered me before.

"I'm pulling up to the site now," I tell Jasper. "Tell me you've got the team finalizing designs for approval."

"They're on it. Should be in your email by the end of the week."

"And the research on contractors in the area? I want the best of the best."

"Also on it."

"Great. Talk soon."

I hang up before I can say something stupid, like, *This is a mistake. I've changed my mind.*

As I drive beneath the wood-framed entrance of the defunct Camp Wild Lake, nostalgia presses heavily on my chest. The sign still hangs at the central point, the paint faded and peeling. This isn't the first time I've been up here since purchasing the land, but it's the first time since seeing Celeste again.

Now I'm struggling to see it for what it is—a business investment, cold and simple. Instead, ghostly crowds of children run screaming down the path to the lake. Firelight plays over young faces sticky with marshmallows as counselors tell age-appropriate scary stories.

The mural-covered side of the Art Barn appears through trees on my left. I look away fast, but my gaze snags on another memory in the shape of a small building. The faded yellow paint by the front door is still legible.

Eagle Cabin.

Eagle Cabin was where Jeremy and I were assigned the summer before our senior year as junior camp counselors. We'd snuck out every night after curfew to meet up with Celeste and a few others, then crept back in before midnight bed checks.

Behind the cabin is another visual trigger: a towering Ponderosa Pine. Jeremy and I were standing behind it the night he told me he was in love with Celeste. That he was going to ask her on a date, thereby destroying six years of perfect friendship among the three of us.

He hadn't known then that I'd already destroyed it.

I park near the Lodge but can't bring myself to get out of my car. Instead, I answer a slew of emails while I wait for the sound of a semi coming up the hill hauling the trailer where I'll sleep and work.

If all goes according to plan, in a few weeks, I'll be surrounded by a hive of activity and construction, and have no time to think about anything, much less the past.

Everything will be demolished, leveled, dug out, to

make way for the resort. While a key feature of my proposal to the city council this morning was a plan to feature some of the original wood from the camp buildings—thereby giving a nod to history—this entire venture will accomplish exactly what both Celeste and I want.

To burn Camp Wild Lake to the ground.

6

Celeste

THE REST of the week is filled with familiar routines that slowly but surely nail boards over the black, endless well of my memory. By the time I leave work on Friday afternoon, I almost feel like my normal self. And while I couldn't escape the rumor mill—everyone and their mother is talking about the camp—there have been no more Lucas sightings in town.

I'm hoping it stays that way. He'll do his thing, wiping Camp Wild Lake off the map, and I'll go on pretending like it doesn't matter.

When I get home from work, I jump in the shower before throwing on fresh jeans and a light sweater. Damien is at his best friend's house for a sleepover, so I have a rare free night. And since Zoey's husband, Ethan, is in New York for the weekend, we get to have a long overdue girls' night out. Not that we have a wild nightlife in Sun River.

Far from it. Our plans consist of dinner, then throwing our feet on my coffee table and watching a movie.

At a quarter till seven, I head out to meet Zoey at Bloom, the only Thai food restaurant in town. She's already there, waving from a booth by the window when I walk in. I veer toward her, skirting around tables. The place is packed, the noise level high.

As I'm closing in on the booth, someone stands from a table to leave. We collide. Strong fingers wrap around my biceps, and my face smooshes against a hard chest. I gasp, my nose filling with a masculine scent that's as familiar to me as the shape of my child's face. After all these years, he smells the same.

In an instant, I realize I've been lying to myself all week. Even if he leaves town tomorrow and never comes back, his reappearance has been the equivalent of a bomb dropping on my heart and head. I'm going to be picking up debris for years.

"Still don't pay attention to where you're walking?"

Lifting my chin, I glare into Lucas's twinkling eyes. "Still wearing the same cheap cologne you had in high school?"

His lips twitch. "I don't wear cologne."

"Then you must take baths in a swamp."

He laughs, then glances over my shoulder at the booth I was aiming for. His hands drop, leaving my arms tingling. "Hey, Zoey. Long time no see."

"Lucas," says Zoey in cool acknowledgment.

His gaze shifts back to me. "I guess that's my cue. See ya later, Peapod." He nods and spins on a heel.

"Don't call me that," I growl at his retreating back.

He throws a grin over his shoulder. "Never gonna happen."

Then he's gone, the doors swinging shut behind him. I slide into the booth opposite Zoey, my gaze veering toward the sidewalk as Lucas appears. My arms tingling where his fingers wrapped around them, I watch him until he disappears from view.

Zoey's voice startles me. "That was interesting."

Flushing, I take a sip of the iced tea she was kind enough to order for me. "I have no idea what you're talking about."

"Oh, really?"

I slump against the cushion. My willpower is no match for her steady, discerning eyes. "Fine. What do you remember about Jeremy, Lucas, and me from high school?"

She frowns thoughtfully. "Not a ton. I remember you guys were popular. That you and Jeremy were prom king and queen senior year." She shrugs. "I was in my own world back then."

I smile softly. "Yeah, I think all of us were, in one way or another. My world... well, for a long time it was the three of us. Lucas and I met when he moved next door right before fifth grade. I'd really wanted a girl my age to move in, so I basically hated him from the moment I saw him."

She smirks. "That didn't last."

I shrug. "He wore me down."

The reality was I never stood a chance of resisting him. I was done for the first night we officially met—a week after he moved in—when I found him wandering in my backyard. It was late; my parents were asleep. I'd come outside to enjoy the cool air after spending most of the evening painting. Before I even saw Lucas, I heard shouting coming from the other side of the fence, then glass breaking. Eventually, a door slammed, and a woman's soft cries faded.

> *"Hey, uh… Can I hang here for a bit?"*
> *"Yes, totally."*
> *"Okay, cool. I'm Lucas."*
> *"Hi. I'm Celeste."*

"And then he became best friends with Jeremy?" asks Zoey.

I nod. "In a nutshell. The three of us were inseparable until senior year."

Zoey hums, her brows pinched. "I'm having a weird memory from sophomore year of a blowup doll hidden in someone's locker and the three of you getting detention. Was that real?" At my wince and nod, she laughs. "Celeste Miller! I can't believe I didn't know what a troublemaker you were!"

I laugh halfheartedly. "Yeah. We kept most of our pranks on the down-low. For the record, it was Lucas's locker I hid the blowup doll in, but he tried to take the blame and ended up getting us all in trouble."

So many pranks. So many embarrassing moments that I thought I'd never live through. So much revenge.

So much laughter.

Covering Lucas's cell phone in an entire roll of tape when he left it at my house, then wrapping it in plastic and throwing it on his front lawn. Taping an air horn behind his bedroom door, perfectly aligned with the doorknob. Googly eyes… everywhere. And one of my all-time favorites—wet cotton balls all over his new car on a snowy night. He'd been pissed about that one for days.

As we got older, the pranks fell off. But we were still misfits, sneaking out in the middle of the night for joyrides in Lucas's Mustang, stealing cans of cheap beer from the fridge in Jeremy's garage and taking them to the lake, where we sipped and talked for hours under the stars.

"So what happened?" asks Zoey.

Luckily, the server chooses that moment to approach and take our orders. My relief is short-lived. Once we're alone again, Zoey stares at me until I wilt.

"Something happened at Camp Wild Lake the summer before senior year."

Zoey hears the waver in my voice and leans forward. "Hey, I'm sorry. We don't have to talk about it."

"No, it's okay. I'm always on you to share your deepest, darkest secrets with me, so what kind of friend would I be if I didn't do the same?" My gaze falling from hers, I rub a finger through the condensation on my glass. "Long story short, I threw myself at Lucas. He rejected me. Then Jeremy told me he had feelings for me."

Zoey sits back abruptly. "Oh, shit."

I smile weakly. "It was a confusing time for sure. But then I fell in love with Jeremy, and the rest is history."

"And you and Lucas...?" She leaves the question dangling, knowing there's more to the story.

"As our relationship progressed, Jeremy became sensitive to how close Lucas and I were. Not that we were that close after the incident at camp. But things changed between the three of us. After graduation, Lucas went off to college. As far as I know, he's only come back twice—once for our wedding, and then for the funeral." I close my eyes. "We haven't spoken since. At least, not until I saw him on Monday."

"I'm so sorry," she says softly. "I had no idea. No wonder seeing him is hard, especially with that chemistry—" She blanches. "I mean chemistry like old friends. It's just, um, obvious you guys have a shared language. Shit, I'm shutting up now."

I force a smile. "It's okay. I get it."

The server returns with our food, and Zoey, in her sensitive way, shifts the conversation away from emotional landmines for the rest of the meal.

But the damage is done. As much as I'd like for it not to be true, she's right. Lucas and I have chemistry. Not the kind Jeremy and I had, which was loving, trusting, and warm as sunlight.

We have the kind of chemistry that science teachers warn you about.

The explosive kind.

AFTER DINNER, I tell Zoey I have a headache. We both know I'm lying, but she lets me off the hook. I head home and try to relax, flipping channels for a while, but eventually, I give up and crawl into bed.

Emotionally exhausted but not tired in the least, I surrender to the tug of the past and relive that disastrous—*perfect, extraordinary*—night at Wild Lake.

I'd snuck Lucas a note during dinner when Jeremy was still in line for food, telling him where and when to meet me, underlining the word alone three times. He read the note at least twice before looking up, and what I saw in his eyes as he nodded made my stomach nosedive.

It was a long three hours until lights out, an even longer forty-five minutes until I crept from my cabin. I avoided the paths patrolled by the older counselors, instead taking the longer route to the lake through the trees. I'd done it so many times that I could probably walk it blindfolded. Good thing, too, because I could barely feel my feet on the ground.

The night was unseasonably warm, one of those following a day where everyone sported a sunburn and we spent every spare minute in the lake. Night swimming was strictly forbidden, but we'd never cared about the rules. And we were smart enough to not get caught.

I finally stepped through the last line of trees before our tiny cove. Away from the main stretch of water the camp utilized, this was the place we'd been coming to since we were kids.

He was already there. Shirtless, in swim trunks, and wet from a swim. My limbs tingled. I couldn't believe I was doing this.

"Celeste."

My footsteps faltered at the sound of my name. He hadn't called me anything but Peapod in years.

"H-hi," I stammered. "Thanks for meeting me."

He nodded, taking a few steps toward me. "I had to lie to Jeremy and tell him I was meeting a girl to keep him from coming—a different girl, obviously. What did you want to tell me that's so important?"

My throat closed. "Can we swim first?" I squeaked.

His head cocked to the side. "Are you okay?"

"Yep." Before I lost my nerve, I pulled off the dress concealing my new—and first ever—bikini and tossed it over a log.

Notice me. Not the girl. The woman.

He did.

"What the hell are you wearing?" he barked.

"A bathing suit, dumbass."

My voice didn't sound like mine, and I could feel his focus intensify. It had always been that way for me—

knowing when he was near or watching me. Sometimes, I was convinced I knew when he was thinking about me.

Ignoring my pounding heart, I picked my way over rocks toward him. He was blocking the path into the lake, so I stopped and looked up. His gaze flickered down, searing my bare skin, my small breasts, the curve of my hips. He dragged both hands over his face, then peered at me over his fingers.

"Me?" he asked.

My heart ricocheted into my throat. "You," I whispered.

His eyes closed, shoulders dropping in either resignation or relief.

"Say something, Lucas," I choked out.

His eyelashes parted, the night turning the blue depths dark. I couldn't read his expression, but he didn't look happy. My body went cold.

I blurted, "Just forget it. We'll pretend this never happened."

His warm fingers caught my arm as I turned, drawing me back to face him. A sigh feathered along my cheekbone.

"Is this what you really want?" he asked with strain.

Swallowing hard, I looked into his eyes. "Yes. But is it what you want?"

He moved a step closer, until his chest, still damp from the lake, grazed mine. An uncomfortable ache unfurled in my breasts, then zinged down between my legs.

"Lucas?" I whispered.

"Shut up, Celeste. I'm going to kiss you now."

When his lips touched mine, the world tilted. The laws

of gravity changed, growing dense at my feet and thin at my head. He made a noise that sent shockwaves through my body, then his strong, bare arms came around me, pulling me up to my tiptoes.

The sweetness of our kiss shifted to something dark and needy. His hand cradled the back of my head, angling my mouth, and the first touch of his tongue on mine lit fireworks in my body. I clutched his shoulders, his back, my hands moving restlessly over muscle and warm skin, overcome with the primitive desire to be as close to him as I could possibly get.

I was glad he was more experienced—that this wasn't his first kiss like it was mine—because I had no idea what to do, no idea anything could feel this good.

Suddenly, Lucas tore his mouth from mine. For three perfect moments, we stared at each other, our panting breaths mingling in the space between swollen lips.

Then his head jerked up.

"What—"

"Shh."

A second later, I heard it—giggling and soft voices, growing nearer. Then we heard the distinctive laugh of a counselor we knew delighted in catching campers doing things they weren't supposed to.

Lucas moved fast, grabbing my dress and tossing it to me. "Go, Peapod."

"But—"

He hauled me forward and kissed me hard, then pushed

me toward the trees. "Hide until they pass, then get back to your cabin. Don't worry, this isn't finished."

Warmth pulsed through me. "Okay."

I went.

Lucas knew the probability of both of us sneaking away was next to nil. We'd be heard. But I was smaller and light on my feet. I hid and listened as the counselors found him. They lectured him on what it meant to be a junior counselor, a role model for the younger kids. Within a few minutes, though, Lucas had them laughing.

I slipped away into the night.

I DON'T KNOW what else happened that night, but something changed. The next morning, Lucas was different. For the first time in our entire friendship, he didn't smile back when I said good morning. He barely looked at me.

And when he threw his arm around Sally Harper, whispering something in her ear that made her blush, I felt a stabbing pain in my chest I've never forgotten.

Not because I haven't felt that pain again in my life—I felt it magnified a thousand times over when I opened the door twelve years ago to two men in uniform. But because we always remember our firsts.

7

Celeste

SIPPING coffee at my kitchen table and absently nibbling a piece of toast, I attempt to clear the fog from my brain by arming myself with memories. Good ones, this time. Of the brief, happy life Jeremy and I shared, but mostly of the awesome human we made.

Saturday mornings without Damien are weird, and it doesn't help that I barely slept. Even weirder, he'll be thirteen soon and entering eighth grade in the fall. It seems like just yesterday he was toddling around in diapers, making mud pies in my parents' backyard and then smearing said mud all over my legs.

My phone buzzes with a text from my mom reminding me that they're driving us to Damien's soccer game. I text her back that Damien spent the night at a teammate's house and will meet us there. Then I tell her I'm leaving in a minute, using the excuse that I'm the snack mom today and we need to stop at the store. Really, I just want out of my too-quiet apartment.

My weather app confirms a cool, clear day, so I dress accordingly. My hair goes into a quick braid. By the front door, I almost step into my Converse, then change my mind and opt for boots because Converse remind me of Lucas.

Then I mentally slap myself and kick off the boots. Lucas—and the stupid memory box he's reopened—can suck it.

The walk to my parents' house goes a long way to restoring my equilibrium. Every step reminds me that the past is gone, that this—now—is my life. It's a beautiful morning, and I love watching Damien play soccer.

My restored sense of self buffers me when, as I walk through my parents' gate and glance at the Alders' front yard, a phantom vision of a boy teases me. He's running through sprinklers, hollering at the top of his lungs. With him, equally energized, are two other kids. Another boy. Dark-haired, with olive skin and a stockier build. And a girl, smaller, with flyaway blond hair and tanned, stick-thin limbs jutting from her jean shorts and baggy T-shirt.

I blink and the vision vanishes, replaced by reality. The little patch of grass is gone, replaced by a flowerbed. Mrs. Alder—in tailored jeans, a navy blouse, and giant sunglasses—is watering the blooms. She doesn't see me and honestly, I'm not sure she ever saw me. At least not until the night she caught Jeremy and me sneaking out of

Lucas's bedroom window. After that, she noticed me, all right, but I still have no idea what she thinks of me.

Not that it's any of my business.

"Mom! Dad!" I call, letting myself inside. Lulu barks and barrels down the hallway toward me. I crouch to give her rubs. "Who's a good girl? The best girl?"

I don't notice the man leaning into the hallway from the kitchen.

"Morning, Peapod."

I try to spring up, but Lulu chooses that moment to jump into my lap. I land hard on my butt, my head thunking against the front door.

Lucas chuckles. My mom hustles around him, wiping her hands on a kitchen towel. "Lulu, no! Are you all right, sweets? Lulu, heel. Sit."

Lulu does as she's told, a doggie grin on her face.

"I'm fine," I grunt, waving off my mom's hand. When I'm standing, I finally look at Lucas. "What are you doing here?"

"I smelled pancakes and hopped the fence."

He says it like it's a given, like it's no big deal. Leaning against the kitchen doorjamb, casual in jeans and a long-sleeved shirt, he looks completely at ease.

My blood boils.

My mom smiles warmly at him, then at me. "Just like old times. We've been catching up, and I told him about Damien's game. He's going to come with—"

"No!" I blurt, my eyes wide on my mom. "He's not coming. No."

My mom flushes, aghast. "What's wrong with you? Lucas is your oldest friend. I'm so sorry, Lucas, I don't know what's gotten into her."

"It's okay, Mrs. M. If Celeste is uncomfortable with me joining you, I won't go."

"I'm not uncomfortable!" I snap, even though I am. Lucas, of course, knows I'm lying and raises an eyebrow at me.

"What's going on out here?" asks my dad, adjusting his glasses as he walks down the hallway, now far too crowded.

"Celeste doesn't want Lucas to come to Damien's soccer game," says my traitorous mother.

My dad peers at Lucas, then at me. I send every ounce of feeling I can through my eyes, hoping he'll back me up. And when his face softens, I relax, thinking I'm in the clear.

Then he says, "Lucas should come," and walks into the kitchen.

My mom nods decisively and follows him, leaving us with, "Pancakes are ready."

Lucas steps away from the wall, his arms falling. "Celeste—"

I lift a hand. "Just don't."

He ignores me, continuing softly, "We aren't kids they can order around anymore. If you don't want me to go, I won't."

A tsunami of old resentment hits. "You asshole." I seethe. "Showing up here? Now? Acting like you want to meet your godson? You're twelve years too late."

"I know," he says mutedly.

"No, you don't!" To my horror, tears fill my eyes, and my mouth spills words I have no control over. "I needed you *then*, Lucas. I needed my best friend. *His* best friend. But you turned your back on me, on us." My voice cracks. "I don't know what you're playing at right now, but if you're looking for forgiveness, it's never gonna happen."

"I don't expect you to forgive me," he murmurs. He drags a hand through his hair, sighing heavily. When his eyes find mine, I can hardly stand the pain in them. Which only makes me more angry.

"I should have been there," he whispers brokenly. "I'm sorry, okay? Peapod. I'm sorry."

For a pregnant moment, I feel the old, sparkling bond ignite. The encompassing sense of closeness and trust that signified our friendship from that first night until the last. Until I ruined it. Ruined everything. The urge to run into his arms is almost overwhelming.

But I'm not a teenager anymore.

"You can come to the game, but you're driving separately. And I want you to leave before it's over. I'm not ready for you to meet my son."

Relief floods his face as he nods. "Deal."

8

Lucas

I MOVED my stuff into my old bedroom earlier this week, after irrefutable evidence that one night spent in the trailer up at Wild Lake was one night too many. I didn't sleep and wound up prowling around in the dark until I ended up in the last place I wanted to be.

The cove. *Our* cove.

I could barely face it, barely handle the punch of self-loathing and misery that hit when I stepped onto the familiar rocks. All I saw was Celeste at sixteen, nervous and trembling as she pulled off her dress to expose her body in that tiny bikini. Baring herself to me—not him, *me*—with perfect innocence and trust.

Kissing her, feeling like every shitty moment of my life was wiped away as her inexpert hands explored my shoulders, was the single best moment of my life until that point. Hell, it probably still is, if I really think about it.

But then, when I got back to Eagle Cabin, I found

Jeremy waiting for me with his confession, unknowing that I had one of my own. I was still dazed, half-hard, baffled, and buzzing with elation. I barely heard him the first time. But he said it again, and that time, he asked me for my blessing. He told me he was in love with her and asked me to let him have a chance. To stand aside. I'd never told him about my own feelings, but he knew.

Second to the phone call from my mom telling me Jeremy had died in the line of duty, that moment ranked as the worst of my life.

And fuck me, but I told him I would. Not because I didn't want Celeste for myself—I'd wanted her for at least two years at that point—but because Jeremy was the better one of us. He came from a happy family. He was generous, kind, and loving. And I knew, deep down, that I'd never be as good as him. I'd never be as good for Celeste as he would be, never make her as happy as he could.

Ignoring her the next morning was fucking torture. Even worse was the devastation on her face when I flirted with another girl in front of her. But her reaction only solidified that I'd made the right decision.

Celeste deserved a white knight.

I was a villain.

Now, as I sit next to Celeste in a camping chair on the sidelines of Damien's game, I pretend I'm not breaking apart inside. That seeing him—this boy on the cusp of manhood whose entire life I've missed—doesn't feel like acid rain on my heart.

He looks like both of them. Jeremy's dark hair and eyes,

Celeste's sun-kissed skin. What I see of his face as he races back and forth is a startling mix of my childhood best friends. His nose. Her mouth. His forehead. Her cheekbones. I almost choke on a longing I don't understand, coming from a place I've spent years burying deep.

When I notice Celeste's questioning glances, I plaster a smile on my face. "He's really good."

She nods. "He's been playing since he was four." Her voice is cool, but pride thickens the words. "Did you ever get married? Any kids?"

I stiffen in surprise, an action she doesn't miss but marks with narrowing eyes. "Uh, yes, but no kids." She glances at my ring finger, which is bare, then frowns. I answer the implied question. "Divorced nine years."

I can see her thinking about timing and want to tell her the truth—that I lost my ever-loving mind after Jeremy died, after seeing her pregnant and grieving. I flew home to Seattle and promptly asked my girlfriend of six months to marry me. Two years later, we parted amicably. While I've had serious relationships since, I've never felt compelled to ask again.

I focus on the game, hoping my voice is casual. "What about you? Boyfriend?"

Celeste snorts. "No time for that."

My gaze snaps to her face. She's looking at me, blue-green eyes frank and challenging.

"Ever?" I ask, shocked.

Celeste is a knockout. Add the kindness, intelligence,

sense of humor, and quirkiness, and she's the top one percent. It's impossible for me to imagine her without someone loving her. She should be worshipped every day.

Unless what she's saying is she does casual hookups only, which is also disturbing. Even more than she deserves to be physically worshipped, she deserves to be loved.

She shrugs, gaze sliding back to the game. "I haven't met anyone who compares to Jeremy. I'm not settling for less."

Beneath my mask of calm, something inside me shatters. It was mostly broken already, held together by memories and old, tired wishes. Its end is surprisingly anticlimactic—a *pop* when I always expected a *boom*.

"Good for you, Peapod," I murmur.

Feeling someone's focus on me, I glance over Celeste's head to find her dad, Jack, staring me down. I've always liked her dad. He looks like Colonel Sanders, has a laugh like a buzzsaw, and a soft spot for lost causes like me. I have no idea what telepathic message he's trying to send me, but his bushy eyebrows are twitching. Eventually, he rolls his eyes and huffs, turning his attention back to the game.

I do, too, just in time to watch Damien receive a pass, maneuver it expertly past two players, and kick it into the top corner of the goal. I'm on my feet almost before Celeste is, hollering like a madman with all the other parents and families.

"That's my boy!" Celeste yells, grabbing my arm and grinning up at me. She's jumping up and down, her body pressing against my side, soft and warm, and the joy on her face feels like sunshine after a thousand years of darkness.

In that moment, my denial evaporates, and I realize why I bought the damn Wild Lake property. Why I came back to Sun River at all.

For her.

But... *I haven't met anyone who compares to Jeremy. I'm not settling for less.*

And I am, by definition, less.

When everyone settles down, I stay standing and touch her shoulder. "I'm gonna go."

A flash of disappointment, then a brisk nod. "Okay. See you around." When I start to collapse the chair, she waves me off. "I've got it."

She doesn't look at me again. I say goodbye to her mom and dad, then weave through the clusters of other families. There are a couple of nods here and there, but overwhelmingly I'm either ignored or given intentionally cold stares.

I don't blame them. If someone came to my town and decided to rip down one of its most beloved landmarks, I'd hate them, too. They don't care that Camp Wild Lake has been empty for three years and that not one offer besides mine was made. They don't care that I grew up here, that I was one of them.

I'm taking a piece of their history and perverting it for profit.

Like I said, I'd hate me, too.

9

Celeste

SUNDAY AFTERNOON, Damien and I head to my parents for our weekly family dinner. While I'm not exactly thrilled to hang out with them after yesterday's little betrayal, I'm also not about to let my personal business mess up my kid's routine. He loves his grandparents. And more than that, I owe them a debt I can never repay.

Without their help—especially in the first two years of Damien's life—I have no idea how I would have survived. My grief was so deep and wide, there were days I couldn't see past it and could barely function as a human, much less a mother.

So despite my lingering annoyance about yesterday, we show up with our usual offering of a pie from Annie's. As we're walking up the path to the front door, an unfamiliar car pulls into the Adlers' driveway.

My skin tingles. Picking up my pace, I ignore the sound of doors opening and closing.

"Come on, bud. We're late."

"Since when do you care about being late?"

"Since right now. Hurry."

Damien throws me an annoyed look, then focuses past me. "Who's that with Mrs. Adler?"

Fuck.

"No one."

Damien slows. Stops. And asks in an odd tone, "Isn't that the guy in all those photos of you and Dad when you were young? The ones in Gram's hallway?"

Double fuck.

I give the front door a final, longing glance, then stop and look across the yard. Mrs. Adler is in the process of finding her house keys in her enormous purse, while Lucas stands nearby holding grocery bags and pretending he doesn't see us. But I know his tells. His fingers twitch against the surface of the bags as he stares pointedly at the sky. Any second, he'll start whistling, which he only does when he's exceedingly uncomfortable.

His lips purse, and the beginning notes of "Sittin' on the Dock of the Bay" float to my ears. In spite of myself—in spite of it all—I laugh.

Lucas's head whips down, gaze clashing with mine. He glances uncertainly at Damien, then back at me. His tension radiates across twenty feet.

I take pity on him. "Hey, Lucas, Mrs. Adler. How are you this evening?"

Mrs. Adler ignores us—it's kind of her thing—but Lucas

strolls across the driveway. He stops on the other side of the low fence. His throat bobs as he swallows.

"We're good," he says in a strangled tone. "Just picked up some stuff for dinner."

"What are you eating?" asks Damien because food is in his top three Most Important Pastimes alongside sleeping and Xbox.

The look Lucas gives Damien makes my chest hurt. He clears his throat. "I'm grilling steaks and some corn on the cob."

"Cool. Gramps is grilling, too. I usually help."

I cock an eyebrow at my kid, who's never helped my dad grill. He ignores me. They both do.

"Nice. I'm Lucas. Damien, right?"

"Yeah. Nice to meet you."

"You, too." His voice wavers, and I close my eyes against a thump of pain in my heart.

"You were my dad's best friend, right?"

He nods and glances at me. "Your mom's, too."

"But then you moved away."

A short pause. "Yeah, I did."

From behind me, my mom says, "Oh, there you are, Celeste! I was about to call you."

She's instantly forgiven for yesterday's mess. Taking the pie from Damien, she gives him a noisy kiss on the head.

He makes a face. "Grams!"

She chuckles. "Hello, Lucas. How are you?"

"Just fine, Mrs. M., and you?"

"Doing great."

"All right," I cut in before my brain explodes. "Nice seeing you, Lucas. Let's go, Damien."

"See ya," he says to Lucas as I usher him up the walkway.

Lucas watches us go. When everyone's inside, I turn to close the door and he's still standing on the other side of the fence. Arms full of groceries. An indecipherable expression on his face. His eyes on mine.

He mouths, "Thank you."

I nod and close the door.

WHEN DESSERT IS DONE, my mom and Damien settle on the couch to watch TV. They're forever bonded by their love of outlandish game shows, the higher the stakes the better. My dad brews a half-pot of decaf coffee—an evening habit of his I'll never understand—and then joins me at the sink.

"I'll take over, pumpkin."

"It's all right, Dad. I've got it."

He snatches the sponge from my hand. "Go on, Celeste. No point pretending. I know the signs well enough."

My heart rate spikes. "What are you talking about?"

My dad levels me with *the* look. I've seen it countless times, and it always means the same thing. He isn't buying my bullshit.

Sighing, I turn off the water and relinquish my spot at the sink. "I won't be long."

He grunts in acknowledgment.

I don't know whether to be touched that he knows me so well—an assumption that would have enraged me as a teen—or embarrassed that apparently now, at thirty-three, it's still obvious when I want to sneak out back.

I snag a beer from the fridge and a blanket from the hook near the back door, then head outside. A breeze drifts around me, marrying the scents of neighborhood grills with pine. The sky is a patchwork of orange, magenta, and fading blue.

Bypassing the chaise, I head for the fence, feeling oddly detached from my own mind.

Why am I doing this?

Before I can stop myself, I step up on a rock and peer over. Lucas sits at an elegant outdoor dining table, alone, his head down as he types on his phone.

"Who are you talking to?" I ask.

To my disappointment, he doesn't scream bloody murder. He must have heard me coming.

"Your mom," he says mildly. He tucks his phone away and looks up. "How was dinner?"

"Excellent. How bad did you burn your steaks?"

"Nice try. They were perfect."

A gust of wind hits me. I shiver. Putting my beer on the top of the fence, I yank the blanket around my shoulders.

"Is that for me, Peapod?"

The words are familiar, but the low, suggestive tone isn't. My stomach dives, taking my pulse with it.

I'm playing with explosives. No matter how well I think I know this man, a lot can change in twelve years.

"Fat chance," I retort. "Get your own."

I hop off the rock and head to the far corner of the yard and the rusty bench beneath a vine-choked garden arch. As I sit to wait, thoughts float just outside my reach. *Go inside. Stay away from him. Nothing good will come of this.* But I can't feel the emotions attached to them. Instead, I feel almost giddy.

The fence creaks. He walks across the yard with an open bottle of beer in his hand and a half-smile on his face. I can't help but notice he moves the same, with fluid, confident steps that made girls swoon and boys jealous. My vision doubles—boy, man, boy, man.

"Scoot," he says, and I move over as far as the bench allows. But it's not large, and when he sits, our hips brush. There's no escaping the heat his body generates or his familiar scent.

I clear my throat, but Lucas beats me to it. "Your dad still drinking that swill?"

I pop open the can of generic beer and take a sip. "You're just jealous."

"That my palate has advanced past that of a fifteen-year-old?"

I roll my eyes. "Just because you drink fancy IPAs doesn't mean you're mature."

We drink in silence for a minute.

"Do you—"

"How is—"

I wince.

He laughs. "Go ahead," he says.

"How's Michelle doing?"

"Good, really good. She's a successful architect."

"Do you see her often?"

"Yep. She's only about twenty minutes from Seattle."

"Your aunts and uncle are out there, too, right?"

Lucas nods, lips quirking. "You're wondering why my mom stays here when the rest of her family is in Seattle."

"Kinda," I admit. "Sorry. I guess I worry about her sometimes. She seems lonely. Mom has tried to engage with her more, especially after—" I falter, heat rising to my face.

"After my dad died," he finishes, then sighs. "She won't leave. We've tried, believe me. Everyone has. But she's okay. She has a grocery delivery set up, and we FaceTime a few times a week to check on her. She just… can't let go, I guess."

I study his profile, the furrowed brow. "Do you want to talk about it? About your dad?"

He glances at me, a dry smile there and gone. "There's nothing to tell that you probably haven't already figured out. Or heard from gossips in the neighborhood."

I snort. "Like my parents are on the gossip circuit."

"Good point." He gives me a searching look, then his gaze falls to his hands. "I know you think I ran away when I left. But I didn't. Or at least, I didn't leave because of you and Jeremy." He takes a long swallow of beer. "Do you remember when my mom broke her leg? About a month before I left?"

"Yeah," I say softly.

I remember it well. Jeremy and I were in my living room and had watched Mrs. Adler being whisked off in an ambulance. The story was she'd tripped carrying a load of laundry to the basement and fallen down the stairs. Although I suspected another cause, when Jeremy questioned Lucas, he hadn't wanted to talk about it.

"It was your dad, wasn't it?" I ask, my voice thick with regret. I hadn't been there for him.

He nods. "Bastard pushed her down the stairs. A few nights later, he was drunk as usual and was laughing at my mom's cast and called her a klutz. I freaking lost it. We got into it. Bad. For the first time in years, he tried to hit me. But I hit him instead."

My chest squeezes. I instinctively reach out, curling my fingers around his tense forearm. "Lucas," I whisper.

His gaze finds mine. "I hit him in all the places he used to hit me. The places clothing hides. I beat the ever-loving shit out of him. My mom's screaming finally snapped me out of it. After all was said and done, he did his usual remorseful routine. She forgave him and took his side when he called me a loose cannon and a psychopath. I couldn't do it anymore. I had to get out."

I count my heartbeats. *One. Two. Three.*

"I have no idea what to say. I'm so sorry."

He shrugs a shoulder. "You didn't know."

"Why didn't you tell me?" I ask, my voice raw.

"A lot of reasons. Things had changed, remember?" Before I can respond, he continues, "Honestly, I think I was ashamed to tell you. I did to him what he'd done to me—I was just like him."

"Bullshit," I say vehemently.

I'm rewarded with a slight smile. "I know. It took a few years to figure out, but eventually I did."

"Good."

He exhales a soundless laugh. "So now the bastard's dead, and no one but you knows that I threw a celebratory party of one."

Giving in to instinct, I grab his hand, threading our fingers together. "I wish I'd been there. I definitely would have celebrated with you."

"I know."

He squeezes my hand, then lets it go. I curl my fingers in my lap, ignoring a flash of hurt.

"Tell me what you've been up to all these years."

His voice is back to normal, if polite interest is normal. Which it isn't—not for us. I'm both grateful for and annoyed by his newfound mastery over emotion.

I attempt to match his tone. "Not much besides being a mom and working. The early years were rough, but I had help from my parents and Jeremy's family. Once I had my feet under me, I got my bachelor's online."

"Art?" he asks, perking up.

"Business Admin."

He nods, looking away. "That makes sense. You still want to take over Main Street Flowers?"

The truth pops out of me. "Not really," I admit in a near-whisper. "I don't know."

"Hey, that's okay. You don't have to know what you want to be when you grow up, remember?"

I roll my eyes. "Says the man who had boatloads of family money to launch himself in the world."

He hums and drains his bottle. "I didn't take any, actually. Even when they offered. I worked my way through school and paid back my loans."

It shouldn't surprise me. He'd worked as a cook at Annie's throughout high school. Jeremy and I never understood why he did, when his parents were rich. He always blew off our questions about it.

But I understand now.

"You wanted to be better than him," I say softly.

"I guess."

"Well, you are," I tell him firmly. "He never reached the level of success you have. Not even close."

A brow tilts my way. "Oh, yeah? You looked me up, huh?"

Unable to maintain eye contact, I stare at a nearby garden statue. The little girl holding an umbrella is over thirty years old and eroded by time.

Just like me.

"Of course I did, Lucas. Just because we weren't friends anymore didn't mean I wasn't curious. For what it's worth,

I'm proud of you." I pause. "Except for the exploiting of small towns and their meaningful, historic properties."

He groans. "Come on. You don't care about that place. When was the last time you were up there, anyway?"

"Damien's fourth grade class had a campout."

"Celeste, if I don't develop it, someone else will. And I can almost guarantee it won't be a company that specializes in sustainable building practices or low environmental impact. They'll clear-cut all the trees and either leave the area to erode into the lake or slap a giant hotel on it."

"I know," I murmur. "I guess I didn't realize how much the place meant to me until I started thinking about it being gone forever."

Lucas shifts toward me, his knee pressing to mine. "Damien has school tomorrow?"

I nod, frowning at the shift in topic. "He has another week before they let out for summer."

Our shoulders bump. "Come up to Wild Lake with me. We can walk down memory lane together and say goodbye."

Nerves bounce inside me like fireflies in a jar. "I can't. I have to work."

"What about Tuesday?"

"I, uh—I'm busy."

He laughs in triumph. "You still can't lie worth a shit. You're off Tuesday. I'll meet you here at ten a.m.? If you say no, I'll find out where you live from your parents and fill the place with balloons. Wall to wall, Peapod."

I gape at him. "You wouldn't."

He grins wickedly. "Oh, I definitely would."

"Fine," I snap. "But we're not driving together. I'll meet you there."

"Fine," he says smugly.

I stand up and glare at him. "Good night, Lucas. I hope you dream about zombies snacking on your fingers."

His laughter follows me back into the house.

10

Lucas

"HEY, Michelle. Now's not really a good time."

"Too bad. What are you doing?"

I'm staring at the lake, its surface glinting in the morning sunlight, and trying not to throw up as I wait for Celeste to get here.

"Nothing," I tell my nosy sister.

Her aggravated sigh makes me smile. "Bullshit. You didn't call me back on Sunday."

"I was busy."

"It's Sun River," she snaps. "The opposite of busy. What were you doing?"

Sitting on a rusted bench with Celeste Miller.

"Cooking Mom dinner."

Her tone shifts, softening. "How is she?"

I watch a red-tailed hawk soaring above the distant tree line. "Perpetually buzzed, as usual. Now that I'm staying with her, she doesn't even bother hiding it."

Michelle sighs. "I never should have told her about that wine delivery service."

"It's not your fault," I say quickly. "At least now she isn't driving to the liquor store drunk."

"Lucas, I know you think there's still a chance she'll come around, stop drinking, and move up here. But it's not on you. She makes her own choices." She hesitates. "Maybe you shouldn't be in that house."

"It's fine. I'm fine. Besides, she's a happy drunk. Shit, it's almost like how it was before... you know."

Before our dad had one failed investment too many, before he lost the respect of his business partners. Before he went from occasionally drunk and mad to always drunk and mad. Before I started putting myself between him and my mom.

"Thank you for protecting us," my sister says softly.

I cough to clear emotion from my throat, then turn at the sound of tires over gravel. "I gotta go."

"Okay. Call me later. Love you, Lucy."

I chuckle. "Love you, too, Michael."

Tucking my phone in my pocket, I walk toward Celeste's car. She stays inside for a few seconds—probably regretting saying yes—before decisively opening her door, stomping out, and all but slamming it behind her.

I bite my lips on a grin as her frowning face swings toward me. I remember this mood well. Jeremy and I would use code words to warn the other when we witnessed it first.

"I'm here," she says acerbically. "Now what?"

"Wait here a sec. I have to grab something from my trailer. Then we can go for a walk."

"Fine. Whatever."

I turn quickly to hide my smile, then jog to the trailer. I grab the bag off the counter, snag a bottle from the mini-fridge, and jog back to her.

She peers at the bag. "What's that?"

Playing it casual, I dig around and pull out a Snickers bar. "Since it's between breakfast and lunch, I thought you might want a snack."

Her blue eyes narrow. She snatches the candy bar from my fingers and rips it open. "Thanks," she mumbles around a mouthful. After another bite, she eyes the bottle of iced tea. I hand it to her. She cracks it open and guzzles, then recaps it with a sigh. "You're weird, Lucas."

My brows lift. "Why am I weird?"

She shakes her head, looking away. "Never mind."

She's weirded out that I remember her favorite candy and drink, and that I knew she'd be hangry when she got here.

The struggle not to smile grows.

I rub the bridge of my nose, looking anywhere but at her. "So, walk?"

"Sure."

Weed-infested gravel crunches under our feet as we take the path toward the Lodge. The breeze stills, and the cloying scent of evergreens and arid earth wraps around us, as familiar as we once were to each other. But the air is also thick, tacky with time that stretches to its breaking point in the space between us.

Melancholy drifts with the pine needles, riding the breeze as it kicks up again.

I should have listened to my gut and canceled.

"Can we get in there?" asks Celeste in a muted voice. She's pointing at the Art Barn.

I swallow. "Yeah. I have the key."

We veer away from the Lodge toward the barn, every step taking us closer to the mural she designed and I helped her paint. I can't remember where Jeremy was that day, but he wasn't there. This project was ours.

I close my eyes against a vision of Celeste's face, young and sputtering and aghast, right after I doused her with a bucket of green paint. At my sides, I rub my fingers together, remembering the feel of slick paint all over me from her revenge.

Celeste walks faster—or maybe my footsteps slow—and she touches the feet of the bald eagle we painted.

"Wow, this is so bad."

It's perfect, I want to say, but I don't.

She looks back at me—the girl who was mine, the woman who isn't—and cocks her head. "What's wrong with your face?"

For once, I can't think of a comeback. "Nothing. Let me open it up for you."

Walking swiftly to the front of the building, I use the master key to unlock the big doors. Then I pull them open and walk inside.

A sensory avalanche flattens me.

"Hey, guess what?"

"What?"

"Chris asked me on a date yesterday."

When I don't say anything, she chucks a paintbrush at my head. I drop my current project—I'm whittling a wooden penis I plan to hide under her pillow—and frown at her.

"Don't go out with that loser."

Her mouth drops open. "What? He's friends with you and Jer!"

"Not really. He's a perv who will try to touch your tits on the first date."

She turns beet red, which amuses me to no end. I don't let it show, though. She's standing too close to heavy objects.

"Seriously, Peapod, you can do way better."

She throws her hands up. "You say that every time someone shows an interest in me! I'm starting to think you want me to stay single forever."

I shrug, looking away. "Maybe you should. Guys are lame."

"You're not lame," she says, trouncing to my side. I quickly cover the penis. "Hey, I have an idea."

"Uh-oh."

She punches my shoulder. "No, it's a good one. When we're old, like in our thirties"—she shudders at the word—"if neither of us is married, let's do it."

"Do what?"

Another punch. "Get married!"

"Sure," I choke past the surge of blood beneath my belt.

"Pinky swear?" she asks, the tiny digit wiggling in front of my face.

"You okay?"

I blink out of the past and look down at her upturned face, the concerned frown and clear blue eyes.

"Yeah," I answer hoarsely. "Sorry, did you ask me something?"

She shakes her head. "You look like you saw a ghost."

The ghost of us.

I can't help myself. She's close enough to smell, to touch. Before I even know what I'm doing, my thumb instinctively finds the little mole on her left cheek, and my fingers sink into her hair. Her eyes widen. For a breathless second, neither of us moves.

Then a car door slams outside. Celeste lurches back, knocking into a table and sending up a cloud of dust, then beelines for the door.

"Celeste, wait—"

She's already gone.

Hands on the top of my head, I clench my fingers in my hair, relishing in the pain. My heart pounds. My blood is on fire. For the briefest moment, I thought I saw need in her eyes.

"Fucking idiot," I mutter.

It was too soon.

Or, as I've always feared, too late.

"What are you doing in here?" asks Billy. "Was that Celeste who just ran by me?"

Arming myself with a deep breath, I face another shadow of the past. Jeremy's brother, younger by two years. He's a man, now, with a family and a successful construction business in nearby Boise. He also looks eerily like how I imagine Jeremy would, were he still alive. Still sturdy and fit, with kind eyes and a generous smile. The kind of man a woman wants when she's done messing around with losers. Handsome, capable, and genuine-hearted.

"Yeah, that was her."

Billy's eyebrows lift. "Bro, she looked pissed." He chuckles. "Some things never change."

"No, they do not," I agree, then glance at my watch. "You're two hours early."

Billy shrugs. "My morning opened up."

I sigh. "Perfect timing, actually. So did mine."

11

Celeste

AFTER DROPPING Damien at school Wednesday morning, I head to Main Street Flowers. My eyes are bleary from poor sleep, I have a pounding headache, and all I want to do is crawl back into bed.

Mom and Dad are already at the shop, unpacking our delivery van. Once a week, they get up before dawn to drive down to their favorite Boise flower market. Back in the day, they made the trip up to three times a week, but now a few local farms supply the bulk of our flowers. I suspect they still make the trip more for the fun of it than out of necessity.

"Good haul," I tell them as I grab a bucket.

"Sure was," my mom agrees with a smile.

My dad squints at me. "Did you shove a fork in a light socket again?"

I stick my tongue out at him and quickly pull my hair into a messy bun. Ten minutes later, the van is unpacked and the work begins. I eagerly embrace the familiar routine of sorting, trimming, treating, bundling. It keeps my mind occupied, away from the barn and *his fingers in my hair*. Away from broad shoulders taking up my vision. His scent around me. Familiar eyes full of longing.

But most importantly, I keep busy to ignore the longing I felt in return. The inner tectonic shift triggered by his gentle thumb on my face, revealing a chasm of want inside me that, instead of closing over time, has widened exponentially.

"Shit." I drop the rose I'm holding and shove my thumb in my mouth.

My dad pulls a Band-Aid from his pocket and hands it to me. His own fingers sport three of them. Mom is the only one who never gets stabbed sorting rose stems and stripping thorns. From the other side of the big table, she shakes her head at us in bemused affection.

"The school carnival is tomorrow, right?" she asks once I'm bandaged and back to stripping thorns.

I nod. "I'm helping with setup, then I'll have a free hour before I volunteer at the face-painting booth from seven to eight. Damien is going over to Caleb's after school and Jane's bringing them. You guys are coming, right?"

"Wouldn't miss it," affirms my dad.

"Oh, look at the time," chirps my mom. "It sure does fly. You two keep working. I'll get the doors open."

I lose myself in the work, in the croon of oldies from a speaker in the office, and before I know it, there are no more flowers in front of me.

Nothing in front of me. Nothing distracting me.

My dad's hand falls on my shoulder. I jerk, blinking, and am surprised when a tear falls to the table.

"Go home, Celeste," he says gently.

"I'm fine," I say quickly, mustering a smile.

"You're not fine," he says, softening the words with a squeeze of my shoulder. "And I'd be shocked if you were. Seeing Lucas again was bound to bring up a lot of memories. We've been here before. If you don't ride the wave, it'll take you under."

He's talking about grief. The ebbs and flows. The sneak attacks. My dad knows better than anyone else what it's like, having lost his parents young. Grief isn't linear, like that famous book told us. No steps or stages lead us to eventual freedom from pain.

The pain never lessens. And even though we grow around it—willingly or not—as life continues, the core of it remains. A cobra primed to strike.

I turn, pressing into the safety of my dad's arms. "I miss him," I whisper into his shirt.

"Of course you do," he murmurs, rubbing my back in soothing, circular motions. "You'll never stop missing Jeremy."

His tone tells me there's something else he wants to say. Something I probably don't want to hear. Stiffening, I lift my head.

"What?"

His mouth droops sadly. "You've missed someone else for a long time, too. I watched you experience a different kind of grief back then. You might have been able to hide it from everyone else but not from me."

I take a step back. "Tell me you're not comparing Lucas abandoning us to Jeremy dying."

My dad sighs. "Grief doesn't discriminate, honey. It's loss. Just loss. Those moments when the world changes under our feet, spinning in a new direction we never wanted. You've grieved Jeremy for the past twelve years, but you never allowed yourself to grieve Lucas."

I don't want to be mad at my dad. I love him. But right now, I'm so angry I can't see straight.

"I'm going home."

My movements jerky, I grab my bag and flee.

JEREMY'S FAMILY moved to Sun River before seventh grade. Lucas and I didn't meet him until the first day of school, and I immediately disliked him. Not because he was mean, or teased me like other kids did for being a year younger. Jeremy was perfectly nice. A bit quiet, or maybe shy. I still didn't like him.

He took Lucas away from me.

Their bond was immediate, as though they had a private language both had known but only remembered upon meeting. Seeing their friendship unfold and solidify was torture.

Lucas was *my* best friend.

"What's gotten into you, Peapod?"

I slam my locker shut. "Nothing."

His finger waves vaguely in my direction. "You're making the face that means something's bugging you but you don't want to talk about it. It's cute that you think it would work on me."

My eyes widen. "Wha—no! That's stupid."

"You're stupid."

I bristle. "Well, you're ugly."

One of his brows cocks. "Tell that to the girls in our grade."

I shove his shoulder, caught between humor and exasperation. "You're so full of yourself."

"You're full of shit."

I gape. "You're full of... STDs!"

He makes a face. "No, I'm not. Ew. You need to stop reading those stupid teen magazines."

"Ugh, Lucas, forget it. Just leave me alone." I head down the hallway, but his arm lands heavily across my shoulders.

"No can do," he says, grinning down at me.

He grew two inches in the last year, and I can't match his long strides anymore. Our hips bump on every other step. When we near a corner, I duck away from him and hustle ahead.

It's no use. He overtakes me in seconds, spins around to face me, and holds up his hands. I know from experience that if I try to walk past him, it'll only get worse. One time he carried me like a freaking baby to lunch.

Sighing, I glance around to make sure no one is in our immediate vicinity. "Where's your new best friend?"

Lucas blinks, confused. Then his expression clears and a slow grin overtakes his face. "Are you jealous of Jeremy?"

"No," I snap, but it's too late.

Lucas is laughing, bent in half in unmitigated glee. Frustrated and hurt, I try to zip past him, but an arm snakes out and catches me in the stomach. Before I know it, that arm is around my shoulders again and he's all but dragging me down the hallway.

"No way you're getting off that easy," he says, grinning down at me. "Don't worry, you'll always be my number one best friend. Forever, okay?"

"You're just making fun of me," I grumble.

Lucas stops and grabs the straps of my backpack high on my chest, shaking me lightly until I look up at him.

For once, his eyes aren't laughing. They're as serious as I've ever seen them. As serious as they are on the bad nights at home, when he escapes to my backyard to avoid his father.

"Peapod. It's you and me. First and forever. Jeremy's cool. I actually think you'd like him a lot. But he's not you. Not us. Understand?"

I nod, horrified to feel an uncontrollable quiver in my lip.

He flicks my chin with his finger. "Quit that. If you start crying, I'll have to hurt whoever made you cry. And I don't want to ruin my pretty face."

I laugh. "You're such a loser."

"You're a bigger loser."

"Takes one to know one."

He presents his pinky between us. "Fine. Best losers for life?"

Nodding, my heart soaring, I link my pinkie with his.

I DON'T WANT to think about the summer everything changed. But my dad's words are like weeds, already rooted and growing inside me. As they spread, they shed spores of shame and doubt and guilt.

Would I have even considered a date with Jeremy if Lucas hadn't rejected me?

I know these kinds of thoughts are pointless. I loved Jeremy with all my young heart. When I said my vows to him, I had no second thoughts. No thoughts at all except how ecstatic I was, how lucky I was to be able to spend my life with him. Even though Lucas was his best man, I barely saw or spoke to him. He came for the weekend then left again. And I didn't care because I had Jeremy and I was happy.

I know those facts are true. I know my own heart.

But in knowing, I'm forced to admit that back in high school, I saw a different path for myself. With Lucas. I imagined adventures and nonstop laughter and prank wars to last a lifetime. But those dreams died when he gave me the cold shoulder on that morning at Wild Lake.

Did I grieve him? The sudden absence of my best friend in the world and the heartbreak he delivered? Or had I let those feelings fuel my headfirst dive into a relationship with Jeremy?

I spend the midday hours on my sofa, my chest tight and my eyes dry as I mull over my dad's words. The doubts growing, multiplying.

Damien comes home from school at four. I pull myself together for him. Make us dinner, chat about his last week of school and the carnival tomorrow. I bribe him with a bowl of ice cream—the price of watching a game show with his mom—and after, he disappears into his room to play video games with his friends.

For him, I pretend that I'm not choking on weeds.

12

Celeste

BY THE TIME families start pouring onto the school's sports fields for the carnival, I—along with the rest of the parent volunteers—are ready for a beer and bed. Soon enough, though, we're swept up in the energy of the crowds, kids running and squealing with excitement to the various games and booths, parents trailing behind with smiles.

I wander around with a bag of popcorn, looking for Damien and my parents, but I spot Zoey and Ethan first. With them is Ethan's daughter, Daphne, who lives in New York with her mom but spends summers in Sun River.

"How's it going, guys? So good to see you, Daphne!"

She grins, a spitting image of her father with dark hair and light green eyes. "Good to be back. I love that my school ends a week before this one so I can come to the carnival." She surveys the crowd, anticipation in her eyes. "Where's Damien?"

I trade a wide-eyed glance with Zoey. "Not sure," I answer, trying not to smile. "Though if I had to guess, he's at the skateboarding ramps we set up out by the baseball diamond."

Daphne's face brightens. "Can I go, Dad?"

Ethan, totally oblivious to what his daughter just revealed, gives her a squeeze. "Have fun, squirt."

Daphne skitters away. Zoey and I watch her go, then make eye contact. We start giggling.

Ethan frowns at us. "What did I miss?"

Zoey leans up and kisses his cheek. "Nothing."

A cheer goes up nearby as some poor soul hits the water in the dunk tank.

"Has she tried to get you into the tank?" I ask Ethan.

He grins. "Every year, but it's never gonna happen. You native Idahoans are nuts. It's like none of you realize it's barely sixty degrees."

Zoey laughs and snatches my popcorn. "Come on, the next sucker is climbing up. Let's go watch."

We make it to the back of the crowd in time to see a man climbing onto the metal seat. He's wearing board shorts and a T-shirt and is currently smiling down at someone below him.

"Isn't that...?" Zoey glances at me.

I nod, sucking in air that doesn't seem to reach my lungs. "Yeah."

The volunteer running the booth lifts a megaphone to his lips. "This is a good one, folks. Former varsity swim captain who brought home three state championships—

Sun River's very own Lucas Adler! You may have read about him recently..." There are good-natured boos from the crowd. "Now, now, none of that! Instead, let's give him the welcome home he deserves!"

The boos shift to claps and cheers. Lucas takes it all in stride, shouting out challenges to those in line. The first three contenders are students and fail to hit the bull's-eye with enough force. The fourth is a burly giant of a man wearing motorcycle leathers.

"Oh, he's going down," murmurs Zoey.

He does. Spectacularly. I laugh at the flash of shock on Lucas's face right before the seat disappears under him. He comes up sputtering and grinning.

"You should get in line," Zoey says, bumping my shoulder. "Weren't you varsity softball?"

Lucas hops back onto the seat, laughing, and pulls off his sodden T-shirt. Goose bumps pebble his skin. There are more than a few catcalls and whistles from the crowd. From his ridged stomach to the flexing muscles of his chest, broad shoulders, and arms, Lucas shirtless is a visual feast.

My mouth dry, I look away.

"Quit drooling," Ethan tells his wife, teasingly tapping her chin.

Zoey, ignoring him, gives me a wide-eyed look. I know exactly where her head is going, what advice she wants to give me.

Jumping into bed with Ethan worked out in the long run for her. Jumping into bed with Lucas? Despite the perking up of my libido, I can't see any outcome but disaster. The all-encompassing kind.

"Cel-este! Cel-este!"

I look around in confusion as my name spreads in a chant through the crowd. A quick glance at Lucas gives me the source. He's pointing at me, a wicked grin on his face, water still dripping from his chin. His finger turns and crooks, beckoning me.

"Don't be a coward, Peapod!" he hollers.

Among the crowd are many familiar faces—including a fair number of our former classmates, who either settled here with their families or never left.

"Get him, Miller!" shouts a former quarterback.

"Dunk him!" shouts his wife, once the editor of our school paper, now the editor of our weekly town magazine.

"Want me to create a distraction?" murmurs Zoey out of the side of her mouth.

I sigh and shake my head, then walk forward to the cheers of the crowd. The line of people waiting for a chance to dunk Lucas applauds as I walk past them. At the front, Miranda Keller, the school principal, hands me three softballs.

She smiles sweetly at me, but her gaze flickers several times to Lucas. "Sounds like there's a lot of history between you two," she says, laughing, but the sound is off.

Then I remember that she's my age and single, and I recall as well seeing Lucas smiling down at someone from the chair. His stupid big smile with the stupid dimple to one side.

"Don't worry, Miranda," I say, rolling the ball in my hand, my fingers absently tracing the seams. "He's all yours."

My first throw misses by a hair.

"Sloppy, Peapod!"

"Why does he call you that?" asks Miranda, still with the big, false smile.

"What did you just call me?"

"Peapod."

Lucas spits a sunflower seed into a cup. His eyes flash to mine, then away. The sunset paints his profile in dusty rose.

"Like two peas in a pod. Only you're the pod and I'm the pea."

"That's ridiculous."

"You're ridiculous. But you're also my Peapod. The place I feel safe."

I stare at him, shocked, my belly full of fuzzy warmth. "That's the nicest thing you've ever said to me."

He grins. "Good. I'm practicing for my date tonight."

"Ugh! You're a shithead." I shove him so hard he almost falls off the roof of my house.

He just laughs.

I narrow my focus to the target, letting everything else fade away, and throw. Muscle memory does right by me. It's a direct hit. Lucas drops into the water with a yelp. The crowd cheers.

I toss the last ball to Miranda and make my way back to Zoey and Ethan.

"You okay?" asks my friend.

"Yep." A glance at my watch brings a sigh of relief. "I'm heading to the face painting booth. I'll be there for an hour. If you see my parents, send them my way?"

"Will do," she says, giving me a brief hug. "We're going to check in with Daphne. I'll give you the lowdown."

I smirk. "Awesome, thanks."

Ethan frowns. "The lowdown on what?"

Laughing, Zoey drags him away.

13

Lucas

AFTER DOING my time at the dunk tank and putting on dry clothes, I walk around the carnival searching for a familiar blond head. It takes me forty minutes to find her due to seemingly endless interruptions from nosy former classmates digging for information on my life and well-meaning but borderline angry townspeople wanting answers about my plans for Wild Lake.

If anyone other than Phil, my varsity swim coach, had stopped me on the street yesterday and asked me to volunteer, I would have said no to avoid this exact situation.

On a positive note, by the time I spy Celeste, my hair is mostly dry and my balls have thawed. I'm also hungry, and if I'm honest, only part of that hunger is for food. The rest is for her.

Always for her.

Since I first saw her that night in her backyard—ten

years old, scrawny, in paint-splattered shorts, with tangled hair and giant blue eyes—some deep part of my psyche had surrendered to her. Needed her.

I'd never been able to explain it. Not then, at least. Where she was, quite simply, was where I wanted to be. I've spent the last twelve years in denial so deep I didn't recognize it. Not until the moment I saw her again.

The line outside the face painting booth is long. Kids leave the booth with wide grins and the visages of various animals and magical creatures, parents trailing behind them looking impressed.

I think of my bedroom at home in Seattle, of the giant canvas over my bed, and a pang of sadness follows.

Do you still paint, Peapod?

No.

She'd wanted more than anything to go to art school, had dreams that ranged from graphic and set design to giant city murals. No one who saw her art, even her scribbles in old notebooks, would question whether she had a shot at living those dreams. The thought of her not painting anymore, even for the joy of it, is physically painful to me, a burn that cradles my heart.

Slowly but surely, I make it to the front of the line.

"Come on over, take a seat," she says, head down as she cleans various brushes and resets her small tray.

The plastic chair creaks as my weight hits it. Her head snaps up, eyes narrowing. "Really?" she snaps.

I shrug. "I'm at your mercy. Paint whatever you want."

Her eyes flare with skepticism, swallowed almost

immediately by mischief. She bites her lower lip, white teeth pressing into the full, rose-toned flesh. I shift in my seat, using every ounce of willpower I have to prevent a tent in my jeans. As I knew it would be, the lure to paint my face is too much for her to resist.

When she reaches for the yellow and blue paints, I smirk. "You can do better than a Minion."

Her eyelid twitches. "Shut up."

I mime locking my lips. She grabs different paints and works fast, covering my face in white before applying lines and shading with smaller brushes. Within a few minutes, she lifts a hand mirror and all but tosses it at me.

I stare at my transformed face and shudder, my skin flashing cold.

"Good one, Peapod," I say, my voice faint. "Ten out of ten."

I fucking hate clowns.

"Oh my God, I'm sorry." She scrambles for a clean rag. "I'll take it off."

"Nah, it's fine," I force out. "But you owe me for this. Big time."

Wide eyes turn my way. "What? No way."

"Yes way." I grin, momentarily forgetting that my face is something out of my childhood nightmares. "I'm cooking you dinner tomorrow night. Can Damien hang with your parents?"

"Absolutely not."

Behind me, Celeste's dad says, "We can watch him, no problem."

Celeste stares over my shoulder, shooting eyeball daggers at her father. Personally, I want to hug him.

"But it's his last day of school! We always go out to dinner."

Mr. M. isn't having it. "Better yet, I'll call Jane Duncan and see if maybe Caleb and a few of Damien's other friends want to come to our place for a sleepover to celebrate."

Celeste grinds her teeth, knowing as well as I do that Damien would rather hang with friends than spend a Friday night with his mom.

"Fine," she grunts.

"Thanks, Mr. M." I stand, grinning down at an angry Celeste. "Then it's settled. I rented a house just outside town. I'll text you the address."

"Wait—what? You're not staying with your mom anymore?" As soon as she asks, comprehension sweeps across her face and the fight goes out of her, confirming that my mom's status as a drunk since my dad's death isn't a secret. "Oh. Okay."

My smile turns rigid. "See you tomorrow, Peapod."

I head for the food area to grab a hotdog, but after the third child under five cries at the sight of my face, I give up and veer for the parking lot. I have plenty to eat at home and more importantly, I have plans to make.

Like what to cook Celeste for dinner tomorrow and how I'm going to convince her to let me back into her life.

14

Celeste

ZOEY ANSWERS her front door on the first knock, a glass of lemonade stalled near her chin. "Are you really wearing that?" she blurts.

I walk past her into the living room, toss my purse on the coffee table, and flop onto a deep-cushioned couch. "This isn't a date," I remind her for the fortieth time. "I was railroaded."

The front door closes, and Zoey rounds the couch. Brown eyes shimmering with concern, she perches beside me.

"What's going on?"

I've been in a funk all day, cycling from uncomfortable anticipation to dread at the notion of eating dinner with Lucas. Plus, I only got to see Damien for less than an hour when he stopped at home to pack a bag. He was beyond excited to head to my parents, where three of his friends are meeting him for a night of pizza and gaming on my dad's ginormous flatscreen.

"I don't want to do this," I say, wincing when the words come out in a whine.

Zoey clears her throat. "If this isn't a date, then why are you acting the same way you do before every date you go on, like someone's walking you to a guillotine?"

I glare. "You suck."

She offers an apologetic smile. "Just try to enjoy yourself tonight, okay? Not a date. Just two old friends catching up."

My brain offers me a flashback to Lucas's long fingers sliding into my hair. The look in his eyes. I squirm on the couch, anxiety pinching my ribs tight.

My voice emerges strained. "I think he has the misguided idea that I've harbored feelings for him all these years. He's stuck in a past that never happened. I don't want to hurt him."

I don't want him to hurt me again.

Zoey doesn't say anything for a beat, my unspoken truth hanging between us. At length, she murmurs, "That's called future-tripping. We don't know what's going on in Lucas's head."

I sigh and haul myself to standing. "You're right. I'm overthinking it as usual." I walk to the beautifully framed front windows of Rose House, the Victorian Zoey's aunt left her. "I still can't believe he's renting the place across the street."

Zoey joins me at the window, frowning at the modern

mansion crouched behind trees. "I miss the old neighborhood sometimes, when the houses were actually occupied by families instead of vacant half the year." She sighs. "At least they didn't cut down all the trees on the property when they rebuilt. I hate seeing that."

"Yeah, me too."

She squeezes my clammy hand. "On a positive note, you can pop over here if you need to escape."

I smile halfheartedly. "Leave the front door unlocked."

"You got it. I already told Ethan and Daphne you might be stopping by later."

I stall for a few more minutes, using the bathroom and pretending it doesn't bother me that I left the house without makeup, in jeans, sneakers, and an ancient T-shirt and even more decrepit sweater. Before I crumble and ask if I can borrow some clothes, I grab my purse and say goodbye to Zoey.

The walk across the street isn't nearly long enough to quiet my nerves. Staring at the buzzer beside the front door, I even consider bailing.

"Don't even think about it."

I spin, my hand flying to my throat. About fifteen feet away, Lucas smiles at me from his seat on a wrought iron bench between trees.

"What are you doing out here?" I bleat.

He shrugs. "Waiting."

Standing, he brushes pine needles from his pants, then strolls toward me. For a few seconds, I'm dumbstruck. I suddenly can't remember the gangly youth with slightly crooked bottom teeth and a lopsided grin. The boy who emptied an entire can of shaving cream in my backpack. Who I watched a hundred sunsets with from my roof, our sunburned knees touching.

I can't breathe. "We shouldn't do this."

He stops a few feet away, head tilting. Evening light caresses his cheekbones, the dark gold stubble on his jaw. "Why?" he asks softly.

My hand flaps in his direction. "Because whatever this is, whatever you want from me, it's not going to happen."

His features still. "And what is it you think I want from you?"

Anger flares. "Quit playing games, Lucas. The inappropriate face touch at Wild Lake? The charming bullshit? Looking at me like... like... *that*!"

His lips quirk sideways, like he's trying not to smile. *"You think I want to fuck you, huh?"*

My jaw drops, then snaps closed. *That* is definitely not something the old Lucas would say. But he's not him. This is a grown-ass man who I haven't seen in over a decade. I have no idea who he is anymore, not really.

"I'm out of here." I march up the path to the street.

Behind me, Lucas groans in aggravation. "Peapod! Stop, okay? I'm not gonna put the moves on you! I'm sorry I used the 'F' word. I didn't realize you'd turned into a Puritan!"

"Fuck you, Lucas."

He catches up to me just as I'm about to cross the street back to Rose House. A touch on my shoulder stops me—

not because it's forceful, but because it's not. Because I felt the tremble in his fingers.

"Please," he says softly, blue eyes direct on mine. "I just want to hang out with you. I miss you."

"That's on you," I say, but without any real heat.

"I'm sorry. Again. I didn't mean what I said that night. I was out of my mind. Believe me."

I actually do believe him. As much as I'd like to cuddle the old resentment for all time, the fact is that grief makes people do crazy shit. I should know. And while I might like to, I can't hold his harsh words to me after Jeremy's funeral against him forever. I said some horrible things to him, too. And to my parents, random strangers, and most notably, the well-intentioned people who didn't know what to say to me and ended up regurgitating tired adages.

You're young. You'll find love again.

He's in a better place.

Better to have loved and lost.

What no one understands is that it isn't the loss that destroys a widow—it's not recognizing the life that goes on. That, and the literal brain trauma that results from the world as you know it ending.

Lucas watches me, patiently waiting for me to come to a decision. He was always the rash one; Jeremy and I preferred to think things through.

"What's for dinner?" I finally ask.

Lucas grins, shoulders relaxing. "Steaks. I think. If I can figure out how to work the grill out back."

"You mean if *I* can figure it out?"

He gasps in mock horror. "No way you're handling my meat, woman!"

I groan.

Maybe he's the same Lucas, after all.

He figures out the grill, a monstrosity set in stone in a giant outdoor kitchen. Beyond is a thick line of trees that whisper with each passing breeze. It's like another world—no neighbors, no traffic. The world of wealth.

I lounge at a glass-topped table with a bottle of beer, my feet on the cushion of another seat, and pretend I'm perfectly comfortable with luxury. The one thing I'm totally on board with enjoying, however, is the fact I was able to discard my sweater and shoes thanks to a giant overhead heater staving off the chilly night air.

As Lucas flips meat and grills veggies, we talk about inconsequential things. Old classmates. Town gossip. I tell him the story of how Ethan Hart, an internationally bestselling author, landed in Rose House and Zoey's heart nearly five years ago.

And eventually, I tell him about Damien.

I thought it would be hard, but it isn't. One, I love bragging about my kid. And two, Lucas's thirst for information and nonstop questions keep the conversation flowing.

"Decent grades?"

"As and Bs, yeah. He struggled with math when he was younger, but I found an amazing tutor. Now he's killing it."

"What does he do for fun?"

"The usual. Gaming is huge. Sometimes I think if it weren't for soccer and skateboarding, or me forcing him out of the house on weekends, he'd live in a cave. But he plays mostly with his friends over headsets, so at least he's being social while staring at a screen."

Lucas laughs. "Can you imagine if we'd had something like that?"

I shake my head, smiling dryly. "We'd have wound up in a lot less trouble."

"Ha! We never got in trouble. We were too smart for that."

I gape. "Are you forgetting the hours upon hours of detention?"

The smile he throws me is wicked. "You mean your hours of detention."

He's right. Lucas always found a way to charm whatever teacher was in charge of us, and nine times out of ten managed to weasel his way into an early exit.

Finally, Lucas closes the grill and brings me dinner. The steak is perfect, the vegetables just how I like them, crispy and full of flavor. After scarfing down the food, I sit back with a groan. Lucas glances at my plate, then looks at me with twinkling eyes.

"I see not everything has changed. You still eat like a caveman."

"Since when are you the food consumption police?"

He grins. "I'm glad you liked it."

I shrug. "It wasn't bad."

He chuckles, pushing his own plate away—which, I notice, is substantially fuller than mine.

"Now you're just shaming me."

"Au contraire," he says easily. "I was nervous-eating all afternoon."

Before I can respond to that, he finally lifts the beer I brought him from the kitchen. I hold my breath, trying not to stare too pointedly, while the soles of my feet tingle in anticipation.

"A toast, Peapod!" he says, voice pitched for maximum drama. "To awkward encounters, old friends, and toothpaste in swim caps!"

My face flames at the challenging gleam in his eye. "You knew that was me? You, uh, never said anything."

He laughs maniacally. "Because I was one step ahead of you. I knew something was coming my way after the tampon incident, so I made sure to clean that thing before every practice and meet."

Remembering a pencil case full of tampons—that I hadn't noticed until after pulling one out for a test—I say mildly, "I never did repay you for that."

"Oh, no." He chuckles, wariness flashing in his eyes. "We're adults now. No more pranks."

"Fair enough." I lift my bottle and clink it against his, then take a swallow. Still eyeing me, Lucas does the same.

Two seconds later, he spits his mouthful all over his plate. I watch gleefully as he leaps to his feet, chair falling backward. Ridiculous grunting noises come from him as his eyes swing wildly. He grabs a glass of water from the table and chugs it. When that doesn't help, he tanks my water, then the rest of my beer.

"What the fuck was that!" he cries, the words thick and slurred.

My grin of victory fades.

His eyes stream with tears and his face is bright red. With a pitiful moan, he pulls up the hem of his shirt and scrapes it over his tongue and around his mouth. My growing guilt hits pause as I stare at his exposed stomach, tanned and ridged, with a trail of dark gold hair disappearing into his low-slung waistband.

The shirt falls and my guilt returns with a vengeance. Sweat drips down his face. He looks truly miserable.

I finally get my ass up and run into the house. I find what I need in the fridge and race back to Lucas, who is panting and moaning piteously.

"Drink this."

I push the half-gallon jug of milk into his hands. He gulps and gulps, milk seeping from the corners of his mouth to drip down his chest. When he finally takes a breath, his red-rimmed eyes lift to me.

"Ten out of ten, Peapod. But you're in such deep shit."

My stomach clenches. I take a few steps backward. "I'm sorry. Really. Bad idea. Out of practice."

"What was it?" he growls.

"Carolina Reaper powder." I laugh nervously, glancing over my shoulder to see how far the door is. "I, uh, found some in the spice cabinet. Split-second decision. Please don't—"

He lunges. A squeal escapes me as I spin and run to the stairs. He catches me right as I cross into the house. I'm suddenly airborne, then my midsection lands with force on one broad shoulder. The air whooshes out of me and I fist the shirt on his back to stay steady.

"Lucas, please, let's talk—"

He slaps my butt so hard I squeak. There's nothing remotely playful about it; I'm one hundred percent being punished.

"Where are you—"

"No talking unless you want to be spanked again."

This time, the low timbre of the words elicits a different reaction in my body, and I become painfully aware that his fingers are gripping right beneath my jean-clad ass.

The trip isn't long. Up some more stairs, through a shadowed bedroom, and into a large bathroom. Lucas strides into the walk-in shower.

When I realize what's coming, I start to squirm in earnest, pushing at his shoulders and shifting my weight back hard. To my surprise, he doesn't fight it, allowing me to slide down the front of him. For a moment, we're caught chest to chest, his arms holding me an inch from the floor.

My heart races, making my words breathy. "I swear, it was just a tiny bit. I didn't know it would be that bad. I'm really sor—"

Before I can finish, he drops me, my feet slapping loudly

on the tile. I stumble back. Lucas darts out of the shower, his hand cranking the dial as he goes.

I screech as freezing water hits me from three angles—overhead, back, and front. Freaking rich people and their showers. I fumble for the dial, cranking it off. But the damage is done. I'm soaked, my jeans heavy on my waist, my hair plastered to my head. Spitting water, I glare at a smug Lucas, safe outside the glass enclosure.

"Okay, we're even," I grumble, reaching for the door. When I try to tug it open, he holds it closed.

He smiles cheerfully. "Nope. My mouth still feels like the sun died in it."

"I said I was sorry, okay? It's cold in here!"

"I noticed."

I glance down and gasp, then cover my chest with my arms. "Creep."

"Tease."

"Ass."

"Degenerate."

I snap my mouth closed, electing to glare. Lucas grins at my discomfort. My stare sharpens.

"How's your mouth feeling?"

His grin morphs into a glower. "Suck it."

I glance below his belt and sniff. "No, thanks."

A different glint flares in his eyes, his smile changing in a way that makes my breath hitch. I shouldn't have said that.

His gaze flickers down my body. "Take off your clothes, Celeste."

An electric bolt of sensation zigzags from my stomach to my core. My face immediately heats.

"What?"

Lucas blinks, then laughs and releases the shower door handle. "Not that I'd object to you naked, but that's not what I meant." He grabs a fluffy towel from a cabinet. I open the door and catch it as it sails toward me. "I'll grab you some clothes."

He strolls into the bedroom, leaving me embarrassed, bemused, and wet in more ways than one.

15

Celeste

NOT THAT I'D *object to you naked.*

"Asshole," I mutter as I peel off my wet clothes and towel dry with rough strokes.

The cobwebs in my vagina are to blame for my flirty words and the insane thoughts in my head right now. There just isn't another rational explanation for why I provoked him. Why I want to tackle him naked and release all this frustration, this humming awareness and energy. Why I shiver as I pull on one of his spare T-shirts and a pair of athletic shorts and his scent surrounds me.

Obviously, my sex-starved body recognizes that he can give me what I want. He's objectively gorgeous: the strength and grace in his body, the jawline, the tousled hair, that sexy smirk and those arresting eyes. If this were a random date, I'd one-hundred percent be rubbing myself all over him. But it's not.

He's *Lucas*.

So damn him and his stupid smile and my stupid body that doesn't know any better.

Armed with enough logic to quell my libido, I finish in the bathroom and collect my wet clothes. I find Lucas in the kitchen doing dishes. He's whistling a nameless tune, a dishrag thrown over one shoulder. Oblivious to my presence. The sight throws me off. Wipes away rational thought.

For a second, I'm flattened by how much I've missed him. Then a bigger wave of emotion hits and wipes the smile from my face before it's fully formed. It's not one of those crippling surges of grief that marked the first few years after Jeremy passed, but softer, gentler. And yet no less potent.

Images assault my mind—*Jeremy* washing dishes. *Jeremy* singing off-key as he wipes the counters in our apartment. *Jeremy* as he kisses my rounded belly. As he kisses me goodbye for the last time.

"Peapod? What's wrong?"

Lucas is in front of me, his expression twisted with concern. He lifts a hand toward me and I flinch back.

"I'm fine." But my voice is weak, my mind spiraling.

"It's me, isn't it. Being near me."

It's not a question, but I nod anyway because he's right and I don't feel like shielding him from the truth. Loss doesn't care about the rules of time. Its roots expand from the past into the future, and we never quite know when we'll step on one.

He sighs, eyes closing. "Yeah. I've been thinking about him a lot, too."

I don't even feel the growing wet spot on my chest from hugging my sodden clothes. My eyes burn as I blink back tears. Of course he's been thinking about Jeremy. We are each other's mirrors in this, Jeremy the ghost just out of sight.

I ache in a different way now. A gnawing, lonely ache—echoes of nights sobbing into my pillow, feeling Jeremy's absence to my bones and wishing more than anything Lucas was there to hold me, to cry with me. Because no one else could possibly understand the emptiness but him.

"Is that why you stayed away?" I ask. *Because you couldn't look at me without seeing him?*

His gaze meets mine. "I was young and stupid. I didn't know how to be present for it." He pauses, inhaling swiftly. "It was too big. Too much. So I tucked it away and ignored it. I'm sorry, Celeste. More than I can ever say."

I swallow hard. "What changed?"

He shrugs one shoulder. "Time, I guess. Life. There came a point when I couldn't ignore it anymore."

I can't help asking, "When was that?"

He laughs; a short, self-deprecating chuckle. "When my dog died at the beginning of last year. Stupid, I know."

My heart squeezes. "It's not stupid," I murmur.

He grunts in doubt, not meeting my stare. "I'd had her since she was a puppy—since just before Jer died. I think she was the only reason I didn't lose my shit entirely back then.

But then suddenly she was gone and that buffer was gone with her. I didn't get out of bed for a week. I'm not proud of it, that it took me so long to actually face losing my best friend."

A wound I hadn't known was inside me closes over at his words. Not that I'd ever admitted it, even to myself, but I'd worried about him over the years. Worried he'd locked away his grief too deeply, that it would lead him down dark paths.

"I wish you'd reached out."

He finally looks at me, his eyes glassy, the blue of them glistening like jewels. "How could I, when I left you to go through it alone?"

Without a thought in my head, I drop my clothes and rush to him, then wrap my arms tightly around his middle. He's different—*we're different*—but in indefinable ways, it feels like coming home. Slowly, his arms lift to return my embrace. He holds me hesitantly at first, but after I squeeze him harder, he finally tightens his arms.

"Much better." I sigh, melting into the familiar heat of him. Time stretches around us, thick and viscous, merging the past with the present.

"Hey, Peapod?" he whispers into my hair.

"Hmm?"

"This is weird. You feel weird."

I know by his tone that we're back on familiar ground. "Oh yeah? Why's that?"

"You have tits now."

I laugh against his chest. "That's what happens when you have a kid, dummy. At least in my case."

I look up, fully expecting to see his smirk, but instead, his expression is soft, almost wistful.

"Don't make this awkward," I warn him.

His lips quirk. "Then you'd better back up because it's about to get awkward."

"Ugh!" I shove his chest and he skips back a few steps, laughing. I scoop my clothes off the floor, then grab the sweater and shoes he was nice enough to bring inside. "I'm leaving."

He's still laughing as he asks, "What about dessert?"

"You think I'd eat any food from you right now?"

He covers his heart with his hands. "You don't trust me?"

"Not as far as I can throw you," I say over my shoulder. "See you later, alligator."

"In a while, crocodile."

The warmth of his voice, the smile in it, stays with me as I walk across the street to Zoey's. As I near the porch, I see that the swing is occupied. My friend looks up from the book in her lap, a mug of tea in her opposite hand. She blinks rapidly as she takes in my ensemble and the wet clothes I'm holding. Then a mischievous grin spreads on her face.

"It's not how it looks," I say through a chuckle. "Really."

"Uh-huh. No way you're leaving here without telling me everything." Standing, she points to the porch swing, then breezes past me. "I'm making more tea."

16

Lucas

I SHOULD HAVE TOLD HER. I'd been planning on it, and I definitely would have—if she hadn't dosed me with fucking Carolina Reaper. Little minx. I'm kinda proud of her, though. It was a savage prank. More than that, it means she's accepting me back into her life.

A man can hope.

Still, she deserves to know what batshit crazy idea woke me up Friday morning before dawn. An idea so outside the rational compass of my life that it skirted positively unhinged. I even took my temperature to make sure I wasn't sick. When hours passed and it was still all I could think about, I started doing research and making calls.

By the time Celeste showed up for dinner, I hadn't even been trying to talk myself out of it anymore.

My plans for Wild Lake have changed.

My plans for *everything* have changed.

SATURDAY AFTERNOON, when I've given it a solid twenty-four hours and my mind is still made up, I make it official with a call to Jasper.

"You can't be serious," he barks, his voice crackling from the spotty reception up at the lake.

I watch a hawk glide over the glistening water and feel like I'm that hawk, gliding toward freedom.

"Dead serious. It's already done. Buy me out or I'll find someone else. You know it would take one call."

Jasper and I have never been friends—he's too cutthroat, suspicious in nature, and manipulative to a fault. All traits that made him an excellent business partner but no one I'd want to chill with on the weekends.

"And the lake site?" he asks, voice calmer as his shock fades and his avaricious brain clicks on.

"I'm taking it with me. That's the deal. Everything else is yours, but Wild Lake is mine."

There's a small pause. "Are you sure you're in your right mind?"

"That's the thing. I feel like this is the first time in ten years I've been in my right mind."

He sighs. "Fine. Can't stop stupid. I'll call the lawyers and get things started."

The hawk lifts on an air current, heading toward the forest. A smile spreads on my face as I hang up. Maybe Jasper is right and I'm out of my damn mind.

I know I can't change the past. My choices. My mistakes.

But I can do this.

17

Celeste

TWO DAYS LATER, I haven't stopped thinking about Friday night. About Lucas's fingers gripping my legs as he hauled me to the shower. About his honesty and vulnerability over dinner and before I left. About his eyes, so clear and direct. The way my body reacts when he touches me, like it knows something I don't.

I'm caught between wishes. One, that time had changed Lucas more, shaping him into a man I didn't recognize so that my heart and body wouldn't ache like this. And two, that he'll leave soon and life will go back to normal. Predictable and safe.

There's nothing safe about Lucas Adler. And there's nothing safe about the dreams that woke me up in the middle of the night and made me reach for my rarely used vibrator.

"Hi, Celeste."

I look up from building a bouquet, blinking in surprise

at the man currently smiling at me. Then a surge of embarrassment hits.

Chris Walker is a perfectly nice, perfectly handsome man. He graduated in the same class as Lucas, Jeremy, and me, though we were never close during high school. After living out west and earning a degree, he now teaches chemistry at the high school.

We went on one disastrous date a few months ago. Not his fault, really. Just timing. He's recently divorced and we ended up talking about his ex-wife, which led me to talking about my dead husband, which resulted in us both going home depressed and alone. He'd called me once a few weeks later, but I hadn't answered.

"Hey, Chris," I say after a too-long pause. "How's your Sunday going?"

He clears his throat, shifting his weight from foot to foot. "Good. I'm good. How've you been?"

"Just fine." I force a smile. I have a bad feeling about why he looks so nervous. "Can I help you with something? Need some flowers?"

"Actually, uh—" He scratches the side of his nose, and the skin beneath his beard flushes red. "I was sort of wondering if you wanted to grab dinner tonight." After dropping that bomb, he rushes on, "I'm sorry I haven't called you. I needed to figure stuff out, you know? But I'd like another shot, if you're willing."

After an internal wince, I open my mouth to let him down gently. Then I hear a familiar laugh, deep and loud. I glance outside and see Lucas on the opposite side of the street, a huge grin on his face. He's standing on the sidewalk with a woman—Principal Miranda Keller. Her face is flushed and pretty as she continues talking and Lucas continues smiling. They're standing close together, matching coffee cups in their hands. Like they spent Sunday morning hanging out.

A burning sensation fills my chest.

"Sure," I tell Chris with a too-bright smile. "I'd love to grab dinner. What time?"

We iron out details, and Chris leaves with an arrogant swagger that annoys the crap out of me. I pick up my phone to text him I've changed my mind, but then I remember Lucas smiling at Miranda.

Jaw tight, I tuck my phone back into my bag.

"That's not the face of a woman excited for a date."

My eyes narrow on my dad as he walks up to the counter. "Were you eavesdropping?"

He smiles. "Definitely."

"I wasn't frowning about Chris," I lie. "I just remembered I forgot a load of laundry in the washer."

His brows lift. "Right."

I ignore that. "Okay if I bring Damien over around six forty-five?"

"Yup."

He studies my face like he can read it, which I'm pretty certain he can. I sigh in defeat. "Just say it."

His mouth opens. Closes. At last he says, "For someone as smart as I know you are, you seem hell-bent on rearranging deck chairs on the Titanic."

I blink, then chuckle weakly. "Wow, Dad."

He winks, a finger tapping the counter before he turns away. "Love you, hon. Have a good date."

WITHIN FIVE MINUTES of Chris and me being seated at Twilly's Café off Main Street, I want to leave. I should be with Damien and my parents, not pretending to be interested as Chris rambles about his hobbies. I'm remembering more about our previous date. Specifically how much he talked and how little he listened.

Even Zoey was less than enthused when I told her this afternoon, and that's saying something. The woman has been trying to find me a man for years.

"...and that's why I took up golf."

"Ah," I say, nodding. "Golf."

A shadow falls over our table. I breathe a sigh of relief, thinking it's our server. But as I'm lifting my head, a familiar scent envelops me. Goose bumps race down my arms and my relief morphs into dread.

"Hey, guys," Lucas says, a sharp smile on his face as his gaze veers from Chris to me. He has a takeout bag in one hand. "Fancy meeting you here."

I think things can't get worse, but then they do.

My date stands up so fast his water glass wobbles precariously. "Lucas! My dude! What's up?"

I grab the tilting glass before it can flood the table, but

Chris doesn't notice. He's too busy snatching Lucas's free hand and pumping it up and down. For a horrible few seconds —that pass in slow motion for me—Chris even moves in for a hug. Lucas takes a smooth step back. Chris fumbles, recovers, and finally gets the hint, releasing Lucas's hand.

Standing face to face, the men couldn't be more different. I feel like a jerk for comparing them but can't help it. Lucas exudes confidence and charisma, a lazy smile on his face, his tanned, athletic body dressed down in jeans and a hoodie. He looks delicious, and Chris looks... less than on every level.

I drop my head into my hands.

"So good to see you, man," Chris continues, his tone only marginally less fanboy-tastic than before. "You moving back to town?"

My head whips up. Lucas glances at me, and for a second, I think there's guilt in his eyes. Then he laughs. "I'll be here for the next few months at least."

"Ah, that's right." Chris nods too many times. "You bought the old camp property. Good for you. That place is such a dump. I'm glad you're tearing it down."

My fingers fist in my lap. "Wild Lake is not a dump," I say, a little too loudly.

Chris sends me a shocked look. "Whoa, sorry."

I've had it.

I grab my purse and stand up. Ignoring the pressure of Lucas's stare on my face, I tell Chris, "This isn't going to work out. Sorry for wasting your time."

I march out of the restaurant and make it half a block before hearing, "Peapod, wait!"

A tiny part of me thrills over the fact he followed me, but I dropkick that impulse. Lifting a middle finger over my head, I pick up my pace. It's a mile and a half to my parents' house, and I'm not dressed for the evening chill, but I'll walk fast. Hopefully by the time I get to my parents, I won't feel so stabby.

Lucas catches up, easily matching my furious pace. "Was that a *date*?" His tone makes me want to slap him.

"Do you have to sound so shocked?" I snap.

"I thought you said you don't have time for boyfriends?"

"It was a date, not a marriage proposal," I retort, then flap my hands. "Never mind. Go away."

We stop at a crosswalk. I gauge the traffic, considering making a run for it, but there are too many cars. I jab the metal button a handful of times, knowing full well it's pointless, and subsequently hear my dad's voice in my head telling me about deck chairs on the Titanic.

"Are you seriously walking all the way to your parents right now? In that short dress and little sweater?"

"I'll be fine," I say through gritted teeth.

"I can't believe you passed on family dinner for that guy. But more importantly, did you really let him pick you up?"

I glance sharply at him. "We've known Chris since middle school. He's not a serial killer."

Lucas frowns. "Yeah, and like I told you back then, he only wants one thing from you."

I blink. "Huh?"

He rolls his eyes. "Sometimes I wonder if you would have survived high school without me."

The crosswalk turns green, but I don't move. "What are you talking about?"

He sighs. "Forget it."

I jab him in the chest, ignoring the hard pec under my fingertips. "Spit it out, Adler."

"All the jocks wanted in your pants," he says tightly. "I had to bat them off every other day. Chris snuck around me and asked you out, anyway."

A vague memory surfaces, then bursts open like a water balloon, flooding me with the hazy light in the Wild Lake Art Barn, the smell of freshly shaved wood mixing with turpentine and paint. Telling Lucas about Chris asking me out, his reaction, and our impulsive pact.

Flushing, I look down the street. "I remember. I turned him down because of you."

He grunts, a masculine sound of satisfaction that sets off a flare of heat in my body.

"It's a good thing Mom requested Twilly's for dinner so I could save you again. Otherwise, you'd still be listening to him talk about the length of his golf clubs. After dinner, he might have asked if he could show you his balls."

I bite my lip. Hard.

He leans toward me, close enough that I can feel his body heat. "You're welcome."

The crosswalk is back to red. Sighing, I turn to face him. "Fine, you win. Where's your car?"

Lucas is uncharacteristically quiet during the short drive to my parents' house. His fingers tap the wheel spastically, and his shoulders are tense.

"What's wrong with you?"

He glances at me before making the last turn. "I'm sorry for ruining your date. I'm a dick."

"You're definitely a dick," I readily agree, then sigh. "But you were right—I should be thanking you. I didn't want to be there, anyway."

He navigates into his mom's driveway and cuts the engine. "Why did you say yes?"

Because I was jealous of Miranda Keller and angry at you, at myself, at the world. Because the longer you're in town, the more insane I feel.

"I don't know." Then my mouth bypasses my brain and asks, "How was your date with Miranda?"

His mouth drops open, then closes. Surprise flashes in his eyes, then something dark and knowing that makes me reach for the door.

"Wait."

I still at the urgency in his voice.

"It was a meeting. A coffee meeting. Not a date."

I pivot to face him, frowning. "A meeting about what?"

"Lucas? Lucas dear?"

The voice turns our heads to the front of the car, where Mrs. Adler stands waving. I gape at the sight of her. I've never seen her less than perfectly coiffed, and she's currently wearing a robe over clothes that sag on her frame, her hair in a messy ponytail. Her face is makeup-free and looks oddly swollen. She's wobbling on her feet.

My heart drops.

"Shit," mutters Lucas. "I have to go."

"It's okay," I whisper. "I understand."

As I'm opening the door, Lucas grabs my arm, fingers searing through my thin sweater to my skin. "Meet me at the bench after dinner."

My heart pounding, I nod.

18

Lucas

MY SKIN FEELS tight and prickly as I wait for Celeste on the bench in her parents' backyard, the sky a dim, dusty blue overhead. I struggled to pay attention to my mom tonight, which I don't feel great about. She barely ate and is currently collapsed on the couch watching a sitcom.

Tomorrow I'll feel like a shitty son, but right now I'm still in knots over seeing Celeste sitting at a romantic little table for two with *Chris freaking Walker*. It had taken serious effort not to throw her over my shoulder and haul her out of there. She had no clue what nasty shit Chris and his friends used to say about her, what they'd talked about doing to her. Sure, chances are Chris isn't the dipshit he was in high school. But I'd still wanted to smash his face in.

At least part of my reaction is rooted in the old, protective urge I've felt since we were kids. But I'm self-aware enough to recognize what else I'm feeling—

especially since I haven't felt it since the day I watched her marry our other best friend. It's jealousy, plain and simple. Break-shit-while-listening-to-heavy-metal kind of jealousy. Dangerous, do-something-stupid jealousy.

I never imagined Celeste stayed celibate all these years. Far from it. In fact, the idea of her not enjoying routine physical pleasure is somehow worse than the notion of her being untouched. But I've also never had to confront evidence of her dating life before.

Since I was old enough to notice, I've been aware of Celeste's innate sensuality, the way she moves like she's at home in her skin. She, of course, has always been oblivious. But not me, and certainly not every straight and horny male in our high school. Her allure isn't superficial, either. She doesn't have to wear form-fitting clothing or makeup or even paint her damn nails. She could be wearing a trash bag and men would still flock to her because she's magnetic. Sexy without effort.

Like magic, she appears, walking toward me on the pathway from the house, a shawl over her shoulders and her hair piled atop her head. She's still wearing the flirty green dress from her date, bare legs on display, Converse on her feet. Utterly clueless about how beautiful she is.

I really don't know how much longer I can pretend. Every time I see her, the urge to confess grows, the words in my heart banging on my throat: *I didn't realize it until I saw you, but I came back for you. I'll do anything to stay by your side forever. You're my home.*

"Is there something on my face?" she asks tartly as she sits beside me.

She's close enough for me to smell her shampoo and the delicious fragrance of her skin. My gaze falls to her lips and my mouth waters. I want to lick every inch of her, mark her with my teeth, scream at the world that she's mine. That she's always been mine.

My jaw clenches as my dick swells in my jeans. Floundering for control, I heave air into my lungs.

"Nope. Nothing on your face."

Except for freckles I want to kiss. A mouth I want to devour. Eyes I want to see hazy with lust.

Unaware of the fact I want to be on my knees with my face between her legs, her eyebrows draw inward.

"Is your mom okay?"

"I can't talk about my mom right now." When her frown deepens, I amend, "I want to talk about it—with you—but there's something else I need to get off my chest."

Wariness fills her eyes. "What?"

Here goes nothing.

"I've scrapped the plans for the resort. I'm reopening Camp Wild Lake."

Her eyes widen. I rush on.

"I met with Miranda this morning about partnering with the school to reach parents and setting up a scholarship fund for underprivileged kids. It seems impossible right now, but I'd like to have the first camps up and running in August. Billy is coming up tomorrow to strategize and get a plan in place for repairs and retrofitting. I'm hoping for inspections by the third week of July."

Emotions flow over her face. Shock is predominant. "But—but—" She shakes her head. "I don't understand."

"I'm selling my company." Now that one of my two big confessions has begun, I can't stop. "I'm moving back to Sun River. Someone has to watch over Mom. Spending time at Wild Lake did something to me. Rewired my brain, or woke it up. I can't let it go. I won't."

I can't let you go.

I won't leave you again.

Celeste jolts to her feet, her gaze pinging wildly around the backyard. I scoot forward on the bench, ready to catch her if she runs.

"Peapod? Say something."

"Why didn't you tell me?" she asks, her voice raw, shadowed gaze swinging to me.

"I was going to tell you Friday night, but then you spiked my beer with hellfire."

To my relief, she sits back down. She's trembling and I don't know whether it's from excitement or disgust or disbelief. Whether she's about to scream or cry or laugh.

I want to hold her so badly.

"There's one more thing," I say slowly.

Her laugh is short and dry. "What?"

Please, God, don't let her run.

"I want to hire you."

Her head whips toward me. "For what?"

"Arts and Events Director. Hiring manager. Head

Counselor. Whatever. All of it, possibly. At least initially. I can't do this without you, and I think—I hope—this project might mean as much to you as it does to me."

She blinks a few times, then her expression sharpens. "Full-time?"

One of the knots inside me loosens the tiniest bit, but I don't allow myself to smile. Not yet.

"Yes. Name your price."

Her shoulders square. "At least sixty thousand."

Internally, I holler in victory. Externally, I scoff. "You're worth more than that. Try again."

"Seventy?" Her voice is smaller now, uncertain.

I finally allow myself a small smile. "How about ninety-five to start? Salaried with unlimited vacation days. Full benefits. Yearly raises. You'll be working your ass off. Make no mistake—I have plans. I want Wild Lake on the map. I want parents raving, wait lists every summer. Failure is not an option."

Her lower lip drops. "You're serious. You're actually doing this."

"One thousand percent serious."

For several seconds—an eternity—she just stares at me. The look in her eyes is almost too much to bear. Relief, hope, and excitement that grow and finally overtake her entire face. My heart bounces against my ribs like it wants to throw itself into her hands.

"Is that a yes?" I whisper.

She launches across the bench, slamming into me with all the grace of a moose. Her knee barely misses my groin.

Her elbow clips my jaw before her arms tighten around my neck in a near-chokehold.

But I don't care.

She's in my arms, delicate and strong, vibrating with joy. Her breath skates over my throat, and there's absolutely no stopping the small groan that leaves me. Thankfully, she's babbling in my ear and doesn't hear it.

"...so many ideas. I can't believe this. You have no idea. Woodworking! Building birdhouses was one of my favorite activities. And I learned how to tie-dye last year—kids would love that. Oh my God, this is so amazing." She stiffens and leans back so we're eye-to-eye. "If this is a prank, I'm going to end you."

Her breasts are pressed to my chest, soft and warm, and if she moves even an inch, she's going to feel exactly how serious this is.

"Not a prank." My voice is raspy, on the edge of a growl.

Celeste gasps, and *fuck*, I'm so over-sensitized I feel her nipples harden, pressing through the thin materials of bra, dress, and my own T-shirt. There's a pause, thick and molten, then she does the exact opposite of what I expect her to do.

Instead of recoiling, she leans in.

She.

Kisses.

Me.

I'm so shocked I can't react to the first brush of her lips. She tenses and starts to pull back. I finally snap out of it and catch her, one arm around her waist and the other hand on the back of her head.

"No take backs," I whisper.

After seventeen years of dreaming about this moment, I finally get to rewrite history. Not as a boy, but as a man.

I claim her lips with mine. Harder than I planned, but I'm so fucking turned on I can't help it. And she *whimpers*. Her mouth opens for me, hot and lush and perfect, and her tongue tangles with mine.

I see fucking stars.

"Mom?"

We jerk away from each other so fast my head slams into the arch hugging the bench and she falls backward, catching herself before she hits the ground. I blink and she's on her feet, half-running toward Damien, whose wide eyes veer between me and his mom. Then he smirks, and I'm gut-punched with how much he suddenly looks like Jeremy.

"Damien, honey! What's up?" Her voice is too high and too fast.

"Grams' show is over. Can we go home?"

"Oh! Okay, sweetie." Celeste throws me the briefest glance. "It was great talking to you, Lucas. Have a good night!"

I would laugh, but there's actually nothing funny about this. "See you guys later." My hand lifts in a super lame wave.

Damien's smirk widens as he waves back. "Bye."

Celeste speeds up, almost dragging Damien toward the house.

I watch them go, then drop my head into my hands. My body vibrates with a need I haven't felt since a moonlit cove a lifetime ago. My head is fuzzy with incredulity.

She kissed me.

I should be buzzing with elation, but I'm not. Far from it. As seconds tick past, incredulity transitions to resignation with a sheen of despair.

Because I know Celeste Miller better than anyone on the planet, and she's going to regret what she did in the morning.

19

Celeste

"WHAT WAS I THINKING?" I ask into my coffee mug, then shake my head. "That's the problem. I wasn't thinking. My brain short-circuited."

Zoey's eyes are fixed wide, her mouth pinched like she wants to smile but knows better. "Maybe it's not the end of the world?" she asks hesitantly.

"But it is!" I wince at my ringing voice and glance at the table next to ours in Books & Beans. An elderly couple frowns at me before going back to their books.

I mutter, "Like you've never kissed the wrong person by accident."

Zoey clears her throat. "Let's focus on the good news. Camp Wild Lake. I can hardly believe it."

My lips tug upward despite my bad mood. "I know." Just as fast, I'm frowning again.

"Did you tell your parents?"

"Not yet. I need to see a contract first, to know this is

really happening. I mean, I know he wasn't lying, and I know he's this hotshot developer with boatloads of money, but what if he changes his mind? What if he realizes this is the worst idea ever and backs out?"

"All understandable concerns." She leans forward, lowering her voice. "But what if he doesn't, Celeste? What if this is all real? Is this what you want? Can you envision yourself running a summer camp?"

A shiver peels down my spine. "Yes," I whisper. "And that's what scares me. That Lucas is handing me a dream so impossible I never let myself imagine it."

Kids at Wild Lake again. Building lifelong friendships. All the drama, bonding, and laughter. The smell of sunscreen and campfire smoke. Wet paint and crinkling paper. Lake water drying on sun-warmed skin. Memories that will stay with them forever.

"I just have to figure out a way to deal with Lucas."

"And how he makes you feel."

I glare at her. "Can you at least try to sound like you're on my side?"

She cracks a guilty smile. "Sorry. I get it, though. This is complicated. He's basically going to be your boss. My advice? Call him before you drive up to the lake this morning. Lay it all out there. The rules or whatever. No touching. No kissing. No flirting. So he knows what to expect."

My heart jumps into my throat. "Yeah, good idea," I croak. "Establish professional boundaries."

"Exactly."

And therein lies the problem. Despite what I just told Zoey, I'm not sure I want any boundaries—or clothes—between us. Kissing Lucas the boy was thrilling. Intoxicating, even. But ultimately, those moments were flavored with innocence and soured by what came after.

Kissing Lucas the man? Fucking mind-blowing. The most erotic, arousing kiss of my life. I can still taste him. Feel his firm lips and demanding tongue. His confident grip on my head as he devoured my mouth.

"You're blushing," notes my best friend.

Shame unfurls poisonous petals inside me, turning my stomach inside out. "It's Memorial Day," I whisper in a choked voice. "I can't talk about this. I can't *think* about this."

Her gaze softens with compassion.

This isn't just about discovering chemistry with the wrong man. This is *Lucas*. My childhood best friend. Jeremy's best friend.

Lucas was my first love, the one who rejected me and broke my heart. And that rejection led me into the arms of my future husband—who made me a mother and ultimately a widow.

No matter how I frame it or minimize it or justify kissing Lucas as a moment of madness, what it feels like is impossible to ignore.

With every thought I have of Lucas, I betray Jeremy's memory a little more.

My call to Lucas on the way to Wild Lake goes unanswered. I spend the drive hyping myself up for the *talk*, reminding myself of all the reasons why what happened between us can never happen again. By the time I drive beneath the framed entrance, I'm brimming with resolve.

The narrow gravel road, bordered by patches of yellow and purple wildflowers, takes me past clusters of cabins, the dining hall, offices, and the infirmary. The road ends in a circular drive, in the middle of which stands an empty flagpole. Just on the other side is the Lodge slash dining hall, where we held assemblies, dance performances and plays, and team-building activities.

Next to the Lodge is a small parking lot, where I spy Lucas's rental car beside a giant truck with black lettering reading *Torres Construction*.

Jeremy's brother is here. My stomach tumbles, then calms. Billy being here is a good thing, reinforcing the necessary boundary between Lucas and me.

As I leave my car, I spot the two men coming out of the Lodge. Billy has a clipboard in one hand. He jots notes and nods while Lucas speaks, his hands gesturing animatedly. I blink, momentarily seeing boy-Lucas, arms waving around as he told one wild story or another.

Shaking my head at the memory, I get out of the car and head for the men.

"Celeste!"

Billy's grin is both contagious and a little jolting—there are strong echoes of his brother in it. He strides to me and squeezes me to his chest. Then he leans back, eyes sparkling.

"Surreal, right? Wild Lake returns!"

"Yeah," I agree. "Surreal." A glance at Lucas shows me he's not paying attention to us; his gaze is directed toward the lake, glittering through the trees. "What are you guys doing?"

Billy gestures over his shoulder. "Just taking a look at the Lodge, seeing how it's held up. Luckily, the initial builders did solid work. Foundation is intact. The structure needs some minor updating and cosmetic work. Nothing major. Plumbing for the whole site is intact as well." He jabs a thumb toward Lucas. "This guy wants to update everything, modernize it, but I've been trying to talk him out of it. Let the kids suffer with creaky faucets and slow flow showers like we did, right?"

I laugh, remembering the misery of the shower situation. Water that was never hot enough. Spray that was never hard enough.

Lucas clears his throat, his gaze briefly meeting mine before focusing on Billy. Whatever I thought I might see in his eyes—some feeling, conflict, or maybe even desire—is absent. His gaze is friendly but businesslike. Detached.

"Now that Celeste's here," he tells Billy, "maybe you can walk her through the timeline and objectives for opening. I have about twenty phone calls I need to make."

"Sure thing." Billy grins at me. "You ready? We can walk back to the entrance and start there."

Lucas leaves without a word to me, heading toward his

car. I watch him walk away, heaviness coalescing in my chest and sliding down my ribs. Maybe we won't need a conversation about boundaries, after all. Maybe he regrets the kiss as much as I do.

I'm not sure why, but the thought doesn't make me feel better.

I tear my gaze away from him and nod at Billy. "Let's do it."

20

Celeste

THE NEXT TWO hours pass in a blur as Billy and I walk and talk. By the time we reach the Lodge again, I'm overflowing with excitement and my brain hurts in the best way, overfull with details and plans.

In addition to necessary updates—replacing old, drafty windows, the porch outside the dining hall, and repairing several roofs—we talk about Lucas's ideas for adding basketball courts behind the Art Barn and expanding the laundry building to include a private kitchen for staff. There are also plans for a volleyball court by the lake, more bathrooms, a cabin dedicated to music, and an outdoor picnic area.

"And we can do all this in just over two months? It seems like a lot."

Billy's nod is all confidence. "Oh, we'll get it done."

We settle on the steps outside the Lodge. A cool breeze

tempers warm sunlight, and birds chatter to each other in nearby trees.

"It's good to be back, isn't it?" murmurs Billy.

"Still feels like a dream."

He nods, dark eyes on mine. "I'm glad you and Lucas are on speaking terms again. In a weird way, it feels like Mom and Dad are back together."

I choke. "Uh, what?"

He laughs. "When we were all kids, you know? It was always you and Lucas. The dynamic duo. Everyone else just orbited around the two of you. Even Jer." My mouth drops, but before I can summon denials, he continues, "He loved you both so much. Wherever he is, he's happy the two of you have buried the hatchet."

Words dry on my tongue.

"Hey, I'm sorry," Billy says quickly, looping an arm around my shoulders. "I didn't mean to upset you."

"It's okay," I murmur, straightening and forcing a smile. "All good. Just a lot of memories here." I clear my throat. "Two months is a long time to be away from Boise, huh?"

His smile is knowing. "Is that your way of asking how my wife feels about it?"

I laugh, glad the conversation is veering in a new direction. "Yes."

"She wasn't thrilled at first," he admits, "but then I had the brilliant idea of bringing them with me. Mom and Dad have the space and are on board. A summer back in Sun River, away from the city, hanging with the grandparents..." He winks. "Macy and I might even get a few weekends to ourselves."

"That's amazing, Billy."

He nods, gaze lifting over my head. "Looks like bossman is wrapping up his phone call." He stands, tucking his clipboard under his arm. "I'll see you tonight at my parents' house, right? Macy and the kids are driving up this afternoon."

Heaviness descends on my shoulders, blanketing my body. My happiness—and distraction—of the last few hours can't withstand the sudden emotional weight, vanishing instantly. The ache of loss and survivor's guilt spreads through me.

I tilt my lips in imitation of a smile. "Of course."

Billy's expression softens. "Great. I'll see you then."

He jogs down the steps and hops in his truck. I watch him drive away.

Lucas's footsteps draw nearer. He's still on the phone, voice pitched low. When I muster the courage to look at him, he lifts a finger with a slight smile. I nod, grateful for the reprieve, and listen to his footsteps fade as he veers around the side of the Lodge. Closing my eyes, I breathe carefully through my nose and out of my mouth until the heaviness lifts a bit, until the urge to cry recedes.

Lucas's voice floats to my ears.

"...come see her if you want to, Michelle. I'm not going to stop you... Not sure what we can do, honestly... Yes, I took her last week, but she wouldn't get out of the car." There's a long pause, then a heavy sigh. "I know, I'm scared, too. She has a doctor's appointment on Thursday. Bloodwork, the full nine yards. Maybe she'll listen to someone with a medical degree… Yeah, I agree." His voice moves closer. "I have to go. Okay. Love you, too."

When I hear his footsteps on the stairs, I open my eyes. My heart is pounding, thoughts of Memorial Day suddenly wispy and indistinct in light of what I just overheard.

I want to say something but have no idea what. Everyone knows Mrs. Adler has a drinking problem, but for the first time, it hits me what that means for Lucas and Michelle. They might lose both parents to alcoholism.

Lucas settles beside me on the stairs, a solid two feet between us. Even with the distance, his nearness sends an electric current over my skin. I can barely look at him. My quick glances only overwhelm me more—his T-shirt shows too much tan, muscled skin. Combined with the tendrils of grief still swimming in me, I feel nauseated.

"So, what do you think of the plans?" His voice is subdued.

I shove my emotions into a mental box and lock it, a well-oiled process I mastered when Damien was a toddler. When he was too young to understand why Mommy was crying.

"Everything is amazing," I say, my voice steady. "I can't wait for construction to start."

"Good. Any input?"

"One thing. I think we should have a garden for growing food."

His eyebrows lift. "Camps only last a week."

"Sure, the campers won't eat the food they grow, and not every camp will plant. But I think the planting itself—and tending to the garden in general—could be a great activity."

"I agree."

Startled, I blurt, "Really?"

Lucas chuckles. "Of course." He stands. "Come on, I want to show you something."

He takes off down a path toward the lake. Off-kilter, I follow, catching up at the first bend. The path is overgrown, bushes encroaching and weeds pushing through old, bleached mulch. Animals have scattered most of the rocks that once formed neat borders.

"Watch your head." Lucas holds a low branch back, releasing it after I pass him. "That will need to come off. Ever used a saw, Peapod?"

There's a grin in his voice and a familiar glimmer in his eye. I think of the phone call with his sister, the heaviness of it, and decide that if banter with me makes him feel better, I'm on board.

"Only in my dreams when I saw off your head."

He barks a laugh.

We round another copse of trees before the path opens up to the familiar beachfront. South of us, a dock stretches over the placid blue water. Sensory memory washes over me, melding the past with the present.

"You don't have to," Jeremy whispers beside me.

Lucas stands at the end of the dock, hands on his hips,

moonlight wreathing his face and the maniacal grin on it. He knows I never turn down a dare.

"It's fine," I tell Jeremy, pulling off my shorts and T-shirt to reveal my one-piece suit.

Leaving Jeremy, I march down the dock. My heart pounds hard, fear spiraling through my limbs. But I don't let it stop me.

"Quiet, Bigfoot," Lucas says as I near him. "You wanna get us busted?"

I ignore him. "To the buoy and back? Winner gets loser's dessert for the rest of the week?"

Lucas nods. Then his smile falters. "You know, maybe this isn't the best idea. Let's do something else."

"No take backs," I snap, and before he can do something stupid, like tell me I'm not a strong enough swimmer, I leap past him and dive into the cold water.

"What are you thinking about?" asks the man-sized version of my childhood best frenemy. "Your eyes glazed over when you looked at the dock."

I shake my head, coming back to the present. Sunlight glimmers on the lake's surface. The old buoy still floats a hundred feet out, its orange faded. It's not far at all—I could swim there and back easily now. But then...

"That time I almost drowned."

Regret flashes over his face. "Man, I was an asshole."

I shrug. "You tried to stop me, and then you saved my dumb ass. Anyway, what is it you wanted to show me?"

Lucas watches me for another few moments, then nods and sets off across the beach. It's more rock than sand, bordered by boulders. There used to be intense turf wars over the larger, flat boulders, nicknamed Sun Rock and Dive Rock.

Over his shoulder, Lucas asks, "Remember that year the counselors had to rope off Sun Rock because those girls kept pushing people off it?"

"Teenage girls are feral," I say, nodding. "But don't forget, the same thing happened to Dive Rock when boys wouldn't let girls jump off it."

Lucas grimaces. "Man, I hope kids these days are cooler than we were."

"We never did that shit," I remind him, then add, "I think you'll be surprised by the younger generations. They're more mature than we were, a little more in tune with empathy and compassion."

He smirks. "Because all their parents are in therapy?"

I elbow him, but I'm laughing. "Maybe."

We make it to the dock, stepping onto the platform that straddles land and water.

"It's smaller than I remember," Lucas says softly.

"You're a giant now," I quip, then move past him, intent on the distant end.

"Whoa!" His arm shoots out, forearm against my breasts for a pregnant moment before I jump back.

"What the hell?"

His eyes are wide. "Jesus, Peapod, did you even look where you were stepping?"

I look down. My stomach turns at the sight of lake water beneath a giant hole. "Oh."

"*Oh?*" he echoes, then shakes his head. "I didn't bring you over here for a buoy race, you menace. I wanted your thoughts on moving the dock to the north side of the beach."

I blink a few times, my brain mush as it processes the tingling sensation from his touch, the fact I could have really hurt myself, and the words that just came out of his mouth.

"North side," I echo.

His lips move around, his eyes bright—too bright. "What's wrong with you?"

And because my brain is still on the fritz, I blurt, "You touched my boobs!"

His gaze drags to my chest, sticks for a few seconds that feel like minutes, then returns to my eyes. All trace of laughter is gone, and I feel like the air just heated twenty degrees.

Then he shoves his hands in his pockets, his gaze shifting to the water. "Just say what you want to say. Kissing me was a mistake and it'll never happen again, right?"

Right.

But for some reason, my mouth won't work.

"I'm not stupid enough to think it meant anything," he continues mutedly. "You were excited about the job and had a momentary lapse of sanity."

I open my mouth and close it again. Even though he's saying exactly what I was prepared to say, it sounds wrong. The words, his stance, the fact he won't look at me.

"Lucas…" I trail off, and finally manage, "I'm sorry."

He nods and even smiles when he looks at me, though it doesn't reach his eyes. "We're on the same page. I get it—I know you, remember? Don't worry. We'll sweep it under the rug, et cetera. Now, about the dock. Let me show you where I think the new one should be."

21

Lucas

NERVES SKATE UNDER MY SKIN, my grip on a store-bought pie punishing as I walk up the driveway of the Torreses' ranch-style home. The collar of my button-down shirt chafes my neck, and even though I'm wearing my favorite jeans, they feel rough and ill-fitting. Like I'm eleven years old again, showing up at a new school with bruises under too-small clothes.

I almost didn't make it here. When Billy invited me to his parents' annual Memorial Day barbecue this morning, I'd been caught off guard and hadn't known what to say. Then, like an idiot, I'd said I'd *try*. The flash of disappointment in his eyes had stayed with me all day, and guilt had worn me down.

The fact is, I owe him and the Torres family. I owe Jeremy to show up for them. Most of all, I owe Celeste for all the years I wasn't here, wasn't facing the grim reality of Jeremy's loss at her side.

I've spent the majority of my life avoiding uncomfortable feelings and situations. Only now, I'm coming to realize the cost of it. Rejecting attachment and all the complications that come from them has left me with nothing and no one.

I'm tired of being alone.

So here I am, feeling more awkward than I have in decades as I ring the doorbell and pray I don't fuck this up.

The door swings open on Billy, whose face splits in a wide grin. "Holy shit, I didn't think you'd come."

I chuckle, the sound strained. "Yeah. Surprise."

"I'm glad you're here. Come on—everyone's out back."

Entering the Torres home is like walking a road into the past. The same furniture, area rugs, curtains. The same wooden picture frames lining the hallway, with a few new additions featuring Billy and his family. But the old photos are there, too.

My eyes burn as my gaze stalls on a familiar one: Celeste, Jeremy, and me, our arms slung around each other, grinning like lunatics. Jeremy's face blurs, disappearing.

There's an anvil on my chest. I can't breathe.

"Hey, man, you okay?"

I focus on Billy with effort, realizing I've stopped, that my hand is braced on the wall next to the photo. He grabs the pie before I drop it, then grips my shoulder.

In a lower voice, he says, "It doesn't get easier, but it does get different. You just keep moving forward. No leaps. Just one step at a time."

Some part of me realizes the gift he's giving me with his

acceptance, while another part of me is deeply ashamed. This family has been through unimaginable grief. They've been processing it and living with it for years, while I did everything in my power to ignore it.

"I should have been here," I say hoarsely. "I'm sorry."

From behind Billy, a familiar voice says, "You're here now."

I look up at Angela Torres, Jeremy and Billy's mother—my second mother, really, who fed me and housed me just as much as my own did during my tumultuous teenage years. She's older, which shouldn't be a shock but is. Her hair is mostly gray. Her face, always expressive, is even more so now, marked by life's cycles of joy and struggle.

Dark eyes glassy, she opens her arms for me. "Come here, Lucas."

Billy moves aside as I half-stumble into Angela's arms. I dwarf her in size, but the strength in her hug makes me feel like a child again.

"I'm sorry," I mumble into her hair.

"I know."

Angela releases me, bringing a hand to my cheek. She studies me with unnerving intensity, finding something I can't fathom.

She finally nods. "We were never angry with you, Lucas."

"I was," mutters Billy.

I suck in a breath, but before I can speak, he winks at me.

"Only for the first five years."

Angela clucks her tongue at him, then returns her gaze to me. A smile lifts the corners of her lips. "I always knew you'd come home. Come, come." She wraps an arm through mine, steering me down the hallway. "Billy, would you be so kind as to put the pie in the kitchen?"

He grumbles something in response that makes Angela laugh. I don't hear it because I can see the backyard now, visible through open French doors. To the right, Mr. Torres mans the giant grill with Celeste's dad—they look like twins in khaki pants and polo shirts, their stocky builds furthering the impression, their heads tilted at the same angle as they discuss the mysteries of meat.

Out on the grass, there's a play structure with a slide and two swings, both occupied by younger kids. Damien stands behind them, looking bored out of his mind as he yields to his cousins' demands for *"Higher, Higher!"*

Laughter draws my gaze to the left, where a group of adults sits around a table overflowing with appetizers. Celeste's mom chats with several strangers, who I assume are neighbors or friends of the Torres family, while Celeste sits next to Billy's wife, Macy.

Like she feels my stare, Celeste glances my way. Shock briefly freezes her face before her expression goes blank.

"She's always been stubborn, hasn't she?" murmurs Angela.

I look at her, surprised. "Who?"

She nods toward Celeste, who has turned away from us to watch the kids. "Our girl." Before I can make sense of the conversation, she pats my arm and releases me. "Give it time. She'll figure it out eventually."

The question *"Figure what out?"* dies on my tongue as Angela strides away, her voice lifting as she asks the grill masters when the burgers will be finished, which generates a chorus of similar, laughing demands.

I want nothing more than to turn tail and run, or find a hole to crawl inside, but instead force myself to approach the table. I've charmed cynical investors and board rooms full of humorless men, but this feels more daunting. I wipe clammy hands on my pants.

Celeste's mom notices me lurking and takes pity on me, coming to my side. She introduces me to the others—I was right, they're neighbors—and forces me into the seat beside hers. She then proceeds to steer the conversation for the next twenty minutes with topics ranging from the weather to a sale on produce at the grocery store, to Damien's soccer camp next week.

Not until Angela announces that the burgers are ready do I realize Mrs. Miller singlehandedly saved me from the inevitable questions about Wild Lake.

"Thank you," I murmur, standing behind her in line to get a burger I'm not sure I'll be able to eat.

She smiles up at me. "Everyone deserves a break."

I'm spared a response by Damien, who slips into line ahead of his grandmother. She chastises him affectionately, ruffling his hair.

The line gets shorter. Plates are distributed. We all grab buns and condiments as the grill gets closer. I almost make a break for it a few times, my heart pattering faster the nearer I move to Oliver Torres.

Angela has always been the forgiving sort—Jeremy's dad has not. Neither of them was big on punishment, not like my dad, but my chest still stings from Mr. Torres's disappointed lectures when Jeremy and I were caught stealing beers from his garage, caught sneaking out his window, caught sneaking back in…

Then it's my turn, and a gruff voice asks, "Cheese or plain?"

"Cheese, please." My voice cracks the same way it did when I was fourteen and he caught me sampling the pumpkin pie before Thanksgiving.

A small, misshapen burger with the cheese half melted off lands a few inches from my bun. I swallow hard, meeting a flinty gaze that strips me bare. Beneath his mustache, Mr. Torres's lips twitch.

"Good to see you, son."

He waves me away. Adrenaline leaks out of me, leaving my knees shaky. I search out a place to sit away from everyone and find it, making my way to a couple of lounges near the side of the house, opposite the bustling table. Angled away from everyone else, I transfer the burger patty onto my bun, smash lettuce and tomato on top of it, and take a bite that tastes like ash.

Mid-chew, a shadow falls over me, then a body plops onto the other chaise. She doesn't wear perfume, but I smell her, anyway. Something light and airy and indefinably her.

She doesn't speak, doesn't even look at me as she eats. I manage a few more bites. She finishes her burger.

Finally, she says in a faint voice, "It wasn't always like this. The first few Memorial Days, I didn't get out of bed except to visit the cemetery. Then, for a long time after, I actually hated today. I understand the importance of it, obviously, and I'm glad it exists, but..." She shrugs. "No one remembers the day he died, but everyone remembers that he died in war. They remember today.

"People would come out of the woodwork like they were checking off a box on a list of How to Be a Decent Human. It was a yearly funeral. *'I'm so sorry,'* and *'You seem happy now!'* or they'd try to make it about politics and tell me he shouldn't have been there in the first place. Like any of it is their fucking business. And then once they checked that box, they'd forget about it, about us, and have their block parties and wave their flags."

She sets her plate down and leans back on the lounge, crossing her arms over her chest. Still without looking at me. Her gaze is unfocused on the early evening sky, watery blue with streaks of pink and orange.

"It's different now," she continues after a moment, her voice stronger and more present. Her gaze flickers to me before returning to the sky. "We come together to celebrate his life. To remember and bring him out of our hearts and into our minds. And we each have our own way of doing things. Angela and Oliver usually spend the morning at his grave. I used to as well, but when Damien was eight or so, he decided he didn't want to go anymore."

"Did you go? Today?" I ask softly.

Celeste shakes her head. "It helps Angela and Oliver. Billy, too. But I don't need the reminder." She pauses. "I mean—"

"I know what you mean."

She carries his grave inside her. His life, too.

I trace her profile with my gaze, seeing the echoes of slightly fuller cheeks and more freckles. A hint of a sunburn on the bridge of her nose. Jaw jutting with stubbornness as Jeremy and I insisted we should give her Beta fish, Josie, a funeral instead of a quick flush down the toilet.

She'd loved that damn fish. We'd thought we were helping. Until she told us: *"Josie is gone, idiots. Who cares where her body goes? She's not using it anymore. She lives in my heart now, anyway, and she'll live there forever."*

Now, Celeste's lips compress as she stares across the backyard. I follow her gaze to see Damien lying on the grass, propped on his elbows as he plays on his phone.

She sighs. "When he was little, he loved hearing about his dad. Watching videos, looking through photos, all of it. But now he gets mad at me whenever I bring up Jeremy. I can't really blame him, either. All his life he's been fed stories, pictures, a million second-hand details about someone he's never met, all with the expectation that he should love his dad as much as the rest of us do."

The words fall softly between us, journeying from present to past, a gift she doesn't know she's giving me. I don't know why she's opening up to me right now, but I won't take it for granted.

"That must hurt," I say.

Celeste glances at me, a hint of surprise in her eyes. "Thanks for not telling me he'll get over it or some other bullshit advice."

Because I can't help it, I say, "But I'm sure he'll get over it."

She rolls her eyes. "Jerk." Then her lips quirk. "You still sweat bullets when you're nervous. When you walked out of the house, I thought you'd just gone for a swim."

I hold back my grin. "Liar."

She doesn't smile, but her stare isn't antagonistic. If I didn't think it was impossible, I'd say it's almost... forgiving.

"I'm glad you came, Lucas. Even if you are twelve years late."

22

Celeste

I DON'T KNOW what it was, exactly, about my conversation with Lucas at the barbecue four days ago, but something shifted between us that night. Or rather, something shifted inside me.

Maybe it was when I realized, after observing him for a bit, how truly uncomfortable he felt being there. I hadn't been lying when I told him he'd been sweating. Seeing him like that—pushing himself into emotionally painful territory despite his instincts—was so out of odds with his younger, devil-may-care self, I had no choice but to accept that, for better or worse, Lucas Adler the man was not Lucas Adler the boy.

The other side of the coin was that his presence—and the way the Torres family welcomed him instead of throwing his ass to the curb—brought forth a wave of memories from the past. The *good* past. When the bond of friendship between the three of us had been its purest and deepest, and that bond had extended to our families. Mine and Jeremy's families, at least. And it was the type of bond that withstood time, heartache, even betrayal.

These truths weren't easy to swallow, dragging on the way down, but when I woke up Tuesday morning, I felt different. Clearer and more peaceful. Angela, Oliver, and Billy welcoming Lucas back into their home had tenderly wiped away the resentment I'd carried for so many years.

The defining moment came when everyone was saying their goodbyes. I'd watched Oliver—stoic to the max—tearing up as he gave Lucas a back-pounding hug. I'd barely held back my own tears.

Now, in that old, raw place inside me is a fresh wound ready for healing. I don't know if I'll ever be able to forgive Lucas entirely for abandoning us, but the acid burn of anger is gone. It took him a long time to come back, to make things right. But he's doing it.

"Care for a swim?"

I look up from the laptop balanced on my knees to find Lucas standing where the path meets the rocky beach, a challenging glint in his eyes. For a moment, I imagine our bodies in the water, skin sliding on skin—a distorted memory from that last summer, when his nearness had felt like a continuous, electric current of want. Before he'd unceremoniously untethered my heart and set it adrift for Jeremy to claim.

I clear my throat. "No, thanks. I'm in spreadsheet hell right now."

He takes a step toward me, into sunlight that teases the

gold tones in his hair. "You know you're allowed to take breaks, right?"

"We're at the end of our first week," I say tensely, "and there's still a ton to get done."

He smiles, unruffled. "Bullshit. You said you have a dozen interviews set up for next week, right? The hiring process is being set up online. Billy and his team are starting Monday. All the rotted furniture is gone. By the end of next week, the roof leak on the Lodge will be fixed and the plumbing upgrades will start. We're in a good spot."

"Yes, but—"

"Peapod. Put the laptop down or I'll unplug our shiny new Wi-Fi router. It's a beautiful day."

It is beautiful, sunlight shimmering and slicing across the mostly still water, the air dry and warm. To the north of the lake, there's a single canoe, two figures within holding fishing lines. Locals, no doubt, since lake access is minimal. It's truly unspoiled nature. Wild and pristine. Quiet, too, since there are no workers at the property today.

I close my laptop reluctantly. "I'm still not going for a swim. I don't have a bathing suit and that water is freezing."

"Suit yourself."

Lucas is in a good mood today. The kind of mood that was impossible to resist when I was young. Even now, its playfulness teases at my edges, fraying my determination and drive.

I've busted my ass all week weeding through online

applications for various camp positions and scheduling both virtual and in-person interviews. My initial worry that there wouldn't be substantial interest quickly turned to awe—hundreds of people, both local and as far as California and Ohio, want to work summers at Wild Lake. With ages ranging from eighteen to their late fifties, they poured out their hearts in the comments portion of the application.

Given the experience of some of the applicants—including a few original Wild Lake staff who I automatically moved to the top of the pile—it's hard not to feel like an imposter every time I sign an email as Wild Lake Camp Director. But I'm getting used to it. Used to the feel of the camp again. Different but the same, as my body has grown along with my mind and heart.

The nostalgia remains a potent force, but there's a newness to it now, a patina of fresh memories on the cusp of creation. Some, too, have already been created.

Like one yesterday: Lucas running out of the Lodge hollering at the top of his lungs, swiping at his head like it was on fire, screeching about bats.

A smile tugs my lips as I remember his utterly juvenile terror, then my expression freezes as he pulls off his shirt and heads for the water. The shoes are next, then his belt clasp. I look away before he can tug off his shorts, but the sight of his naked, muscular back stays, a double exposure every time I blink.

"Last chance," he taunts with a grin.

I look down only long enough to confirm he's wearing

boxers—black cotton—then wave him into the water. "Have fun."

"Party pooper."

He wades out, making pitiful sounds as the water rises to his knees, then thighs. A few seconds later, there's a distinctly masculine yelp of affront.

"Told you!" I call.

He squints at me in annoyance. "It's definitely colder now than it was twenty years ago."

I can't help but laugh. "Oh, yeah. That must be it."

He flashes a quick smile, then turns and dives, disappearing into the dark water. My lungs tingle as I wait for him to surface. I remind myself he's always been at home in the water and can hold his breath for close to two minutes. Or he used to be able to. I still wilt with relief when his head pops up, looking small, already halfway to the buoy.

He begins swimming, a clean, hypnotic breaststroke. Past the buoy, around, and back toward shore. I'm compelled to watch, barely blinking, and not because I'm wowed by his form. I'm captured by the same instinct I have when I don't see Damien for hours, or when I don't hear from my mom and dad. I watch because I need to know he's safe. That he won't disappear beneath the water between one blink and the next, never to be seen again.

PTSD is a bitch who has only mellowed slightly with age. She's saucy at the moment, rejuvenated by Memorial Day and everything it represents.

I breathe another sigh of relief as Lucas reaches the

shallows and stands, shifting a bit as he finds his place on slick rocks. His back is to me, his hands on his hips as he looks out over the lake. Relaxed and contained, a master of his domain.

Meanwhile, my insides are thrumming, my armpits prickling with a flight or fight response that has nothing and everything to do with him. And it's fucking irritating.

The more time I spend with him, the more it feels like I'm shifting toward the open door of an airplane with tissue paper for a parachute. All the work I did over the years pushing him from my mind has come apart at the seams in the last few weeks.

While I worried about Lucas from time to time, that worry never attached itself to the trauma of losing Jeremy. Now it has. The proof is the faint tremor in my hands, my still-elevated heart rate.

I know what it means—and that's the scariest part. I care about him. Still. *Too much.*

Lucas eventually turns, peaceful expression shifting as his eyes lock on my face. Then he's out of the water, half-running to my little outdoor office consisting of a blanket under the shade of a tree.

"What's wrong?"

He looms over me, dripping water on the edge of the blanket. His voice is sharp, demanding, his gaze scanning my features. My face feels like wet plaster as I shift it into a smile. His wince tells me I failed in my efforts.

"I'm fine."

His gaze narrows, dissecting me before he glances back

at the lake. When he turns to me again, understanding and sympathy swim in his eyes.

He knows.

I can't stand it. Can't stand that he can read me so well. All these years later. Like nothing has changed between us, like we're kids again and I'm pretending my feelings aren't hurt because a girl in our class told me I'd always be flat-chested like a boy.

I reach for my laptop to pack it away, my movements jerky, but before I can carry out my hissy fit, Lucas says, "Get your shit and meet me in the Art Barn."

Without waiting for a response, he strolls toward his clothes.

23

Celeste

THE AIR in the barn is cool and musty. I took my time following Lucas, and by the time I step inside, he's pulled on shorts and shoes sans socks. His hair drips on his bare shoulders, which flex as he drags open the back doors to let in more light and a fresh breeze.

Still a bit off-center, I look around. Dust motes dance in the stale air. Five of the six central worktables are covered with drop cloths, their surfaces lumpy from protecting who knows what the last few years. Probably junk.

To my right is the 'expert only' area, a fenced space with a padlock that used to hold two old kilns, along with saws, drills, and paint. Basically anything sharp or toxic. It's empty now, the gate hanging open and listing toward the ground.

The left wall of the barn used to be a staging and display area for art in the drying process, but now piles of trash obscure it. Chunks of wood, broken furniture, old paint cans, rotting sheets and towels. My nose wrinkles at the sight of animal droppings and about a billion spiderwebs.

"Should've ordered another dumpster," I note as Lucas approaches me.

"We will," he assures me.

I look up at him, feeling a jolt when I find his gaze already on my face. "What are we doing here?"

He smirks. "Unwrapping presents."

He rips off the nearest drop cloth, sending a ton of dust into the air. We both sneeze and say, "Bless you," at the same time. I have a coughing fit and he pounds my back.

"Ugh, Lucas, what the hell!"

He chuckles and sweeps an arm toward the table. "Ta-da!"

Eyes watering, I blink at what's been revealed. Small cardboard boxes, sagging and half disintegrated, with faded marker on the sides denoting years. I immediately look at the oldest boxes, with buckled and warped sides, the cardboard almost paper at this point. Then I find it. Our year.

Not the last one, the one where everything changed, but the one before that. Our sophomore summer. The golden year.

Lucas sees it at the same time I do. His arm brushes against mine—warm, electric connection that makes me twitch—as he pulls the box from the table. It's heavy, his biceps straining as he carries it outside and puts it down carefully in the sunlight, on the small cement landing before the barn.

Then he plops down cross-legged in front of the box and grins up at me. "Do the honors?"

I nod eagerly and sit opposite him to peel back the loose layers of the box top. Even half-knowing what I'll find, my jaw still drops. "I can't believe these were kept."

He grins and picks up one of the eight-by-eight painted and glazed tiles. There are roughly twenty in the box. Without speaking, we begin to remove the tiles, lining them up side by side on the cement. Every tile is different, the artists' techniques ranging from blobs of colorful paint to intricate geometric designs to animals of varying realism. Each is signed and dated by the creator in the bottom right corner.

Lucas chuckles as he holds up a tile. "You hated mine."

I grab the tile out of his hand, my fingers sweeping fine dust from its surface. Lucas isn't an artist; he never has been. But I'd demanded he make a tile with me.

My thumb traces the three interlocking circles. A simple, two-toned design. Green background, applied unevenly, with the terracotta showing through in areas. Black circles drawn with the help of an empty can and pencil before the lines were inexpertly overlaid with black paint. His name is barely legible in the bottom corner beside the year.

When I'd seen his finished product, I'd been merciless. I think I called him a colorblind kindergartener. He'd just laughed and told me he hadn't wanted to do it in the first place. He really hadn't, but he'd done it anyway, turning down a boys' canoeing trip.

Jeremy, on the other hand, had never blindly acquiesced to my constant demands. The day the tiles were made, he'd chosen to go canoeing. But Lucas was always there. Always with me.

I blink dry eyes and glance up. "Why did you always do whatever I wanted?"

His eyes darken, deepen with memory or emotion. For a second, I feel like the world is about to rip in two. Then he shifts, relaxing, and gives me an easy smile.

"It was easier than the alternative. Temper tantrums for days."

I duck my head so he can't see my lack of smile. My aching uncertainty and fear. My thumb falls again to the circles. Three. Bound forever.

Tiles shift as Lucas resumes his task, removing and lining them up beside us until the box is empty, the tiles forming a square with one missing piece. He holds his hand out and I give him his tile, which he places in the open corner. It isn't until I scoot closer, wondering why he didn't give me mine, that I see it. Right beside his.

Nearly two decades later, I notice what I didn't then—he'd copied my color scheme. Mine is varying shades of green, with a bit of orange and blue, a depiction of leaves falling. The minimal background space was done in textured waves of black.

The past folds around me: Lucas standing beside me at one of the worktables, chatting and laughing with other kids while I concentrated. His voice a consistent playlist in the background of my life.

"Are you crying? Shit." Lucas leans forward, his hand cupping my shoulder. "Peapod! I'm sorry. I thought this would be a happy memory. I'll put them away."

I swipe a tear from my face, sniffing back the rest, and grab his hand as he's reaching for the tiles. He stills at my touch, and I snatch my hand back.

"No, it's a happy memory. Really. It's fine. Thanks for showing me these."

His worried eyes meet mine. "What's wrong, then?"

I shrug and choke out a laugh. "Just feelings. They happen." Wanting the forced intimacy to end, I lie, saying what I know will reset our boundaries. "I'm PMS'ing."

Expecting Lucas to react like his teenaged self had, with utter horror and immediate evacuation of the area, I'm wholly unprepared for his actual response. He leaps to his feet and grabs my arm, hauling me up with little effort.

"Come on, I have snacks in the trailer. You need chocolate."

Blindsided, I don't even react when his hand seizes mine, our fingers interlacing, or when he tugs me across the camp to the rectangular work trailer sitting past the Lodge. He finally lets me go as he enters first to open the blinds and crack a window. There's a folding table covered with papers, a single chair, and a tired-looking sleeping bag in the corner that I recognize as the same one he used when he was young.

The rest of the space holds camping equipment, all

decades old and obviously pilfered from his mom's garage. A single butane stove. Gallons of water. A cooler. Lantern. Tent still in its bag. Mixed in are grocery bags full of chips, pretzels, ramen, and candy.

"This is sad," I remark, craving a return to normalcy. My palm still burns where his was pressed against it. "I can't believe you were sleeping up here."

He laughs. "I lasted one night."

"Why the hell didn't you set up in one of the cabins? They probably have more insulation than this place."

He shudders comically. "Spiders."

I snort and walk to the back window, pulling up the blinds as he rummages through grocery bags for chocolate. I don't stop him—chocolate actually sounds heavenly at the moment.

My gaze roams the forest behind the Lodge. I can just see the glitter of the lake through the trees and the hint of a manmade structure in the distance.

"What's that building out there?"

Lucas appears beside me, leaning down to squint out the window. His breath warms my neck, raising goose bumps. Then he straightens and hands me a chocolate bar that just so happens to be my favorite. I unwrap the end and take a bite.

"Didn't you ever sneak over there at night?" he asks in surprise.

"No!" I say with affront. "You went without me? Rude."

He chuckles. "It's not that impressive, honestly. That's the original lake house where the owners lived before they built the camp. When they moved to Florida, the year-round caretaker lived there."

I look at the house again. "Why didn't you set up there? It has plumbing, right?"

"It does, but it's uninhabitable at the moment. A tree fell and took down half the roof."

"I bet the view is beautiful, though," I say as I munch on chocolate, lost in imagining a charming lake house with a private dock and a big porch, smoke piping from its chimney.

"It really is," he agrees, but when I glance at him, he's not looking out the window. Steady blue eyes are locked on my face.

My breath gets caught between a gasp and a laugh. I want to punch him, tell him how unbelievably cheesy and horrible that line is, but at the same time, heat captures my face and spirals downward, robbing me of my voice. Eyes wide, probably panicked, I fight to look away.

He finally breaks eye contact, glancing out the window. "You want to go see it?" His voice *sounds* normal, but his shoulders are tense.

I'm definitely curious about the house, but at the moment, I'd rather jump into the middle of the lake without a life jacket. Fight or flight kicks in again, and this time I don't hesitate, jerkily lifting my watch-encircled wrist.

"I need to pick up Damien from my parents soon. In fact, I should get going." My voice, unlike his, is high with anxiety. I back awkwardly toward the door. "Do you need me to help you clean up the tile?"

Lucas watches me with an unreadable look. "Nope. I got it."

"Thanks for the chocolate." I hold up the bar, waving with it.

A small frown puckers his brow. "Celeste—"

"Bye!"

Heart pounding, I flee to the Art Barn to collect my laptop bag and purse, then jog to my car. Thirty seconds later, I'm driving down the gravel road. Although I'm almost afraid to, I glance in the rearview at the trailer, expecting to find him watching me.

The doorway is empty.

24

Lucas

"MOM, DRINK SOME WATER, PLEASE."

She bats at my hand. "I don't want it. Stop badgering me."

Swallowing a sigh, I set the glass on the coffee table and collapse into the chair opposite the couch where my mom lies with an arm over her head. Pretty sure she's wearing the same thing she wore yesterday—a floral print pajama set and a silk robe with wine stains on the lapels.

It's three in the afternoon on Saturday and she's drunk. She was drunk yesterday, too, when I drove straight from Wild Lake to bring her dinner. I should have stayed the night, but she'd seemed okay when I left, having finished most of the food. Looking at her sallow face and frail limbs now, I wonder if she slept at all. If she's eaten anything today besides the ice cubes in her wine. If she gives a shit at all about the fact she's killing herself.

The buzzing of my phone snaps me from a downward

spiral. When I see the caller ID, I stand and head upstairs to my old bedroom, answering as I open the door.

"Michelle."

"Hey, big brother, sorry I didn't get back to you last night." She pauses. "Did the blood work results come in?"

I sit heavily on my old twin bed, hunching forward like I can protect myself from the memories—and pain—that happened within these walls. Like I can protect myself, too, from the words I have to speak and everything they mean.

"Yeah, they did. Yesterday afternoon."

Right after Celeste left Wild Lake, which in retrospect was either the worst or best timing possible. I wince as I remember the mess I made in the trailer as I vented my frustration on the folding table and chair.

From Michelle's silence, she knows—just as I did—what it means when a doctor calls within twenty-four hours of a test. Bad news.

"And?" she finally whispers.

"Not that it's a surprise, but she has all the indicators of chronic alcohol abuse." I clear my throat, allowing myself one more second before telling her the worst of it. "They'll need to biopsy her liver to confirm, but based on her symptoms and the blood test, she has second stage liver disease."

"What does that mean, exactly?" she demands.

I summon the voice of the doctor on the phone yesterday, his words precise, his tone surprisingly gentle. "Fatty liver is usually the first sign of long-term alcohol abuse. She's past that, with the beginnings of alcoholic hepatitis. If she keeps drinking, she'll get cirrhosis of the liver, which is irreversible and generally fatal."

It's also what killed our father.

My chest squeezes at the sound of my sister's soft sob. "Why?" she whispers. "Why is she doing this?"

"I don't think she has much of a choice at this point," I murmur, closing my burning eyes. "She's physically and mentally addicted. Her only chance to undo the damage is to stop drinking permanently and as soon as possible. And I don't think she can do it alone."

"How do we get her to rehab, though? An intervention? She'd laugh us out of the room. She won't even admit she has a problem!"

"If an intervention doesn't work, we'd have to go to court," I answer morosely. "Have her declared a danger to herself. That's the only way we can involuntarily commit her. But I'm not sure we can control where she'd go. It might be a state-run psychiatric hospital."

"Fuck," she hisses.

"Pretty much."

Michelle releases a harsh breath. "Did you tell her the results?"

"Not yet."

"Okay, okay. We'll do it together. I'm getting on a plane tonight. An intervention armed with the results might be our only chance of fixing this."

I don't say what I'm thinking: that there might be no way to fix what's wrong with our mother. I won't take away Michelle's hope, though, just like I'll never tell her the extent of what it was like being the sole focus of our father growing up. There isn't much I can do to protect my little sister now that we're grown, but I can do this much.

"Before you book a ticket, maybe we should talk to Aunt Kathy, Aunt Claire, and Uncle Justin? See if they'd come? If we're doing this, let's to it the right way."

"Yes, of course. Good idea." There's a long silence. "Aren't you angry? I'm so angry at her."

Emotion clogs my throat. "Yeah," I admit. "I am, Michelle. Sometimes I can't even look at her. Or I have to leave the room because I'm disgusted. Sometimes it takes everything I have not to unload on her. Blame her. Hate her for all the times she failed."

I hear my sister's soft sob through the line, and I know she understands. Feels the same way. There's something deeply disturbing and uniquely painful about acknowledging the humanness of your parent. Especially a mother who repeatedly chose her own needs and those of her abusive husband over us. And who also tended our wounds, sang us to sleep, hung our bad school art on the fridge, and comforted us when we were sick.

Whoever said love and hate can't coexist never experienced what we have.

"I hate her, too," Michelle says finally. "And I love her and don't want her to die. So this is it, then? She's going to kill herself or we're going to stop her?"

My heart squeezes. "No, baby sister," I say firmly. "It's not on us. Not on you or me or anyone. This is between our mom and whatever demons live inside her. All we can do is try to be heard, to let her know she's loved and that we'll support her if she wants to pick a different path. It's up to *her*. Remember that."

She exhales a tired laugh. "How'd you get so wise?"

I snort. "Hardly wise. I've just done a lot of Google searches on how to deal with an alcoholic parent."

"I'm sorry," she says mutedly, "that you've been dealing with this—with her—alone."

Her guilt echoes and magnifies mine. We both left Sun River as soon as we could and barely looked back—our reasons different and yet the same at their core. And now we feel like we failed our mom by not being more present for her after our dad died. For allowing our anger over our father's treatment of her and us to keep us away, to keep our emotional guards up so high we didn't recognize the signs of her deterioration.

"I'm not alone," I tell her. "You've been with me every step of the way. We'll get through this. It's not too late."

"But there are no guarantees," she murmurs.

"No," I admit sadly. "But there are no guarantees for anything. Life is messy and complicated. People are the same. All we have to do is our best. To try to do what's right."

To my relief, she issues a tired giggle. "Again with the Yoda vibe, Lucy. You're ruining my impression of you."

"Very funny, Michael." But I'm smiling. "Let me know what everyone says?"

"Will do. I'll call them now."

I SPEND the rest of the afternoon cleaning the kitchen, changing the sheets on my mom's bed, doing laundry for her, and ordering groceries she probably won't eat.

I stare too long at the wine in the pantry, the box of it in the fridge, battling the instinct to pour it all down the sink and hide her car keys. It wouldn't matter. She'd find a way. Either she'd order a delivery on her phone or walk to the liquor store.

So I leave her booze alone.

Mom wakes up around six. I coerce her into eating grilled cheese and tomato soup and drinking a full glass of water. She's subdued, bleary-eyed, and for once has an appetite.

By the time I take our plates to the kitchen, though, that familiar, restless energy is building inside her. Stopping on the threshold of the living room, I notice the fine tremor in her hands.

Pity surges through me, followed by a spark of resentment, then guilt. All the research I've done has been pretty clear on one count: her compulsion is outside of her power to control at this point.

She may not want to drink. She may hate herself for it. But her addiction owns her body and brain.

"You can go, Lucas," she says, not meeting my stare.

"Why don't you take a shower?" I ask, hoping to redirect her. "Then I'll make popcorn and we can watch a movie."

Her face flushes, angry eyes snapping to mine. "You seem to be confused about who the parent is. I don't need your help."

Even though I'd expected a reaction along those lines, it burns. The helplessness. The anger. Why am I even trying to help this woman who turned a blind eye to my father's beatings? Who took him back when he pushed her down the stairs, breaking her damn leg? What sick, small part of me still believes she can be someone she isn't? A loving mother who protects her children.

I want to unload all my vitriol on her shoulders. Instead, I clench my teeth so hard pain spikes through my jaw. "Fine. I'll be back in the morning."

I head for the front door, but her voice stops me. "Why did you even come back here?" she demands. "I know it wasn't for me. It's that Miller girl, isn't it?" Her chuckle is sharp and grating. "She marries your best friend but still has you wrapped around her little finger. You think she's going to love you? Marry you now and have your kids? She pities you. It's pathetic. Your father would be ashamed of the man you've become."

Each syllable is a blow that echoes against old scars and healed bruises. It isn't the first time she's said these things, but it's the first time since realizing what Celeste means to me. The first time I don't have a layer of apathy to protect me.

My stomach knots with the need to lash out. Rage tunnels my vision, electrifying in its potential—and so utterly terrifying it instantly drains from my body. I gulp in air, release my white-knuckled grip on the doorframe, and walk slowly to the front door. Grab my keys. Close the door without slamming it. Walk to my car.

"Lucas?"

Her voice, coming from her parents' front yard, makes me flinch. Cuts me deep. Long, riotous blond hair and a concerned expression in my peripheral. I keep walking. I can't, *can't* see her right now.

"Hey! Are you okay?"

She's moving closer. I move faster, unlocking my car and all but jumping inside. I fumble with my keys, finally getting them in the ignition. I back out without looking, them slam on the brakes as a car honks.

Fuck. Keep it together.

My breath hisses through my teeth, which I can't seem to unclench. Celeste is at the end of the driveway, her eyes huge and worried.

I check all my mirrors, then reverse carefully into the street and drive away. Two miles below the speed limit. Extra-long stops at stop signs. Careful and safe.

Inside, I'm a dying star. Imploding into nothing.

25

Celeste

SOMETHING IS VERY wrong with Lucas.

I watch his taillights disappear around the corner, then glance back at his mom's house. The soles of my feet prickle. My chest tightens.

I recognized the look on his face, though seeing it on a grown man somehow hits differently. She hurt him. Not physically. No, this was worse than a punch or a kick.

Before I fully realize what I'm doing, I'm pounding on Mrs. Adler's front door. I give her ten seconds to answer, then twist the knob and walk inside.

She's leaving the kitchen and jerks to a stop when she sees me. "What the hell are you doing here?" The wine glass in her hand shakes. Red drops splatter onto her robe. "Get out!"

"What did you say to him?" I demand. I don't even recognize my voice, dark and snarly.

She wobbles precariously. Her face shines with sweat and her eyes are glassy, feverish.

"Get out or I'll call the police!" she screeches.

"Do it," I growl. "I'll be happy to tell them I heard a crash inside the house and came to check on you, only to find you drunk as a skunk and getting ready to drive somewhere. How does a night in a cell sound? Who do you think they'll believe, Linda?"

The color flees her face. I honestly don't know if it's from the threat or the fact I called her by her first name.

"You'll never be good enough for him!" she screams. "Uneducated and crude. The worst type of woman! You made my son chase you all those years, then you married his best friend. You ruined him!"

My jaw drops. She sways precariously, then sags against the wall. All at once, I realize how stupid this is. *Rearranging deck chairs on the Titanic.* Lucas's mom isn't who I want to be in the same room with, no matter how much I'd like to throttle her.

I take a breath, fighting for calm. "I feel sorry for you," I tell her evenly. "You're a lonely, sad person."

Her eyes close. "So is my son," she mumbles. "Because of you."

I back away, my skin prickling, and make a beeline for the front door. I slam it behind me. Outside, I lean forward, hands on my knees, and take deep breaths until the urge to scream at the sky fades.

When I straighten, I see my dad standing on the other side of the short fence. By the expression on his face, I know he heard what Mrs. Adler screamed at me. The whole neighborhood likely heard.

I swallow until I find my voice. "I have to go."

He nods. "Damien and your mom are starting a movie. If you're not back by the time it's over, we'll get him sorted in your old bedroom."

"Thanks, Dad."

"LUCAS! OPEN THE DAMN DOOR!"

He's not answering my calls or texts, but I know he's here. His car is in the driveway. There's a light on upstairs.

My hand hurts from pounding on the thick wood of his rental's front door. There's a doorbell, but it doesn't make any sound that I can hear, and the fence around the property is too high to climb without risking serious injury.

Giving my hand a break, I kick the front door repeatedly with my sneakered toe, jabbing the doorbell with one hand while I call him with the other.

When the front door suddenly jerks open, I'm mid-kick. I freeze, phone extended in one hand, finger of my other hand jammed on the doorbell—which, incidentally, does work. I can hear a continuous, soft chime coming from the back of the house.

Lucas gapes at me. "What are you doing?"

He's wearing sweatpants that ride low on his hips. No shirt. His hair is damp and disheveled. My brain, suddenly sluggish, puts the images together and concludes he was in the shower.

For a few beats too long, I stare at the deep divots of muscle bracketing a trail of dense gold hair that disappears into his waistband. Then I wrench my gaze to his face.

"I came to check on you."

My voice is breathless; his eyes narrow, scanning my face, no doubt registering my burning cheeks.

He takes a shallow breath and a half-step backward. "I'm fine." After a moment's pause, he adds, "This isn't a good time."

To my shock, he starts to close the door. I dart forward, blocking the swing with my shoulder. "No way. Don't shut me out. That was the rule. When hard shit happens, we tell each other the truth."

His jaw hardens. "We're not kids anymore, Celeste. I don't need to cry on your shoulder."

I flinch but don't back down. "What did she say to you?"

"It's not important."

"Like hell it's not."

Shoving past him, I plant my feet and cross my arms over my chest. With a sigh and a shake of his head, he closes the door.

I should feel some sense of victory, but all I feel is unsteady. The fierce protectiveness I felt when he walked out of his mom's house tonight—wearing that eerily familiar, brave mask—hasn't faded. Even though I know he's right, and we aren't kids anymore. But I can't help what I feel.

Since that first night in my parents' backyard, when he opened up to me about what it was like in his house, I've cared.

When he doesn't say anything, just watches me with jaded blue eyes, I bite my lip. "I, uh, told her off. After you left."

His brows skyrocket. "What?"

I wince. "Not my finest moment."

Humor flares in his eyes, then fizzles. "Why are you really here? I don't need a cheerleader anymore, someone to tell me my mom sucks and I'm awesome." He points at his chest. "Grown man, in case you hadn't noticed."

"Literally impossible not to notice," I mutter, then screw my eyes shut like I can teleport myself away. "Forget I said that."

"Nope." There's a smile in his deep, silken voice.

My eyes snap open to find him a step closer, staring at me with an intensity that turns my insides to jelly.

"Lucas?" I whisper, either a plea or denial.

"Why did you come?" he asks again, but there's too much golden skin filling up my vision and too many *muscles* everywhere and my brain isn't working.

I shake my head helplessly. "I-I don't..." Words fade on a sigh as something inside me, some tension or angst or maybe denial itself, disintegrates. And I know why I followed him. Why I'm here. There's no point fighting it.

I want him. Innately. Undeniably. With every fiber of my being.

Connected as we've always been, a new awareness blooms in Lucas's eyes. His jaw tenses, his gaze so vivid and concentrated that I tremble a little. My gaze flickers across his chest, broad shoulders, trim waist. My fingers burn with the need to touch him. My cheeks and chest flame with heat, my pulse patters fast, and my breath comes short and shallow.

"Celeste." My name isn't a question anymore—my face and darting eyes have already revealed my secrets.

He takes two steps forward, close enough that I can feel the heat of his body on mine, feel the ephemeral cord that connects us grow heavy and taut.

Blood beats a thick, demanding cadence between my thighs. *Is this really happening?* The errant thought comes and goes, whisked away by the all-consuming present.

His eyes scan mine, expression unreadable to anyone who hasn't known him a lifetime. But I have, and so I see the need held in check by iron will. The uncertainty, too.

The beautiful eyes I've loved and loathed in turn drop to my mouth. "This is your choice," he murmurs, the gravelly words clenching muscles low in my body.

My skin twitches and tightens in anticipation and maybe a little fear. There's still rationality somewhere inside me. Enough to know that this will change everything.

But I can't seem to care.

My hand lifts and presses to his warm chest over his

heart. His tall frame shudders, his eyes burning brighter, the blue searing. My chin lifts at the same time his head lowers, and our kiss feels like the first and last, a mingling of our breath and souls.

The gravity of it is too much, almost physically painful, so I do the only thing I can think of and close the final distance between us. The moment my breasts brush his chest, his restraint snaps.

One hand anchored in my hair, he tilts my face for a better angle. Our kiss turns deep and hungry, an artless frenzy of teeth and tongue.

Overwhelmed by the sensory onslaught, my knees weaken. Powerful arms wrap around my waist, supporting me and sealing our bodies. The thick, hard line of his arousal presses into my stomach. Sensation jolts through my core, quick and almost violent as my body cries out for him.

The kiss softens, his tongue flicking against my top lip followed by a gentle nip of teeth, then his mouth drags across my cheek. Hot breath fans my ear, making me shiver, and he rains kisses beneath my ear and down my neck.

His arms loosen, hands flowing up my back, down and across my stomach before grazing and cupping my breasts. I gasp, my nipples tightening to tender points.

Lucas stills, his mouth lifting from my neck. My eyelids flutter open to find him gazing down at his hands like they belong to someone else. He squeezes my breasts gently together, thumbs brushing across the peaks. The friction makes my breath catch.

Warmth cascades through me and his erection, tucked tight against my stomach, hardens to steel. My own hips jerk forward instinctively, that yawning ache inside me intensifying.

"Breast man, huh?" I manage.

A wicked grin curls his lips as his eyes lift to mine. "Just these breasts. Give me a second to live out my favorite teenage shower fantasy."

The words trigger another flood of heat at my core. The thought of a seventeen-year-old Lucas fantasizing about my breasts is weirdly, excessively erotic.

"You wanted me," I whisper, almost disbelievingly.

With a final squeeze, his hands leave my chest. I almost moan at the loss, but then he clasps my neck, gripping tenderly as he lifts my face toward his. His eyes are stark with desire, simmering with an emotion that makes my breath catch.

"I've wanted you since the summer before sophomore year. Probably before then, if I'm honest, but that's when I started having to jack off every morning before seeing you or risk sporting wood all day."

My laugh is soundless, a rough exhale tinged with an unexpected bite of pain. I can't help but remember that last summer at camp, our single, stolen kiss and the searing burn of his rejection the following morning.

My gaze lowers. I bite my lip, a pang of old hurt curling through me. "You sure hid it well."

"Hey. Look at me." I do, and his eyes scan mine, his chest heaving on a deep breath. "Whatever you may think, I've *never* not wanted you, and what I felt then is nothing to what I feel now. A match flame to a forest fire. Hate me tomorrow, Celeste, but give me tonight. I don't deserve it, but I'm still asking. *Please*."

The last word is a whisper. A plea wrenched from a dark, lonely place inside him that mirrors the same place inside me: the echoing cavity left by his absence in my life.

The past melts away in the heat of the moment, the tension in his body, the flickering need in his eyes, the spasms of his fingers on my neck and in my hair.

I touch his face as I've always, *always* longed to, tracing his temples and cheekbones, the sharp line of his jaw, and finally dragging my fingers across his lips. Going to my tiptoes, I press a soft kiss to that beautiful mouth.

"Yes."

26

Celeste

HE GUIDES me by the hand. Down the hall, up shadowed stairs, and into a dim bedroom. The only light comes from the bathroom, the door half-closed. A gentle glow reaches the bed.

I swallow hard, my heart drumming with anticipation and sudden nerves. I've only been with three people in my life, and two of them were mistakes. Lucas, on the other hand, exudes that particular magnetism of a man experienced in the bedroom.

He doesn't flaunt it. I know he'd never brag about it. But... us women just know.

"Come here," he murmurs, tugging me the final few steps to the bed. He sits on the edge and draws me between his legs, his hands clasping my hips as mine fall naturally to his shoulders.

Then he looks up at me and smiles—a subtle curve of lips that makes my stomach flip.

"The thought of you at my mercy is"—he sucks air through his teeth, then blows out hard—"almost enough to make me nut right now. But if you want to be the boss, I'll let you. Fuck, you can do whatever you want to me and I'll love every second."

My voice, it seems, was left downstairs with my shoes. All I can do is make a small, pitiful sound. His smile widens, those enchanting eyes on my face even as his thumbs begin tracing circles on my hipbones. My cotton pants might as well be invisible, my body so sensitized it feels like he's touching bare skin.

"Does that mean you want me to be in charge?" he asks.

There's so much tension beneath my hands, his shoulders rock hard in stark contrast to his fingers, which remain gentle.

"Nod or shake your head, Peapod."

Maybe it's the use of my nickname that does it—a reminder that this is Lucas—but my inhibitions fly out the proverbial window.

I nod, sharp and graceless.

Some of the tension in him eases, his head bowing toward my chest. A warm kiss presses between my breasts. Farther south, his fingers deftly untie the drawstring of my pants. With little fanfare, he tugs the material over my hips and sends it to the floor.

"Well, isn't this a lovely surprise."

His gravelly voice sends a bolt of heat straight to where he's looking: at the flimsy, bright red, lacy underwear cradling my sex. His gaze flashes up, so full of desire, of all the things he wants to do to me, that my thighs squeeze together helplessly. He notices, of course, and to my immediate horror, his head lowers again toward my belly, and he drags in a heavy breath through his nose.

"Fuck, you smell divine."

Sweet God.

I'm trembling in earnest now, my knees liquid. "Lucas," I whisper with strain. "Enough foreplay."

He chuckles, soft and dark. "Nice try. No way I'm rushing this. You can kiss me, though, while I play with you."

Fingers splayed over my pelvis, his thumbs trace across the front of my panties. I jerk forward, seeking, but he evades touching me where I want him.

When his head lifts, I take out my frustration by slamming my mouth to his. I can taste his surprise and pleasure as I devour him like he devoured me downstairs. And then he's *right there*, his thumbs dipping down, tracing the borders of the soaked lace between my legs.

I gasp, the seal of our mouths breaking just as a finger dips beneath the lace and drags through my wetness.

"All this for me?" he murmurs, spiraling a finger at the opening of my body, spreading me with a sound that makes me blush furiously. It's not enough—not nearly enough. I drive my body down, wanting penetration.

His finger retreats. "Uh-uh."

My growl is lost in his mouth. He nips at my lips, then leans back. A second later, my shirt is pulled over my head and tossed to the floor. A second after that, rough fingers tug my bra cups down. There's a pause, a swiftly drawn breath, then his mouth descends to one nipple as his hand covers the other.

I clutch his head to my chest, panting as his tongue circles and flicks the sensitive skin, squirming at the pinch of his teeth. He cups my breasts together, raining kisses over them, tasting and sucking them into his mouth.

Never in my entire life did I imagine I could orgasm simply from someone fondling my breasts. But I'm close, my core fluttering, swollen and primed for release.

"I'm going to fuck these someday." I've barely registered the words before he shifts, grabbing me and flipping me onto the bed. I land on my back, his arms caging me.

I've had enough. I yank his sweatpants over his hips, kicking them down his legs, my hands diving for what I want. He grunts as I fill my hands with him, tugging the soft skin forward and back, swirling one palm over the blunt, flared head.

Much like every other girl in high school who stalked his swim meets, I've seen him in a speedo. I always had some idea of what he packed in his pants. But the reality far exceeds my expectations. He feels fucking incredible, and I already know having him inside me will wreck me.

"Naughty woman," he whispers. "You'd better stop before I come all over your stomach."

I stop immediately, which results in a soft chuckle.

"Lucas." I don't even care that my voice is a pitiful whine. "Please."

"Not yet."

With little effort, he shifts my body up on the bed while he stays where he is. Hot breath fans over my stomach before his lips touch down, mouth and tongue trekking across my abdomen. I squirm, abruptly self-conscious. The skin on my belly isn't as firm as it used to be, and it's patterned with stretch marks. I push at his head, but he grabs my hands and plants them on either side of me.

"Don't," he says, gaze lifting to mine. "You're perfect. Any man who made you feel otherwise should be castrated."

He doesn't wait for a reply—not that I have one—before licking a path down to my panties. My wrists are released. My underwear is tugged from my hips. He lowers to his knees on the floor and grabs my legs, sliding me toward his mouth like he's starving and I'm a banquet.

There's no time for me to prepare, either emotionally or physically, before his mouth covers me. His tongue spears my center before retreating to circle around my clit. A finger dives inside me, tugging downward, a knuckle curling against a spot that presses a scream against my teeth.

Three swipes of his tongue. That's all it takes before I'm bucking against his mouth, chanting his name as a universe explodes behind my eyelids.

27

Lucas

CELESTE in the throes of an orgasm is hands down the most exquisite sight I've ever beheld. That I'm the one who caused it fills me with searing pride.

She pants, boneless, legs splayed and one arm thrown over her face, and barely twitches as I pull my finger carefully from her pussy and lick the taste of her from my lips.

God, she's perfect.

My cock jerks impatiently as I crawl over her and plant a soft kiss on her mouth. She comes alive beneath me, her arms encircling my neck, her eyes opening, afire with want. Her hips buck against mine, and a grin overtakes my mouth at her impatience.

"I'm perfectly happy stopping now," I lie, peppering kisses across her nose and cheek. "Unless…"

She growls, fierce hands gripping my biceps. Her teeth

clamp on my lower lip, leaving behind a sting as she says the magic word, "More."

Savage need sparks inside me. My mind blanks of everything but the consuming desire to fill her body with mine. Scooping up one of her legs, I shift until the head of my cock meets the wet heat of her center. *Fuck.* Even the merest contact makes my balls hard and tight.

I sink inside her one inch, then two, so slowly, and the deepest, most male part of me revels in how her body reacts as she stretches to accommodate me.

She feels glorious. Made for me. So hot, clenching me so tightly I have little hope for lasting more than a few minutes. Gathering the shreds of my patience, I wait until the tiny frown on her brow smooths, until her body relaxes and her fingers clench urgently on my shoulders.

"God, Celeste. You feel…" I shake my head helplessly. "Like everything I've ever wanted all at once."

Breath pants from her lips, her eyes wide and crazed with desire. With utmost care, I draw back, then sink inside her again. Deeper this time. I stop when she winces.

"Oh, fuck," she whispers. "Tell me that's all of it."

My ego swells even as a breathless laugh leaves me. My forehead drops to hers. "Not quite."

A soft whine leaves her throat. "Seriously?"

A grin still curling my lips, I give an experimental roll of my hips. Celeste gasps, then moans, the sound tingling down my spine and straight to my groin. Her sudden spike of arousal sends warmth gushing around my cock. I lose the fight, my body jerking forward to claim every last inch she has to give. Her back arches off the bed, nipples grazing my chest, a cry in her throat.

I kiss her forehead, her cheeks, and finally her open mouth. My tongue drags against hers as I suck down her little gasps. And when her hips do their own little swivel, her pussy fluttering around me, it's all over.

I make love to her like I've always dreamed of doing, with everything in me. Everything I have to give.

She's a storm beneath me. Writhing and meeting me thrust for thrust. Every time she whispers my name, it feels surreal. Like a dream. Like this can't possibly be happening.

But it is.

Then she stiffens, whimpering and trembling, big, surprised eyes staring into mine as her pussy clamps down and pulses around me. A strained mewl escapes her.

"Fuck yes," I growl, losing what little restraint I was hanging on to. I thrust once, twice. Fireworks ignite behind my eyes, blazing a path down my spine. A tidal wave of sensation slams into me and detonates at the place we're joined.

I have no idea what comes out of my mouth—I only dimly hope it isn't the words on repeat in my head. Lowering my face, I suck her tongue into my mouth. The kiss is sloppy and perfect. And for a few seconds, there's nothing in the world that's wrong. Everything is exactly as it should be.

Then, as I knew it would, something dark and painful crosses Celeste's face. Guilt or regret or something equally fanged. Whatever it is, it launches like a serpent into my chest, slithering and tightening around my heart.

I pull out of her—probably too fast, as she gasps—and roll onto my back at her side. Before she can move away like I know she wants to, I roll again, trapping her with an arm over her stomach. I nuzzle her shoulder, kissing the sweat-damp skin, and send a silent prayer into the uncaring sky.

"Please," I whisper. "Just a few more minutes."

Her breath is short and choppy, her body growing stiffer by the second. That coil around my chest tightens again, nearly cutting off my air.

"We didn't use a condom," she gasps, her head whipping toward mine, eyes wide with horror.

Horror.

I swallow hard, my limbs turning as stiff as hers. "I got a vasectomy three years ago, and I'm clean. I'm sorry I didn't say anything. I'm—I got carried away."

Shifting back, I sit up, swinging my feet to the floor. As my fingers trail down her leg and off her body, I wonder if I'll ever get to touch her again.

Fabric rustles as she sits up. "Not your fault. Seriously. I'm equally responsible. I, uh… don't have any STDs, either."

Glancing over my shoulder, I see her sitting with her back to me, legs off the adjacent side of the mattress. I can't decipher any emotion in her voice, which only hurts more. It's detached. Empty.

Anything else would be preferable, even her screaming and crying.

But I knew. As much as some small part of me hoped this would end differently, I knew what I was getting myself into.

"Do you"—I swallow the lump in my throat—"want to stay?"

She's still for a moment, then shakes her head. "Damien is at my parents' house. I need to go."

"Okay."

I'm not good enough at hiding the emotion behind the word because she suddenly spins toward me, golden hair rioting over her shoulders and around her breasts. She's so beautiful, so fucking perfect and *not mine*, that I flinch.

"Lucas," she starts.

I hold up a hand and look away, unable to stand the apology in her eyes. "Don't. It's okay. We both know that was a long time coming. It doesn't have to be more than an itch we scratched."

I think I'm giving her an out—doing the right thing—but instead, *she* flinches.

That tidal wave rises again, but instead of promising bliss, it's poised to deliver extinction.

"Celeste—"

"No, you're right." She smiles, brave and false. "That was great." She gives a little laugh. "Thanks."

I almost throw up in my mouth. Before I can think of something to say to fix this, she lurches off the bed, grabs her clothes, and disappears into the bathroom.

I'm still sitting on the bed, elbows on my knees, head in my hands, the scent of us all around me, when the door opens and she reappears fully clothed.

She breaks the strained silence. "I'm sorry I can't…" Her voice trails off, but the intended continuation of her thought floats between us for a moment before falling like lead to the floor.

Be what you want.

Love you back.

And I realize with a sucking, sinking feeling that she heard the words that escaped as I climaxed inside her.

Three damning words.

"I'm sorry," she whispers, and then she's gone.

28

Celeste

"MOM? ARE YOU OKAY?"

I close the photo album in my lap and hurriedly wipe my wet cheeks. "Y-yes. Fine. Hungry for lunch?"

My son's eyes narrow, a familiar expression of exasperation on his face. Sighing, he crosses my bedroom to plop onto the edge of my bed.

"You're such a bad liar." His gaze falls to the album still perched on my knees. "Dad?"

Before I can respond, he grabs the album and opens it. Frozen, I can only watch as he flips through the pages, his eyes reflecting first surprise, then curiosity. The ancient plastic sleeves crinkle under his fingers as he takes in the series of photos I haven't looked at since before he was born.

"He seems like a nice guy," Damien says at last, lingering over a photo of Lucas and me sitting at the edge of my parents' roof. We're grinning, a bright orange sky behind us. My mom had taken the photo.

"You guys were super close." Damien's eyes meet mine. "What happened? Did you and Dad have a fight with him or something?"

I clear my throat, wishing I could sink into the mattress and disappear. "Nothing like that. We just grew apart, and when your dad died, Lucas, uh... it was hard for him to see me. Us."

Damien's gaze shifts to another photo. Lucas at sixteen, sitting on a crowded couch at a house party, a plastic cup balanced on his knee. His hair was longer then, flopping into his eyes. He's not quite smiling in the shot, but there's a soft look in his eyes as he stares straight at the camera.

At me.

"You know I'm not stupid, right, Mom?" asks Damien softly.

I blink at him, my throat squeezing as my stomach drops. "Of course I know that! What are you talking about?"

My son. My beautiful, smart-as-hell son, watches me with his father's dark eyes. I brace myself for his condemnation, but he only sighs and closes the album. Standing, he walks toward the door.

A million words press to my teeth, but none emerge.

Pausing in the doorway, he looks back. "I didn't know my dad, but from everything everyone's told me about him..." His head hangs for a moment, then lifts. "You're allowed to be happy again, Mom. He'd want that."

My breath stills.

"I'm gonna make a sandwich and meet the guys for a skate sesh in a bit." His gaze darts away and a flush blooms on his cheeks. "Then, uh, Daphne wants me to come over and watch a movie. Can you drop me off at Rose House? Around five?"

I nod numbly.

He smiles. "Thanks." As he heads into the hallway, he throws back, "I'll make a sandwich for you, too. Eat it!"

When I hear the fridge door open, I snatch my phone off its charger and call Zoey. She answers on the second ring.

"Let me guess," she drawls, "Damien asked if he could come over tonight."

I can't help but laugh. "Ethan's okay with this?"

"I mean, does he *like* it? No. If it was anyone but Damien, I'm sure he'd be blowing a gasket."

I settle back onto my pillows, my grin faltering as the shift wakes up soreness I'd rather pretend didn't exist.

"So, is this a date? What did Daphne say? She's so awesome—I never would have had the nerve to ask a boy out at her age, much less invite him to my house."

Zoey laughs. "She's more confident than we were, that's for sure. As for a date, I think it's more of a *hangout*, whatever that means. Nothing official. She wanted us to drop her off at the movie theater, but Ethan put an axe to that idea. I made him swear that we'll give them space tonight, though."

Feeling lighter than I have all day, I giggle. "This is amazing."

"It is, isn't it?" she gushes. "You should just stay after bringing Damien. Have dinner with Ethan and me." Her voice drops to a conspiratorial murmur. "We can spy on the kids."

I groan. "Damien would murder me."

"Then at least do something fun. Is Lucas free? You can have dinner over there and I can text you updates."

My stomach rolls and drops. "Yeah, that's not gonna happen."

Zoey's quiet for a beat, then whisper-hisses, "I saw your car over there last night. What happened? Tell me right now, woman. Did you guys kiss?"

I pull the phone from my ear, listening until I hear Damien closing a cupboard in the kitchen. Then I sigh and admit, "It was way more than a kiss."

I wince at the screech that comes through the phone, then smother a laugh as Zoey coughs and forcefully sobers. "Are you okay?" she asks carefully.

"Yeah." Then I whisper, "Not really."

"Oh, Celeste." Her concern drips through the line. "Do I need to buy a shovel?"

I snort. "You own ten shovels. But no. There won't be a body to dispose of. He was… it was…"

Amazing. Perfect. The most intense sexual experience I've ever had.

Until he whispered those words in my ear. Until I freaked out. Until guilt and shame and self-loathing swallowed me, smothering every ounce of pleasure his touch had brought.

"I don't need details," Zoey says softly, "but I'm here if you need someone to listen."

"Damien suspects there's something going on," I blurt. "He saw me crying and looking at old photos of Lucas. He told me Jeremy would want me to be happy."

Zoey's silent for so long I check the phone to see if our call dropped. Then she says, "That's the problem, isn't it? No matter how many people tell us we deserve happiness, no matter how many times they say it or how sincere they are, it means nothing until we think we deserve it ourselves."

Fresh tears spring to my eyes. "I feel like I betrayed Jeremy," I whisper, my eyes on the empty doorway. "I can't explain it, but I'm sick about it. I've never felt this way before, after... you know. But with Lucas, it's so different. How could I do that to Jeremy? I know it's stupid, but I can't stop thinking it."

I don't tell her the worst part. That with Lucas, I forgot. I *forgot* Jeremy. There was only him and the way he made my body sing. The way he'd felt—so right—and the way I'd felt in his arms. Treasured and safe, and so, so wanted.

A small part of me can admit that when Jeremy and I were together, we were young. Still kids, really. Inexperienced and fumbling, still learning what the other liked. Whatever awkwardness we had was always made up for by the love we bore for each other.

Comparing the two men is absolutely pointless and

serves no one. But unfortunately, my heart doesn't give a shit what my logic center knows, preferring instead to burn with guilt for enjoying last night so much.

"It's not stupid," Zoey says gently. "You didn't choose to be a widow so young, Celeste. And it was sudden. There was no closure, no preparation or a slow goodbye—not that those scenarios are any less painful, but they're different. Be gentle with yourself. And please remember that falling in love with Jeremy, marrying him, being happy with him... it didn't erase the bond you had with Lucas."

I stiffen. "I hope you're not suggesting—"

"I'm not," she says quickly. "I know you were madly in love with Jeremy. It was obvious to everyone, even in high school. But Jeremy and Lucas are very different men, and the history you have with Lucas didn't magically go away when you fell in love with Jeremy. All I'm saying is that you shouldn't beat yourself up."

My breath sounds harsh in my ears. "I hear you," I finally say. "But I don't know... I can't—"

Damien fills the doorway. "Mom, I'm heading out." His eyes narrow. "Eat the sandwich I left you."

I smile faintly. "When did you get so bossy?"

He smirks. "You made me this way. I'll be home in a few hours."

He disappears, and I hear the front door open and close.

"Celeste?" asks Zoey.

"Yeah?"

"Letting go of the past isn't something that happens

overnight. It's a long process of rewiring the brain with new—and oftentimes uncomfortable—thoughts."

"Whoa, am I talking to Zoey or Alana?" I quip, referring to her psychologist mother.

She doesn't laugh, though. "Do something for me."

"What?" I ask warily.

"The next time your thoughts go to a dark place, I want you to tell yourself what everyone has been saying for years. That you deserve to be happy. That you deserve love."

I scoff even as my heart squeezes. "I don't think—"

"This isn't about Lucas," she says sternly, correctly guessing where my head went. "This is about you. I'm not saying jump into a fling with Lucas. I wouldn't even blame you if you wanted to quit working at Wild Lake just to get space from him. But I'm your best friend, so I'm not going to bullshit you. You deserve love. Chemistry. Happiness. And mind-blowing sex."

I take a deep breath. What feels like the first one in hours. "Thanks, Zoey."

"Always." Then her voice drops. "I'm sorry, I know I said I didn't need details, but I have to at least ask—how was it?"

I laugh through a squeeze of pain. "Mind-blowing."

29

Celeste

THE WATER of the lake is cold on my toes, the sun warm on my back as I sit on my folded sweatshirt on the rocky shore of the beach.

I've been in the same spot since just before eight this morning. It's nearing ten now. Past the trees behind me, there are sounds of saws and hammers as the porch outside the dining hall is replaced. Truck engines growl, beeping as they reverse. I think Billy's team is also clearing and leveling the ground for the new volleyball and basketball courts today, but I can't remember. Maybe it's the additional bathrooms? Or possibly both.

I haven't checked my phone calendar. Or my laptop, which sits untouched in my bag by the tree line. Frankly, I don't even know what I'm doing here. I should be working from home, filling the final interview slots for this week. It's too loud and distracting on the property for phone calls.

But I drove here anyway, right after dropping Damien off for his first day of soccer camp at the high school. I think some part of me longed for the old magic of the lake that made things clearer when I was near it. Magic that used to settle and soothe.

Magic that died a long time ago, if my current state is anything to judge by. My thoughts haven't been soothed, and they certainly aren't pleasant.

Well, most of them aren't. There are a few that shimmer with light. Sparkles of brightness in a knotted mess of dark memory yarn—like the unguarded happiness on my son's face when Daphne answered the door last night to welcome him in.

I didn't stay at Rose House after dropping him off, and I didn't go over to Lucas's, even though his car was in the driveway and my traitorous body screamed for him.

Instead, I went home, took a bath, read a book, and pretended nothing was wrong. That I didn't still feel him with every step and movement. That I wasn't sucker punched with flashbacks every time I closed my eyes.

His scent and his body inside mine. The flex of his arms, his hips. The strokes of his hands. The look in his eyes. His tongue in my mouth, on my breasts, between my legs. His sheer masculine power. His vulnerability.

"I've never not wanted you."

"Hate me tomorrow, but give me tonight."

"You feel like everything I've ever wanted all at once."

And the words he whispered as he pulsed and filled me. Words I can't escape, that have burrowed under my skin where they spark and smolder with every breath I take.

"I love you."

He didn't mean to say them. I know that much. But I have no idea what to do with the information. Was it real? Or just manufactured by the moment, by our intimacy and long history? Did it even mean anything? Why?

Why did he fucking say that to me?

He can't be in love with me.

He just can't.

I didn't tell Zoey, just like I never told her the details of how Lucas and I parted after Jeremy's funeral, what he said then in his rage and grief. It doesn't feel important now. Nothing feels important but those three words.

Words I can't fathom. Don't understand. Words I can't tell my best friend because I can't even admit to myself what I'm feeling.

He didn't mean to tell me he loved me. It was reflex. An accident.

"We both know that was a long time coming. It doesn't have to be more than an itch we scratched."

Which words do I believe?

"Hey."

His voice comes from behind me, carefully void of emotion. It still hits me like a physical jolt, whipping my head around and shortening my breath. If he notices the heat I feel blazing in my face, he doesn't say anything.

His eyes lift to the water. "I thought you were working from home today with all the construction going on?"

My tongue is stuck to the roof of my mouth. Pebbles shift as he moves nearer to me. Eddies of time swirl and tighten between us as he lowers to his heels a few feet away. He picks up a pebble and tosses it into the water.

I don't want to look at him, but I make myself. Mussed hair. Unshaven jaw. Pinched mouth. Furrowed brow and shadows beneath his downcast eyes. They're not seeing anything, though. Their blue is disturbingly flat.

And suddenly my inner freakout doesn't matter. Every horrible, conflicting thought I've had in the last twenty-four hours doesn't matter.

"What's wrong?" I ask, shifting to face him. My fingers ache with the need to touch him, but I hold back. "Did something happen?"

His gaze spears me, one eyebrow cocked. The blue isn't empty anymore but a thousand leagues deep. My face heats again. My *whole body* heats.

I stammer, "Besides… you know."

Lucas huffs a soundless laugh and rocks back until he's sitting, arms clasped over his raised, jean-clad knees.

"I'm not sure I want to tell you," he says at last.

I bristle, dread firing up its engines in my stomach. "What? Why? Is it something about the camp?"

"No," he says quickly, with a brief glance of apology. "Personal stuff."

"Your mom?" I guess.

He nods but doesn't say anything else.

"I'm still your friend, Lucas," I say, the words full of conviction.

Despite everything, I can't *not* be his friend. Once upon a time, before a stupid kiss and Jeremy dying and twelve years of silence... he was my whole world. And I'll never not love that boy who jumped my fence to escape his father's fists.

Finally, he speaks. "Michelle and my aunts and uncle are flying in Thursday night and Friday morning. A private rehab facility in Boise is going to work with us to stage an intervention Friday afternoon. My mom is, uh... she's pretty sick. If she doesn't stop drinking, she's going to die."

My mouth drops. I grab his arm, barely feeling the muscles tense under my fingers. "Shit."

His lips curl. "That about sums it up."

"I'm so sorry." I want to hug him but have no idea what the boundaries are between us right now. What it would mean. What I'd want it to mean. So I focus on what I can do. "What do you need from me right now?"

He shakes his head before dropping it between his knees. "A dangerous question, Peapod."

My body flashes cold, then hot. "I was thinking along the lines of a buoy race. Or better yet, I'm sure there's stuff in the Art Barn we can destroy with hammers."

He looks up, a sad smile twisting his lips. "I know. Forget I said that." He sighs and stares at the water. "I haven't been sleeping much."

I swallow a hard knot of worry. "You should go home. Get some rest. Billy doesn't really need us here, anyway."

"I can't. I need to work. To do something."

I'm at a loss until I look north along the shore, spying a

glint of glass. Sudden adrenaline brings me to my feet. Pins and needles attack my right foot, which I shake spastically until Lucas's eyebrows lift.

"I've been sitting for hours. Let's go for a walk."

Lucas blinks up at me. "A walk?"

I nod decisively. "I'll drop my laptop in the trailer, and then you can show me the old caretaker's cabin. No work. Just walking. Then you're going to go home and sleep."

He stares at me another moment. "Feeling bossy today, are we?" His voice is dangerously low. I ignore the sizzle of heat down my spine, swirling in my breasts and between my legs.

Surprisingly, I'm not daunted. His teasing is familiar ground.

I smirk. "I've always been bossy."

With an exaggerated sigh, Lucas stands. "Ain't that the truth." He bows, waving an arm with flourish. "After you, your majesty."

I smother a smile. "Weirdo."

I'm halfway to the path when his murmur catches up to my ears.

"Your weirdo."

My chest compresses, pinching my heart.

I keep walking.

30

Lucas

AFTER FIVE MINUTES OF WALKING, I realize I have two options: either distract myself from the frankly pornographic thoughts I'm having about Celeste—who walks next to me blissfully unaware of how many times I've unclothed her in my head—or distract myself.

"So... do your parents hate me?"

She jerks a little, like the sound of my voice surprised her. I try and fail not to wonder what thoughts she was lost in. Is she wishing she were anywhere else but with me? Was the best night of my life her worst?

Between the uncertainty of my mom's future and the clusterfuck of my relationship with Celeste, I'm a fucking wreck. I didn't lie—I've barely slept the last two nights.

"Of course not," she answers, frowning, her eyes darting to mine for the barest moment. "Why would you ask that?"

I duck under a low branch. The path we're on can barely be called that, mostly reclaimed by the wild in the last years, but it's leading us unerringly toward the cabin ahead of us.

"I stole you from Main Street Flowers."

Celeste laughs, a shadow of the usual, lighthearted sound. "I think they were relieved, honestly. They've never said anything, but I think they know by now that I don't want to take over the shop when they retire."

I chuckle. "Retire? They'll never retire."

This time, her laugh is almost normal. "Yeah, probably not. But no, they don't hate you. I'm sure they're grateful for the opportunity you've given me." Her voice lowers as she ducks her chin. "I'm grateful, too."

I hear what she's not adding to that sentence—that she's afraid what happened Saturday night has messed it all up… that she's worried we won't be able to handle running the camp together. That all of this will blow up in our faces.

I wish I could tell her it won't.

"You signed a two-year employment contract," I tell her instead, unable to help the disgruntled rasp in my voice. "Unless you decide to stop showing up, I can't fire you. If I did, you could sue me for wrongful termination. But it's a moot point. I'm not firing you, Celeste. We're adults. I think we're both mature enough to maintain a professional working relationship."

When she doesn't say anything, I glance up to find her eyes on mine. I can count on one hand the number of times

I haven't been able to read her expression in our lives, and this is one of them.

"What?" The word comes out more harshly than I intend for it to, but there's no helping it. I want to touch her so badly my fingers curl into fists at my sides.

Instead of answering, she just shakes her head and hurries forward. The cabin is close now. From this direction, it looks intact, if a bit sad. Dark, dusty windows. Leaf and debris-strewn porch and a small dock. The other side, I know, is far worse where the tree fell, concaving a section of the roof. It was a damn good thing the place was vacant when it happened because it flattened what used to be the bedroom.

It takes another twenty steps before I realize what Celeste's inscrutable look was for. What it meant.

Just as I know every nuance of her face and voice, she knows mine.

And what I revealed is exactly what I felt saying those words to her. I don't want to maintain a professional working relationship.

What I want is her.

Once Celeste peers through a few windows to see the destruction inside the cabin, she gives up on her mission of getting inside. I trail behind her as she walks the short path to the dock.

"What do you think about having local kids repaint the

side of the Art Barn?" she asks, toeing loose rock and dirt a few inches from the waterline. "Giving them a chance to make their mark on the camp that will be theirs?"

Raising a hand to shade my eyes from the sun, I stare at the side of her face. My tongue is bitter and wants to ask if she's trying to erase what we created. But at least I'm self-aware enough to keep my mouth shut.

Nothing that's bothering me is her fault. Not my ex-business partner trying to squeeze more money out of our deal. Not my friend who's house-sitting for me in Seattle wondering when the fuck I'll be home. Not my mom and the cold shoulder she's been giving me the last few days.

Not the sheets I haven't washed yet because they still smell like Celeste...

"Sounds good," I manage, then walk a bit south along the shore.

Turning my face to the sun, I close my eyes and suck the dry air into my lungs. The gentle lapping of the water against wood and rock is its own kind of music. Lulled by the sound, I close my eyes and let time wind backward. I hear young voices laughing, squealing, giggling. Arguing in the dining hall, chatting in the line for the showers, whispering in the dark, trading secrets, expelling their hopes and fears...

A little bit of the heaviness inside me shears off.

"Feel that, Peapod?" I take another deep breath. "Summer is right around the corner."

"Too bad the lake never warms up."

I snort. "You're such a wuss. Always have been."

The last word is barely out when a spray of freezing water hits my back, immediately soaking through my T-shirt to my skin. I spin, only to get another spray of water from her wily foot, this time aimed higher. Droplets spatter over my face and chest. I'm so shocked, I hardly register the crazy grin on her face.

"You did not just do that."

She cackles, drawing her leg back for another kick. I'm faster.

Two leaping steps and I tackle her, hoisting her onto my shoulder with barely any effort. She wails in affront, hollering obscenities and threatening to cut off my balls if I do what she thinks I'm going to do.

She's right, of course.

Cold seeps through my sneakers first, then socks, up my calves, past my knees. When the water is thigh-level, I throw her into deeper water. Oh, she tries to hang on, but I'm motivated and I know all her tricks, peeling her fingers easily from my hair before I release.

The splash is impressive.

More impressive?

A soaking wet Celeste, sputtering and spitting as she surfaces, incandescent with rage.

31

Celeste

OUR SNEAKERS SQUELCH and squeak over pine needles as we trek back to the camp. My arms are crossed tightly over my chest for modesty's sake. Not helping my nipples thaw is Lucas's broad back, muscles flexing with each step, every dip and swell visible through his thin, soaked shirt.

Who knew watching someone walk could be so erotic? Definitely not me.

I shake away the thoughts, reminding myself that Saturday night was an anomaly that can't happen again. As vehemently as my lady bits disagree.

"I'm appalled at your behavior, Lucas Adler. More than that, I'm disappointed."

He merely glances back at me with a grin, despite being as wet and miserable as I am. I'd wrestled him into the water and dunked him twice before he'd stopped laughing long enough to escape my punishment.

"I thought you wanted to cheer me up?" he asks,

blinking innocently. A droplet of water rolls down his tanned neck, disappearing into the sodden cotton of his shirt.

I look away. "With a walk, asshole."

"I seem to remember you starting it."

I grunt. "Yeah, well, unlike you, I don't carry around spare clothes in my car."

I regret the words as soon as I speak them. Since middle school, Lucas has always carried a backpack with a change of clothes and basic hygiene products—toothbrush, deodorant, et cetera—in case he needed to crash at Jeremy's or in my parents' spare room because his dad was on a bender.

Eventually, both of our families insisted he leave extra clothes at our houses, but it took a few years for Lucas to comply.

"I'm sorry," I whisper, shaking my head and unable to look at him. "I shouldn't have said that."

"Eh, you're not wrong." He doesn't sound angry, and when I hazard a glance, he's smirking. "The habit has served me well in life."

His meaning is immediately clear—*unexpected overnights*—and I grimace to cover a pang of something uncomfortable in my chest.

"Gross, Adler."

He shrugs.

We keep walking.

Squeak. Squelch.

Each step is like an added layer of paint on my inner

canvas, only instead of color, it's emotion. Primarily shades of orange irritation with a patina of green.

"You've, uh, gotten around since high school, huh?"

Lucas bursts out laughing, stopping in the middle of the path and facing me. "Mission successful, Peapod. You've officially cheered me up."

Red-faced and wanting to kick myself—or him—I settle for staring fixedly at a nearby tree. "Whatever. Shut up." I should take my own advice, but verbal vomit overflows my lips. "I was probably a lousy lay. I don't—I mean I haven't been with—" I finally pull my head out of my ass and fall silent.

When he doesn't say anything immediately, to my utmost horror, my eyes prick with tears. A second later, he's in front of me, his fingers pinching my chin lightly and lifting it. I blink hard, staring past his shoulder.

"Celeste Miller, you ridiculous, maddening woman," he grinds out. "Look at me."

Drawing on inner strength I didn't know I possessed, I meet his burning gaze. We're too close, but I don't know how to step away. Don't know if I even want to.

Lucas's gaze drops to my lips, then snaps back to my eyes. "If I thought for one second you'd give me another night, I'd fall to my knees right now and beg. You were my first crush." He swallows. "My favorite fantasy. And believe me when I say no woman has ever compared to you, either real or in my imagination. You'll always be the most beautiful, sexy woman on this planet to me."

The words unravel me. End me.

Because he means them.

"Then why?" I cry, wrenching backward and almost tripping over a tree root. "Why did you kiss me that night at the lake, then snub me the next day? You fucking broke my heart!"

His teeth clench. "I know."

The old hurt roars through me. As fast as I moved away, I launch forward, shoving him with all my strength. He barely moves, which only makes me madder.

"Tell me why, you asshole!"

Something snaps in him. He grips my shoulders, anguish and anger blazing in his eyes.

"He told me he was in love with you," he growls.

I gape. "What?"

"Jeremy. After I came back from the lake that night. He said he loved you. What was I supposed to do? I didn't deserve that kiss. But Jeremy? He did. *He* deserved you."

My mind melts. Turns to dust. "That doesn't make any sense. You two, what, played fucking Rock Paper Scissors for me?"

"No," he snaps. "I never told him I kissed you. He gave me this whole speech and asked me to stand aside. So I did what I thought was right—for both of you. And it was, wasn't it? You and I both know that if he hadn't fucking died, you'd still be happy together. I did it so you could be happy!"

I'm shocked. Horrified. Beyond hurt. My heart bleeds its pain into my chest and arms, all of me throbbing.

Lucas's hands fall away, robbing me of an anchor I

desperately need. Unmoored, I sway, then prop myself up with a palm against a tree. My fingernails dig into the pitted wood.

Rough bark.

Cold toes.

Itch on my back.

Lungs fill. Deflate.

Still here.

Alive.

Without even trying, I revert to the survival mode that got me through the first months after Jeremy's death, when I existed in suspension between the endless void of grief and the painful markers of life.

"Celeste," Lucas whispers, my name a broken sound.

I feel blank. Colorless inside and out as I look at him, at the pleading in his eyes.

"I'm going home." My voice is flat. A smooth, endless lake of darkness. "I'll be doing interviews all week and will email you my final thoughts and decisions by Sunday. I'll be back here next Monday and we'll reconvene then."

He heaves in a deep breath. "You're not quitting."

I don't meet his gaze. "Of course not. Like you said, we're adults. I hope the intervention is successful and that your mom gets the help she needs." I force the next words, which feel like broken glass in my raw throat. "And for what it's worth, I agree—you did do the right thing. Jeremy was the love of my life."

I ignore the flash of devastation on his face as I walk past him.

Squeak go my sneakers.
Splat goes my heart.

Lucas leaves before me, his car tearing out of the small parking lot as I'm squeezing water from my socks on the steps of the Art Barn.

I clench my teeth to keep from racing after him.

I shouldn't have said what I did. As painful as it was to hear the truth of why he rejected me, there's no excuse for kicking someone when they're down.

Especially him.

"Whoa, he okay?"

I look over at Billy, standing a few feet away with a water bottle halfway to his mouth. There are workers all around us, sprawled in the sunshine as they rest and eat lunch.

No, he's not okay.

"I dunked him in the lake."

Billy chortles, eyeing my wet hair and jeans. At least my upper body is dry—I used the privacy of the barn to peel off my wet shirt and bra and pull on my dark, oversized sweatshirt.

Billy shakes his head chidingly. "Some things never change."

I force a laugh and gather my wet clothes, which is becoming a theme after being alone with Lucas. "I'll see you later, Billy. The new porch looks great."

He grins. "Thanks. See ya."

The drive back into Sun River doesn't take nearly as long as I want it to. Before I know it, I'm approaching the turn that leads to Rose House. And Lucas's rental house.

My knuckles turn white on the steering wheel as I pass the street. Almost unconsciously, my foot lifts off the accelerator.

You need to apologize.

"I'll call him later," I tell my inner critic.

Now.

The impulse hijacks my body, which jerks the car into a small parking lot in front of a real estate office, makes a U-turn, pulls back onto the main road, and then takes a sharp left.

Trees press close on either side of the street. A yellow Narrow Roadway sign warns me in my peripheral. I almost laugh at how appropriate it is.

Even as I stick to the pavement, it feels a lot like I'm driving toward a cliff.

32

Celeste

I ONLY HAVE to ring the doorbell once before Lucas opens the door in a surreal parallel of last time: wet hair and shirtless. But this time his jeans are wet, too, goose bumps pepper his chest and arms, and he looks miserable.

"I'm sorry," I blurt.

He shakes his head. "It was the truth, so you have nothing to apologize for."

I swallow past a dry throat. "That's the thing. How do I know?"

He frowns. "Know what?" Then he steps back. "Just come in. You're not wearing shoes and my nuts are ice cubes."

I follow him into the house, closing the door behind me. Lucas veers to the right, stepping off the foyer's area rug to stand over a heating grate. After a full-body shudder, he sighs in relief. Unable to resist, I move next to him and bump him with my hip, stealing half the vent. Hot air funnels up my legs.

"That's good stuff." I sigh.

He snorts. "Look, I appreciate you coming by, and the apology, but you don't have to—"

"What if Jeremy wasn't the love of my life?" I ask, cutting him off.

Lucas inhales sharply.

"I'm not saying I didn't love him," I add quickly.

"I know you loved him."

I nod, then clear my throat. "I mean… I guess what I'm saying is, there's a chance he was, you know? That I'll never experience what we had again. And really, no matter what, I know I won't. There'll never be another Jeremy for me."

"No," he agrees softly, gaze trained on the floor.

"But that doesn't mean there'll never be another… someone." Flushing, I shift from side to side. "Either way, I shouldn't have said that. And thank you for telling me why you acted that way. It gives me some closure. At least now I know it wasn't because I sucked at kissing."

"Jesus, Celeste—"

"I'm kidding," I cut him off. I'm not actually kidding—that whole thing really fucked me up and made me super insecure until enough time with Jeremy convinced me otherwise.

I step away from the grate and turn to face him. He still won't look at me, which gives me the opportunity to study him. Really *see* him.

A swell of affection courses through me—for the boy who stepped aside for his best friend because he didn't think he deserved me, who wanted me to be happy above all. And affection for the man he's grown into: sensitive, kind, and still so funny. Strong, successful, and smart. Not to mention heartbreakingly handsome and sexy. Even his bare feet are lovely, the nails neatly trimmed and clean.

My gaze trips up his bare torso to find him watching me. Pale blue eyes seal my feet to the floor, and my next intake of air stumbles over the speed bumps of my rapidly pulsing heart.

"Anyway," I say, the word nearly breathless. "I didn't want to leave things like that with you. And I want to be there for you, in whatever way you need, while you're going through this stuff with your family this week."

"Celeste," he rasps, the tone full of raw longing.

Heat floods my body, eclipsing the effects of the vents around us. All rational thought flees. We move toward each other at the same time, my arms lifting to encircle his neck as his lock around my waist and lift me against his chest. There's no pause before our open mouths meet. No words as he backs me up until my spine connects with a nearby wall.

He angles a leg between mine, pushing the seam of my jeans against where I throb. I moan, my hips circling, searching for friction.

Lucas's mouth dips to my jaw, then to my ear. "Tell me to stop," he whispers.

I pause in my exploration of his throat. He immediately

stiffens, his arms dropping as he takes a step back. His eyes are closed, his hands up and his entire body trembling.

"You should go," he manages.

I should, but I won't. And I don't care to examine why.

I close the distance between us and grab his waistband, popping the button from its sodden denim hole. His eyes snap open.

"Peapod?"

"What?" I ask, feigning distraction as I carefully take down the zipper.

His hips jerk forward. "Are you—"

"Shut up, Lucas," I say as I yank his jeans over his hips and my hand dives beneath the elastic waist of his boxer briefs.

The feeling that fills me as I close my fingers around his hard length? Ecstasy. Relief. Sharp-edged desperation.

"I guess the itch isn't scratched yet," I murmur, pumping him once.

Lucas pants, his chest bumping against mine. Lowering his head, he tugs on my earlobe with his teeth, then licks the offended skin. I melt back against the wall, momentarily losing my purpose.

Then I remember and cup his balls, tugging them *somewhat* gently.

"Fuck," he growls. "You really are a menace."

A startled laugh escapes me and I look up, only to have my lips ensnared by his. He whips my sweatshirt over my head, groaning at the sight of me naked beneath it. My hands are captured next, handcuffed by his to the wall on either side of me. He feasts on my breasts, neck, and mouth until my legs turn to jelly and I sag into a pulsing, wanton mess.

"My turn," he whispers.

Before I can protest, he lowers to his knees. In seconds, my jeans are undone and tugged roughly down my thighs. To my embarrassment, he immediately presses his nose to my secondary pulse and breathes deeply, his chest rumbling with approval.

"What is it with you and doing that?" I gasp.

His grin flashes upward, my only reprieve before he pulls my underwear down and spreads my legs as much as my pants allow.

The first touch of his tongue wrings a cry from my throat. My hands flutter helplessly and finally find purchase on his shoulders. He laps me with long, sure strokes, which gentle as they swirl around my clit.

Dear God.

It's torture. Not enough and altogether too much. I ache with emptiness, poised on a fence of sensual overwhelm and an innate craving for more.

With a growl, Lucas yanks my pants off completely, then pulls my left leg over his shoulder. "Hang on to me," he demands right before burying his face in my pussy.

This time, two long, skilled fingers sink inside me, curling into and massaging a spot that makes my head thud against the wall, my eyes close, and stars explode across a dark canvas.

My raw, helpless moans fill the house as I undulate

shamelessly against his face in an effort to find what I need. And then I do. I sob as I come apart, my orgasm a full-body molecular massacre that makes me black out for a few seconds.

When I next open my eyes, the only thing holding me up is Lucas. His firm hands on my waist. His shoulder still angled beneath my trembling leg.

He blinks up at me, licking his glistening lips. His eyes twinkle merrily. "Did I break you?" he asks. I smack him on the head, but he just laughs. "I'm serious—I called your name like four times."

I roll my eyes and shove him. He isn't expecting it, toppling backward atop the foyer's area rug. His legs splayed as much as the jeans still tangled around his knees allow, he lifts onto his hands.

For a moment, I merely appreciate the sight beneath me, then I follow him down and straddle his hips.

"Get rid of these," I say, snapping the waistband of his underwear.

He chuckles and folds his arms behind his head. "You're closer."

I bite my lip on a grin, then play along, moving on all fours and lowering my head until I have the elastic band in my teeth. I look up, watching his face—grin faltering, swallowed by need—as I peel the damp material down.

Once his cock is free, I waste no time, grabbing the base with one hand and licking a line from my fingers to his tip. I swirl my tongue, tasting the salty nectar, then take him into my mouth as far as I can.

He groans, his fingers cradling my face before tangling in my hair. "Celeste, stop. Stop before I come in your mouth."

I take a break long enough to say, "I'm in charge right now, and I want this."

His sigh mingles with a gasp as I marry my pumping, twisting hand to the movements of my mouth and tongue. His hips begin to jerk, small upward thrusts, and I exalt in his unraveling control.

His helpless groans.

His tender, filthy whispers.

His fingers spasming in my hair.

"Celeste, I'm—"

I already know, having felt him swelling, growing even harder against my tongue. I give him no quarter as his body stiffens, as he cries out and his release coats the back of my throat. I swallow him greedily—and with a surprising lack of gag reflex.

When he relaxes, I give him a final kiss and sit back. A gratified smile teases my lips at the sight of him: limbs lax, chest heaving, and eyes closed.

"Aww, did I break you?"

One blue eye opens. "Touché, Peapod." The other eye opens, and his soft gaze snares me. "Can you stay a while? At least until you have to pick up Damien from camp?"

For the first time since Lucas Adler barreled back into my life and turned it upside down, I feel zero conflict. No panic. No uncertainty or fear.

"Yeah, I'll stay." His smile crinkles the edges of his eyes and fills me with effervescent warmth.

The moment shatters when his stomach growls loudly. Like it's answering a mating call, mine growls, too.

Laughing, Lucas sits up. His arms trap me in his lap, and I squirm a little at the feel of him half-hard against my inner thigh.

He gives me a slow, lingering kiss. "After I make you lunch, I'm coming inside you. As many times as possible." My breath hitches and my thighs clench. Then he frowns. "In a bed, though, because I'm not a teenager anymore and my knees are killing me."

I smirk. "You should have thought of the rug, like I did."

He nips my chin. "Brat."

I sniff. "You like it."

His eyes spark. "So do you."

He's right, of course. I really, really do.

As we disentangle and Lucas tugs me upstairs for dry clothes before lunch, I count the faint, beautiful freckles on his broad back and wonder why I don't feel ashamed for what just happened.

But even when I look for the feeling, it doesn't come.

33

Lucas

CELESTE IS naked in my bed. Her head rests on my chest, one leg draped over mine. She fits against me like a dream, all soft curves and long limbs. Sweat lingers on our skin, and I know she needs to get up soon. She'll want to shower before picking up Damien.

But I cling to her, anyway.

I'll cling as long as she lets me.

Drained of tension—and most of my body's water—after spending an hour lost in her, my mind wanders into a fantasy that the past fifteen years were a bad dream. Instead, I told Jeremy the truth that night behind Eagle Cabin. I told him that Celeste had feelings for me and I had feelings for her.

Maybe our friendship would have survived it. Maybe his life would have followed a different path. Or maybe it wouldn't have, but Celeste and I would have weathered his loss together.

But as soon as the fantasy floats, it capsizes. Without Jeremy, there'd be no Damien. And no matter how much I might long for a way to rewrite history, I can't imagine a world without my best friend's son in it, or a world wherein Celeste isn't his mother.

I don't regret the path my own life has taken, either—however radically different it was from anything I envisioned as a kid. Despite carrying around a suitcase full of emotional baggage into adulthood, I've managed to have several meaningful relationships with amazing women. I even have a decent group of friends, most of whom I met in college or shortly thereafter. And I've had a challenging career, not to mention massive professional success.

But something was always missing.

Two somethings.

One, I doubt I'll ever have again: a male friendship so close it was brotherhood. And the other… the other, I'm going to do everything in my power to never let go of because she's the gravity that keeps my feet on this rock hurtling through space.

Even if I don't deserve her. Even if she never feels for me what I feel for her. If I can give her pleasure now, maybe a little joy, but primarily the support and friendship I robbed her of for the last twelve years, maybe someday the grossly imbalanced scales of my karma will equalize.

"What are you thinking about?" she asks.

I kiss her head and breathe in her scent. "Honestly?"

Her snort puffs against my chest. "No, lie to me."

My lips twitch. "I was thinking about the scales of judgment."

Celeste props her chin on my chest, her eyes wide and laughing. "Since when do you believe in a Higher Power?"

"Since when does someone need God in order to have a moral compass or a sense of personal accountability for one's actions?"

She squints at me. "Did you hit your head?"

I chuckle. "Must have been the orgasms."

For a few pregnant seconds, she scrutinizes my face. I resist the urge to squirm beneath the old, familiar feeling that she knows exactly what I'm thinking.

"Why'd you get a vasectomy?"

I blink, then exhale a rusty laugh. *Not* what I'd been expecting.

"Sorry," she says quickly.

"No, you're not."

She winces. "Yeah, I'm not. I'm too curious. Back in the day, you wanted lots of kids. I think the term you used was an *'army of misfits.'*"

I force a small smile but can't repress the slight tightening in my body, a ripple of tension she senses. Before I can think of something to stop her, she sits up. Thick, unruly blond hair falls forward, curtaining her breasts.

"My eyes are up here, champ."

I grin, unrepentant and relieved as the tension of the moment passes, even as I recognize the stubborn tilt to her chin.

"You really want to know?" I ask, hoping she'll change her mind—knowing she won't.

Her cheeks flush slightly and she looks down. "I mean, you don't have to tell me. I know we haven't been, uh, close for a long time—"

"Of course I'll tell you," I interject before she can write a story I don't want her to. "I'm an open book, Peapod." *At least to you.*

Tucking an arm behind my head, I shift my gaze to the ceiling. This will be easier if I'm not looking at her.

It doesn't occur to me to evade the question or sugarcoat the answer. She's the only woman I've ever been completely, brutally honest with about my thoughts and feelings. The only one I've ever fully trusted. Even with our years apart, there's no undoing the foundation we built so long ago. I can't find it in me to give her less than the unfiltered truth.

I owe it to her a million times over for the one lie I told with my actions—that I didn't want her—and the betrayal of abandoning her.

"This is going to be a downer," I warn.

"Basically your M.O."

I don't smile, instead lowering my gaze to hers. "You're not allowed to jump up and run after I tell you."

Her gaze turns wary. "Uh. Okay? I mean, I'll do my best."

I lift the hand closest to her, waggling the smallest digit in her face. She rolls her eyes but finally complies, linking her pinkie with mine.

"I pinkie swear not to run."

I take a moment to summon courage. "I went through a breakup four years ago. We had been pretty serious. She was hinting at wanting a ring, talking about kids. All of it. I was thinking about it. Even went to a jewelry store."

Out of the corner of my eye, I see a familiar blankness steal over her features. I want to grab her, kiss her back to life, but I'd be lying if I said I didn't also feel a glimmer of satisfaction. A pinch of hope that maybe what she's feeling is jealousy thinking about me with another woman. That maybe she wants me to belong to her.

"Did you buy a ring?" she asks, her voice odd.

I shake my head. "I actually got a phone call when I was in the store. A buddy of mine. He told me that another friend of ours, Eric, had just lost his wife in childbirth."

"Oh, God," she whispers.

"Yeah." I clear my throat. "The baby lived, thankfully, but obviously Eric was devastated. A day before, he'd had a wife and a baby on the way, and now he had a newborn and he was alone. We got a group together and helped him manage shit the first few months until his sister moved across the country to help him."

I shift again, old emotions stirring at the memory of holding a bottle to the mouth of a tiny, red-faced human while my friend lost his ever-loving mind in the next room. The ropes of past and present overlap, and I feel what I felt then: the crushing guilt of not having shown up for Celeste the same way when she was experiencing something similar.

When I look at her face now, there's barely concealed pain in her eyes, and I know she's thinking about it, too. Her struggle. My failure.

I focus on the ceiling fan above us. "After that happened, I decided I couldn't risk… I didn't want… You know—" I swallow the rocks in my throat. "I was terrified."

"That your wife would die in childbirth?" she asks in a small voice.

"Yeah," I say hoarsely. "Or that I would die and my kid wouldn't have—" I choke off, unable to finish the sentence.

After a moment, she asks, "And your girlfriend left you when she found out?"

"Yeah."

"I would have, too." When she turns toward me, her eyes are fiery, her lips pinched. "That was incredibly selfish of you, to make that decision without her, especially if you loved her and wanted a life with her."

I nod slowly. "I know. I guess that was the problem. I didn't want to spend my life with her. I wasn't thinking about her at all."

I was thinking about you. About Jeremy. About your child.

Her laugh is short and stilted. I'm losing her, so I do the only thing I can and haul her back onto my chest, wrapping an arm tightly around her waist. She's stiff as a board for close to a minute before a miracle happens: she melts against me.

I send a silent thank you into the universe for the power of a pinkie promise.

"I should shower," she mumbles into my neck.

"Okay," I whisper back, trailing my fingers down her spine and across the delicious curve of her ass.

Her breath goes choppy against my throat, her skin warming against mine. My dick stirs, oblivious to the emotional undercurrents of the last minutes.

"Lucas?"

"Mmm?" I barely keep a growl out of my voice.

"Can we have sex again? In the shower?"

Shock freezes me for a second. Then previously dormant superpowers awaken inside me and I'm off the bed and striding across the bedroom with a laughing Celeste draped over my shoulder.

I MAKE her come twice in the shower, and by the time we kiss goodbye at my front door—our hair wet and our legs wobbly—I can't think of any reason why we shouldn't be doing this all day, every day.

I also can't think of a reason why I'm not following her. Not picking up Damien with her, going home with her. But I retain enough sanity to keep those questions to myself.

I spend the afternoon catching up on work emails, touching base with my assistant, and finally calling Amanda, the saint housesitting for me in Seattle. When I tell her I'm not coming back, it feels final in a way it didn't before.

"You can take the plants if you want."

"Wow. You're serious."

"Yep. I'll probably put the condo on the market at the end of next month."

"You're coming back to pack, right?"

I wince. "Don't think so. I found one of those moving companies that does everything for you. I'll pay you through next month to give you time to find a place. Sorry if this throws a wrench in your summer."

"It's fine."

She clears her throat, a habit of hers that means she's about to speak her mind whether or not I'll like what she has to say. I rub my temples while I wait, knowing I probably deserve whatever's coming.

"We both know you're not giving up your whole life to open a summer camp and spend afternoons fly-fishing. Does this mean the terminally unavailable Lucas Adler has finally fallen in love?" Her voice is a smidge too tense, and guilt pinches in the vicinity of my solar plexus.

Amanda has been a friend for a long time; sometimes, she's been more. Outside of the three longer relationships I've had, she defines what my love life has looked like: casual, friends with benefits situations.

Only now, Celeste's voice rings in my ears.

"That was incredibly selfish…"

I have been. I was.

I am.

"I'm sorry, Amanda, if I ever made you think—"

"No!" she yelps, then laughs. "Please don't. Honestly."

I laugh uncertainly. "Okay."

She sighs. "I'm not in love with you, Lucas. Sure, I've

enjoyed our time together and was maybe looking forward to more, but we're friends first. Are you going to tell me now? Did you fall in love?"

I recall a conversation we had a few years ago, after too many margaritas on both our parts, wherein she diagnosed me as incapable of falling in love. In her words: *"I've known you since college and met every one of your exes, and believe me, a woman knows. You cared about them, sure, and showered them with respect and loving behavior, but you never looked at them like a man in love would. Like the world could end and as long as you were holding them, everything was okay."*

I'd called her a hopeless romantic with a demented bent and dismissed the words as booze-born bullshit. We'd laughed about it, after. Now I wonder if she was right.

Scratch that—I know she was.

"Yeah," I manage after a too-long silence. "I'm in love."

I never fell out of it.

Amanda sighs a bit too dramatically for it to be congratulatory. "Lucky woman."

If only it were that easy.

Even after we hang up, the conversation lingers as a pit in my stomach.

So I text Celeste.

> How was Damien's first day of soccer camp?

When she doesn't immediately respond, I busy myself with starting a load of laundry—including sheets this time

—and pulling a steak from the fridge that's been marinating all day.

I check my phone too often over the next hours, as the light outside dims, as I watch mindless television, overcook the steak, and undercook asparagus and a baked potato.

I send her two more texts, neither of which she answers.

> Thinking about you, Peapod.
>
> Wish you were lying next to me, even if it means getting your hair up my nose.

And finally, as I collapse in bed near midnight with an anchor dragging my heart down to my balls, I send her a final message.

> Sweet dreams.

34

Celeste

WHEN I WAKE up Tuesday morning, the familiar colors, shapes, textures, and smells of my apartment are more vivid. Richer, sharper.

Sounds are different, too, almost like there's a resonance I was never aware of before, or an echo just outside my range of hearing. My alarm is less grating than usual. I'm hyperaware of birds outside, their normally raucous calls a soothing symphony. Even Damien's choice of morning music is less jarring.

My first cup of coffee tastes like heaven. I drink it slowly, savoring when I usually gulp it like a fiend. My normally utilitarian morning shower is instead a decadent sensory overload, my skin flushed and burning despite cranking the temperature down until I shiver. The sight of teeth marks, pink and fading, on my breasts overwhelms me. I touch myself, orgasming in three quick strokes.

I wait for shame, but all I feel is relief.

Over breakfast, Damien gives me a funny look and tells me I look pretty today, then in the next breath asks if he can hang out with Daphne after soccer camp. I dismiss the rare compliment as a tactic of negotiation but say yes anyway.

Then, when I drop him off at the high school, two of the other moms tell me I look amazing. They ask about my skin care routine and hair products.

That has never happened before.

At home, I pause before the mirror inside the front door and appraise my face. I look exactly the same. Wild blond hair that I hated as a kid but have made peace with as an adult. Faded freckles over my nose and cheeks. Eyes somewhere between green and blue, my lashes and brows closer to brown than blond. The same imperfections greet me—tiny scars, faint lines.

I don't get it, but nevertheless, I *feel* it.

I clean off the kitchen table and do the breakfast dishes, then gather my laptop and notes for today's interviews. All the while, I feel strangely disconnected from my body, but in a peaceful way. Like I'm floating a few inches in front of myself, unattached to the everyday stresses of life.

A loud, sudden knocking doesn't even make my heart jump. After checking the time and seeing I have twenty-five minutes before my first Zoom interview, I calmly walk to the front door and open it.

Blue eyes. Messy hair. Pinched mouth.

Broad shoulders: tense.

Hands: clenched.

"Peapod."

My ears ring, and with a *snap*, my brain returns from its vacation. My pulse jumps, then races.

"You're ignoring my texts."

My tongue too thick for words, I nod.

"Why?"

"I don't know," I whisper.

But I do know. And so does he.

"Liar."

I swallow. Lick my lips. His gaze narrows on my mouth. Without thinking about it, I say, "We have twenty minutes until my first interview. Is that enough time?"

He surges toward me. The door closes a second before long fingers grip my neck and his mouth covers mine. I whimper at the taste of his tongue—mint and coffee and *him*. We shuffle backward. Hit the table in the entryway. My shirt sails over my head. His belt clatters on the floor.

"Where?" he mumbles into my mouth.

"Don't care." I gasp, then lick his lower lip and bite it.

He groans. "You're killing me. Hold tight."

I lock my arms around his shoulders as he hoists my legs to his hips. I clamp my teeth onto the side of his neck and he hisses, fingers squeezing my ass and hip.

"Are you wet for me?" he asks, his voice low, rough against my ear.

I nod.

"Good. Because I woke up hard for you, and I have to be inside you right now."

He presses me against a wall—I don't even know which

one. All I can think is how grateful I am that his mouth is back on mine. I'm doubly grateful for my long, flowy skirt as he drags the fabric up. My underwear is yanked to the side and his fingers unceremoniously sink into me.

"So sweet. So warm," he murmurs into my lips. "I'm going to fuck you hard and fast. Okay?"

My answer is a breathless moan of assent. I hear a zipper. A whisper of denim as it drops to his feet. Then his blunt head teases me, dragging between my legs, dipping inside me a little before retreating.

My hips jerk downward. I'm rewarded with shallow penetration. But it's not enough. Not even close to what I want—to what I know he can give me.

"Lucas!"

"I know, baby," he whispers against my jaw. "Tell me what you want."

My head thuds against the wall.

"Say it," he growls. "Tell me you need me. That you want me filling you up. That you want my cum dripping down your legs."

An unhinged sound escapes me, and my eyes open involuntarily. His gaze lifts from my mouth and narrows with a familiar, uncompromising expression.

"You want to pretend I don't exist when we're not together, Celeste? Fine. Friends with benefits? An itch to scratch? All fine." His voice is sharp, almost brittle. "But when I'm fucking you, don't even think about holding back or lying to me. You give me everything, or I give you nothing."

If I wasn't so out of my mind with need, I'd probably slap him. Maybe have a mental breakdown.

Instead, I say, "I need you inside me. I need you to fuck me. I want your cum dripping down my legs. I want to feel you for the rest of the day."

His eyes shutter, his forehead dropping to rest lightly against mine. "Good."

He adjusts me in his arms, jerking me down as he thrusts into me. I'm so primed there's barely any resistance, just the before and after—empty; full. My flesh spasms around him, greedy and single-minded. *Keep him. Keep him.*

"Holy fucking shit," he mumbles, then his tongue dips into my mouth as he circles his hips against mine, hitting spots inside me I didn't know existed.

Words tumble from my mouth to his, breathless gasps of, *"Please,"* and *"Yes,"* and *"Right there, don't stop."*

He doesn't stop. Not until I fall apart with a ragged cry against his shoulder. I'm still reeling with bliss as he quickly pulls out of me and lowers my feet to the floor. Chest heaving, I sag against the wall, then watch in a swiftly fading stupor as he pulls his jeans over his hips, tucking his erection in with a wince and a hiss before zipping up and rethreading his belt.

"Wha—Why?"

It's all I'm capable of saying.

His eyes flash to mine, full of heat and unfulfilled need. Then he glances at his watch. "You have ten minutes before your first interview. I'll be working from home today, so email or call me if you need to touch base."

My afterglow burns down to embers before igniting with a different kind of heat. His cum is *not* dripping down my legs like it's supposed to be.

I cross my arms over my chest and look meaningfully below his waist. "You didn't finish."

An eyebrow lifts. "Oh, did you think you deserved what you wanted today?"

I gape at him. "What the hell?"

In two long strides, he's before me, lifting my face to his. His teeth clamp on my lower lip before releasing it with a *pop*. He licks the burning spot, then whispers, "Be good today, Peapod."

He gives me a soft smile, then grabs his car keys from the floor in the entryway and lets himself out. I stare at the door for another minute before it occurs to me that another emotion is eclipsing my irritation.

I'm hurt.

I want him to come back.

I want *him*.

His nearness and touch. His pleasure. His voice, laughter, sighs, and groans.

It's then I realize how truly fucked I am. Because I'm not rearranging deck chairs on the Titanic anymore.

I can see the big picture now, and I know exactly what's coming my way.

I SOMEHOW MANAGE to get my head on straight in time for my three Zoom interviews, two of which are with former Wild Lake counselors who've moved away.

The first, Alice Jenkins, is an immediate rehire. Not only did she work at Wild Lake when I was a kid, she put in another six years before moving to Ketchum to be closer to her adult children. Her excitement over the camp's return is contagious, bolstering me enough to deal with the next two interviewees—both of whom spend most of the call bemoaning all the rules and regulations governing kids' overnight camps and waxing poetic about the "good old days."

I sign off the last interview and update my notes on the candidates, then make myself a quick sandwich for lunch. The urge to call Lucas is nigh overwhelming, but after finishing lunch, I force myself to pivot, grabbing my purse and making the short walk to Main Street Flowers to visit my parents.

I almost turn around when I see Jen chatting with Darla Templeton outside the shop, Hercules the Pomeranian murdering a chew toy at their feet. Instead, I picture Zoey's face and hear her voice saying, *"Fuck the Lilac Ladies."*

"Hi, Jen, Darla," I say as I pass the point of no return. I'm smiling so hard my face hurts.

Darla purses her lips, squinting at me like I've been body snatched. I wonder what she sees—if it's the post-orgasm glow to my skin or the shadow of impending doom hanging just outside it. Somehow, I imagine she sees the latter. Negativity is her worldview, after all.

Jen grins and gives me a hug. "Celeste! I wasn't expecting you. What brings you by?" Her face turns toward my ear and she whispers, "Save me."

By the time she pulls away, I'm ready. Adopting an air of gravitas, I ask, "Did you forget? We're supposed to go over the new ordering software."

Jen grabs her face. "Ohmygosh, I totally forgot!"

She won't win an Academy Award, but it does the trick.

Darla sniffs. "I'll let you working girls get back to it. Come, Hercules."

Jen and I watch her sashay away in her orthopedic sandals.

"Thanks," Jen says, sighing. "I know she's lonely, and I usually don't mind chatting with her, but she was extra today, going on and on about how the town is changing and selling out."

"She's been saying that for twenty years—about the same amount of time she's been slipping the 'working girl' comment into conversations with any woman who earns a paycheck."

Jen laughs. "She's such a trip. So, what are you actually doing here? Your parents are at lunch." She glances at her watch. "They said they'd be a few hours."

My brows lift. "A few hours?"

She nods in agreement with my surprised tone. "I know, right? I'm proud of them. I hope they're napping or—"

"Don't say it," I warn, aghast.

She laughs. "I won't. By the way, you look amazing today. Did you do something different with your hair?"

My face heats. Even my eyeballs feel warm. "Uh, no. But thanks."

I have a vivid flashback of Lucas pulling out of me, hissing as he tucked himself back in his pants. A move as blisteringly hot as it was aggravating.

"Oh, did you think you deserved what you wanted today?"

To punish me for ignoring him, he punished himself.

Did he know that doing that would knock my head sideways?

Probably.

Did I like it?

Unfortunately, yes.

God help me, I loved it.

35

Celeste

AFTER CHATTING with Jen a few more minutes, curiosity gets the better of me. I say goodbye and walk to my parents' house, sending my mom a text on the way so they can put on clothes if necessary.

With my new schedule, I haven't seen as much of them as usual, and I miss them. Plus, hours-long lunch breaks are not the norm for them, so naturally, I'm worried.

Despite what I told Lucas, I know my decision to leave Main Street Flowers for good affected them in ways they're not telling me. How could it not? While they've never said outright that they want me to take over the shop when they retire, I can't help but think they must want me to. Right? It's the business they've spent their lives cultivating, and I'm their only child.

Or maybe they're totally fine—everything is fine—and I'm a worrier who projects worst-case scenarios onto everything. That, or I'm creating an issue where there isn't one because I'm avoiding thinking about other, *larger* issues affecting me. Like the situation with Lucas.

Sometimes I think life would be more peaceful if I'd never done therapy.

On the off chance my parents are, in fact, naked, I ring the doorbell. The sound sets off Lulu, whose barks grow closer to me every second. I grin as I hear my dad's voice nearing as well, muttering about muzzles, the words belied by the affection in his gruff voice.

When the door swings open, I'm thankful to see that my dad is fully clothed and doesn't look red in the face. He does, however, look a bit shifty. Before I can process that, he grabs me in a hug. Lulu dances around us, knocking into our legs.

"What a nice surprise! What brings you by?"

"Just wanted to come say hi. Where's Mom?"

"She's, uh, in the kitchen." He scratches his bearded cheek. "It may not be the best time."

My eyes narrow, and I mentally hold up my heart to keep it from dropping to my toes. "Why not? What's going on?"

"Nothing. Everything's fine."

My voice lifts. "Then why can't I come in?"

Clearly sensing that I'm pedaling toward a freak-out, he comes to a decision and opens the door wider. With a grave expression that does fuck-all to alleviate my nerves, he waves me inside.

"Go on and see for yourself."

I barely breathe until I walk into the kitchen and see my mom looking perfectly healthy, though her smile is a bit too wide. Her eyes flicker nervously past me. Then she squares her shoulders and gestures to the paperwork all over the kitchen table.

It takes me a good thirty seconds to make sense of multiple piles.

One pile is brochures for RVs—the giant, house-on-wheels kind. Another pile looks like articles printed from the internet about road travel. Where to go, what to pack, best national parks, dog-friendly campsites…

And the final pile: legal documents.

"What are those?" The question comes out in a whisper, but I'm suddenly scared to look closer, to read the tiny print.

There's a full ten seconds of silence before my dad breaks the seal, and then they're tag-teaming bomb drops.

"We found a buyer for Main Street Flowers, honey. It's time. We're ready to move on to the next adventure."

"We're going to buy an RV and travel around the country for a few months this fall. We've always wanted to."

"But don't worry, we'll be back by Christmas."

"And before you ask, we're not selling the house."

"Well, we might. But that's down the road. Nothing to worry about now."

"We know this is a shock, Celeste."

"We weren't trying to keep anything from you, honey. It all happened pretty fast. We really just finalized things today."

"We were going to tell you either tonight or tomorrow."

Itch on my heel.

Lungs fill. Deflate.

Still here.

Everyone is fine.

Alive.

"This is great news," I say.

My dad grimaces at my tone, and my mom's eyes fill with sympathetic tears. "We're so sorry to spring this on you."

I clear my throat, avoiding eye contact as I move steadily toward the door. "No, no. That's silly. Really, don't worry about me. I'm happy for you guys. You deserve to do all of this. I just need to… um, process, you know?" A laugh bubbles out of me. "You know me! I'll be fine. Have to head home now, though. Work to do. Okay, talk later!"

ONE OF THE greatest lessons loss taught me is one I'd rather not know. But I didn't have a choice in the matter.

Love is grief.

When Jeremy died, all the love I had for him suddenly had nowhere to go. That, I've learned, is what breaks a heart. The pressure, the too-fullness, and finally, the rupture. All that excess love reshaped my organs. My cells. My entire inner world.

Mothers feel echoes of this: looking at your child sleeping one night, a twang of melancholia hits. That uncomfortable truth unfolds inside us: we cannot live forever. We will eventually slip away from this moment—this love—either in old age or suddenly, and our child will be left without us.

If you've been rewired by loss, though, it's my experience that instead of an amorphous sadness at the thought of leaving our children behind, or even just the sense of time's inexorable passage, what we feel is crystal-bright and razor-sharp.

Crippling, staggering fear.

All because of one moment—or a series of them—wherein our brains decided that love was equal to loss. And now every moment in which we experience the fullness, the brightness, of deep love... we simultaneously experience the future loss of it.

In some alternate reality where I'm the bravest human, I suppose I'd naturally lean into this knowledge instead of letting it cripple me. I'd fling my arms wide and embrace the singular tragedy and miracle of life: it's impermanence.

But I'm not the bravest human.

Not even a little bit.

By the time Damien and I walk up the porch steps of Rose House late that afternoon, I've buried my parents' news somewhere beneath the memory of the time in middle school when I started my period in the middle of a test and the teacher wouldn't let me leave to use the bathroom.

As Damien crosses to the front door, I veer to the side and make a show of checking my phone. What I'm really doing is forcing my almost-teenager to do something scary without me as a buffer. My heart pulses, tired and tender, trying to make me feel love as loss.

I ignore it.

Everything is fine.

"Mom," Damien hisses.

Holding the phone like I'm listening to a voicemail, I whisper back, "Just ring the bell."

The tips of his ears turn red.

I give him a goofy smile and a thumbs-up, which earns me an eye roll but also mellows him out. He rings the bell, and Zoey answers the door with an equally goofy grin.

"Hi." His voice cracks. "Is Daphne, uh, here?"

"She sure is!" answers Zoey too loudly. I catch her eye and make a slashing motion over my throat; thankfully, she dials down the crazy. "She's out back. Go on through, Damien."

My son gives me a brief glance, and for a moment, my heart swells because I think he's going to ask if I'm sticking around—implying he wants me to—but then he takes a deep breath and says, "Bye, Mom," and walks into the house.

Zoey catches my expression and makes a sound of sympathy, which I quickly wave away. "It's fine. I'm fine. He's almost thirteen, after all."

Her eyes light up. "His birthday is next week, right?"

I nod, stuffing down a sudden urge to cry. "On Wednesday. We're having a party Saturday afternoon, but I've been slacking on sending out invites. Barbecue at Phillips Park—the one with the skate ramp right outside town. Can you guys make it?"

"Of course. Do you want to stay? We can have lemonade out here so the kids won't think we're spying on them, then we can slowly sneak around the side of the house to, you know, spy on them."

I laugh. "Nah. I know you're on top of it."

Zoey and I had a detailed conversation about the rules for Damien and Daphne's "hangouts," including no closed doors. Basically, they don't get any privacy at all. I'm really not worried—I know Zoey checks on them often. Besides, Damien is equally terrified and in awe of Ethan, whose wildly popular young adult fantasy series he read last year.

"Mmkay." She glances over my head. "Lucas is home! Crazy."

I scowl, but I'm fighting a laugh. "Subtle. What time should I be back?"

Zoey huffs dramatically. "It's really too bad Damien is a boy. Otherwise, I'd tell you in the morning."

My sigh contains a groan. "*Zo.*"

"Fine, fine. It's four now, so, eight? I'll feed them dinner and they can watch a movie with Ethan and me."

"Okay, great. Thanks."

My efforts at not letting my relief show fail, and Zoey grins evilly. "Go on, wild woman. Get out of here."

My laugh is strained, my heart suddenly fluttering in my chest. I thank Zoey again, then walk off the porch and pull out my phone to text Lucas. What I need is a distraction, and there's only one distraction I want.

> Just dropped Damien off at Rose House. Want company?

His reply comes seconds later and melts the hair off my head.

> Come here right now

I wonder if he's still mad at me for ignoring him yesterday. If he's still in the mood to punish me. I kind of hope he is, a fact I refuse to examine. My skin feels too tight, my nerves strung to the point of breaking.

I need the release he can give me.

I walk faster, crossing the street at a jog, only to pull up short at the end of the driveway. There's a familiar black pickup truck parked behind Lucas's rental car. My steps slow just as the front door opens on a petite brunette with a big smile: Macy, Billy's wife.

"Celeste! I was so glad when Lucas said you were joining us. I'm making cocktails in the kitchen. The men are out back. You're staying for dinner, right? We brought stuff for fajitas."

I return her enthusiastic hug, my smile strained at the edges. "Good to see you! Um, sure, I can hang for dinner."

It should be good to see her. I hate that I'm disappointed. I hate that when I walk out back and see Billy —his familiar smile landing like a spike in my chest—I realize that perhaps Lucas is still punishing us both.

36

Lucas

CELESTE WANTS TO MURDER ME.

I sort of want to murder myself, so I can't really blame her. She's barely looked at me since she got here, which isn't a surprise but still makes my chest feel heavy and tight.

I fucked up when I didn't warn her that Billy and Macy were here. I don't even have a good excuse. I wasn't thinking about anything but wanting her close to me.

And now I've thrown in her face everything she can't stand about what's happening between us, which boils down to the fact that I'm not Jeremy.

Not the right man.

Whereas I can see Celeste's polite mask crumbling slowly to dust over the course of dinner, Billy and Macy only see what she presents to them: her usual bubbly, chatty self, all smiles and charm. Or maybe they sense something because not long after dinner is cleared, Macy delivers the exit line common to parents the world over: they have to put the kids to bed.

No one voices the fact that the kids are in the perfectly competent hands of their grandparents.

We all hug and smile and wish good nights and good lucks, and Celeste and I walk them out. I'm a little surprised that she doesn't leave with them—a little suspicious, too.

Billy gives us a long look and a giant smile before driving away.

"So," I start.

"Shut up," she says, then stomps back inside.

I bite my lips and follow her to the living room, where she flops down onto the couch and stares blankly at the opposite wall.

Feeling very much like I'm treading on thin ice, I settle a few feet away from her.

"You're upset with me," I hazard.

She shakes her head, still with the empty, glazed-eyed expression. "It's not your fault," she whispers.

"What isn't?"

"Everything."

Tears fill her eyes and spill over, even as her expression doesn't change.

Alarm bells ring in my head and race down my nerve endings. I scoot closer to her. "Peapod, talk to me."

She shakes her head again, then sniffs and wipes her cheeks with her palms. Finally, she looks at me, and the pain in her eyes lands like a knife to my chest.

"It's all fucked up, Lucas."

The air in my lungs crystallizes, then shatters like glass. My numb lips miraculously shape words, make sounds. "What is?"

"Everything." She stares blankly at the fireplace. "I don't... do well with change."

As hard as it is, I keep my mouth shut and brace for the worst.

Finally, she says, "My parents are selling Main Street Flowers and buying an RV. They're leaving this fall to travel around the States. I know I should be happy for them—I am happy for them. Hell, I've dropped hints for years that they should retire and travel. They've always talked about it, and I think they would have done it years ago if it hadn't been for..."

For her. For Damien.

"Anyway, I'm a selfish asshole because now that it's happening, I don't want them to go. I want things to stay the same." She sniffs and sits upright, her shoulders squaring. "It's immature, I know."

"Come here, Peapod."

I open my arms, half expecting her to reject my offer of comfort, but to my surprise, she shifts and sags against my chest. The ache in my heart magnifies—and impossibly, also eases—as I wrap my arms around her. Giving in to temptation, I bury my nose in her hair and kiss her head.

"It's not stupid. It's perfectly understandable. Change is scary, especially when you've lived through what you have. There's no rule that says you have to be brave all the time."

"I don't feel brave," she whispers, and I know she's talking about more than her parents leaving. She's talking about us.

"Neither do I."

When she tries to lift her head, I snuggle her closer. She eventually gives up, relaxing again. Her sigh warms the area over my pounding heart.

"What are we going to do?" she whispers.

My thoughts race. I know exactly what I want to do, but she's not ready for it. Might never be. So for now, I say, "We take it one day at a time. How about after your interviews tomorrow morning we pick up whatever supplies we need and repaint the Wild Lake sign?"

There's a long pause. "Okay." Then another sigh. "Lucas?" She sounds sleepy now, her voice soft as spring rain.

"Mmm?"

"I missed you so much. I missed my best friend."

A tsunami of emotion—joy, grief, hope—roars through me. My eyes burn, and my chest convulses as I fight back tears.

"I won't leave you again," I whisper hoarsely. "I promise, Celeste. I'm never leaving again."

After a few moments of silence, I peek down to see her eyes closed, her lips slightly parted. Asleep.

It's okay, though.

I'll tell her as many times as it takes—asleep or awake—for her to believe me.

She sleeps for about an hour. I don't move an inch, even

though my right arm goes numb at the twenty-minute mark. It's worth it because when she wakes and looks up at me, for the briefest moment, I see everything I've ever wanted in her eyes. The same love I feel for her.

Then she blinks, and it's gone like it was never there.

I make myself smile. "Feel better?"

She nods, those aqua eyes holding all the mysteries of the deep sea as they roam my face.

When she kisses me, I kiss her back because I can't help it. Because I'm a fool worshipping at the altar of a goddess whose heart cannot be touched by a mere mortal. And when she straddles my waist and her hands undo my belt and lower the zipper of my jeans, I let her stay in control.

I let her take what she wants, even if she wants to consume all of me and leave nothing behind.

37

Celeste

THE INTERVIEWS WEDNESDAY morning go well. So well I'm beginning to feel like we might actually have a competent staff in the making. They do run longer than anticipated, though, so it's after lunch by the time I make it up to Wild Lake.

As I near the entrance, I see Lucas already at work. Shirtless, perched near the top of a ladder that looks about ten seconds from kindling, he's systematically sanding away at the faded letters of the sign. I park behind his car, then cut the engine and just watch for a minute.

I half-expect panic to rise in my chest, like it does most times I think of what's happening between us. But it doesn't. Maybe it's because nothing can dent my good mood.

When Damien and I got home last night, we had a long talk—a rare exposure of his inner thoughts that I've missed terribly over the last year or so. We chatted about soccer camp and friends, but mostly about Daphne.

Listening to him dance around admitting his giant crush brought back the best kind of nostalgia—not for his dad, for once. For Lucas. For those first magical months of sophomore year when I realized being around him felt different. Electric and tingly.

When he looked at me, my heart pounded a little harder. When his arm brushed against mine, my breath stuttered and my skin came alive. I began to notice all the little details that had never mattered much before. His mouth—the bottom lip slightly fuller than the top—and the slight dimple to the right of it. The sparse freckles on his tanned nose. Even the color of his eyelashes and brows, several shades darker than his hair.

I didn't quite know what to make of it, at least not until I woke up achy and hot with Lucas on my mind. While I didn't have a female best friend, I had enough girlfriends and had read enough of my mom's magazines to know what it meant.

I had a crush on Lucas.

My aggravating, funny best friend, who half the girls in our class already had a crush on. Who'd grown two inches since freshman year and gotten over a brief bout with acne. Whose quicksilver grin and deepening, melted-butter voice charmed adults, too, and got him out of detention more times than I could count.

The man in question pauses in his task to wipe sweat

from his face with the back of his forearm. When my eyes lift from his flexing stomach, I find him watching me with a smug grin.

There's no stopping the flush that surges up my neck to cover my face. The truth is a gentle wave that sweeps me up and cocoons me.

I have a crush on Lucas.

Sighing at the mingled tragedy and comedy of it all, I finally turn off the car and get out. At twelve, I would have been mortified to be caught ogling him. At thirty-three, I'm too old to care.

"Hey, Peapod. Enjoying the view?"

I pointedly check him out, settling on his ass in a pair of beat-up jeans. "Very much so."

Surprise flashes briefly on his face before he chuckles and climbs down the ladder. I resist the urge to run forward and brace the bottom, but still breathe a sigh of relief when his feet hit the dirt.

"You're not afraid of heights, are you?" The tone is teasing, but the look in his eyes is anything but.

"No, but if you expect me to get up there to paint, you're going to be standing on the ladder the whole time."

"Duh."

He strides to his car and pops the trunk, giving me a delicious whiff of his warm, sweaty body when he passes me.

Stepping back, he waves his arm with a flourish. "I wasn't sure what colors you wanted, so I got a variety."

"Holy hell, Lucas!"

The trunk is full of bags stuffed with paints, reusable palettes, and brushes of varying sizes. When I gape at him, he shrugs. "I figured whatever you don't use will go to the Art Barn mural and general stock for the camp. It's mostly latex paint. The lady at the store said that was best for outdoor wood signs."

I nod absently as I rummage through the bags and quickly pull out a selection of colors. "These are great."

"Good. Do you want me to sand the original sign down completely?" He hesitates. "I wasn't sure if you wanted to do something new or just refresh it."

"I want to keep the old design." It's simple but classic: two-toned block font with minor flourishes.

The hint of a smile twitches a corner of his lips. "I figured."

Holding the thick tubes of paint to my chest, I look up into his clear eyes and feel that same feeling from twenty years ago. Tingly skin, shortness of breath, achy awareness.

"Lucas?"

His eyes narrow at my breathless voice. One eyebrow cocks in question.

"Can I have a kiss?"

Emotions play over his face like a slideshow, most too fast to name. Then he does as I asked—and exactly in the way I want—tilting my chin and placing the sweetest, most gentle kiss on my lips.

I'm still floating in the sensation of the past and present

merging when he smacks my ass and says, "Now get to work."

On a Tuesday night in September, two weeks into our sophomore year, I hear yelling through my cracked bedroom window. The path of my highlighter stills as I angle my head, waiting to see if it will escalate or taper off.

There's a muffled thump, then a feminine cry. My mouth turns down and I squeeze my eyes shut.

It's been weeks since their last fight. Weeks in which I've seen the ever-present knot of tension inside my best friend slowly unwind.

Tossing my highlighter to the side, I close my textbook and grab the blanket off the end of my bed. Mom and Dad are watching a show in the living room. I glance in as I walk past, meeting my dad's gaze. Knowing exactly what the look on my face means, his eyes darken and he nods.

I know my parents—and Jeremy's parents, too—really struggle with Lucas and Michelle's situation. Three times, my mom has called the cops. Twice when Lucas showed up with visible bruises on his arms and once when there was a crash next door so loud we thought a car had wrecked outside. And three times, nothing came of it because Mr. Adler has clout and money and is friends with the major.

They feel helpless, and so do I. But at least I can do this: support my friend when he needs me.

Outside, the sky is clear, the air crisp even while the ground holds tightly to the vestiges of summer. My footsteps crunch over gravel and mulch as I pick my way to the bench.

Lucas is already there, shivering in a T-shirt, his eyes wild with helplessness as he stares toward his house. A nearby solar light highlights half of his face and the goosebumps on his arms.

I sit beside him and wrap half the blanket around his shoulders, keeping the other half anchored around me. Like a computer rebooting, he shudders and takes a deep breath.

"You smell good, Peapod."

"You smell like feet."

He doesn't, actually. He smells like leftover chlorine from swim practice and that slight earthiness that's indefinably him.

The barest smile grazes his lips. When his head turns, his eyes meeting mine, I feel a strange jolt in my stomach. His arm lifts around my shoulders, tugging me flush to his side. This time my stomach tries to crawl out my throat.

I make myself relax. Remind myself this is standard for us. We hug. We lean. We shove and pinch and high-five. Physical connection had always been a part of our friendship, and there's no reason for it to get weird now.

Even though it feels different. New and a little scary.

We both stiffen when the back door of his house opens, slamming against the siding. His father's voice reaches our ears, low and drenched in rage.

"Where is that little fuck?"

There's a muffled sob, then his mother's voice. "Maybe he went for a walk? He didn't mean to leave the freezer open. Nothing was spoiled."

"That doesn't matter," growls Mr. Adler. "He still needs to be taught a lesson."

Their voices lower and the back door slams closed.

A few moments of thick silence later, Lucas says, "I didn't leave the freezer open."

My chest squeezes, my heart dropping as I process what he means.

He continues, "There's a bottle of vodka hidden in the freezer. Hers. That shit about vodka not smelling like anything? It's bullshit. I smell it on her sometimes when I get home. I smelled it tonight."

I don't want to say the words but know I have to. "She's blaming you for something she did?"

He grunts an affirmative.

"Lucas…" I whisper, swallowing past a dry throat. I want to tell him so many things. I want to make it okay. But I've learned over the years that he doesn't want to hear it. There's no fixing this. So I say, "Want to stay here tonight?"

His eyes find mine and linger. "Can I sleep in your bed with you?"

I blink. Blink again. My mouth drops open, then closes. Lightning streaks under my skin, zinging from my stomach to my fingers and toes. I'm grateful for the shadows because I'm sure my face is bright red.

"I'm kidding, Peapod." But his eyes stay on mine, and they aren't laughing. Finally, he looks away and sighs. "But yeah, I'll stay. If it's okay with your parents."

"You know it is," I manage to say.

He nods.

I shift restlessly. "Is Michelle okay?"

"Yeah, she's okay. We have a system. Whenever he starts ramping up, I go in her room and give her my tablet and headphones. She knows not to take them off until Mom comes to tuck her in."

"Are you okay?"

His arm tightens around my shoulders, smooshing me against his body. He's warm now. It's almost too warm under the blanket, but I don't say anything.

"I'm always okay when I'm with you, Peapod."

"Stay right there."

A quick glance down reveals Lucas aiming his phone up at me. I roll my eyes and turn back to the final flourishes on the last letter of the sign.

My arms are burning like the flames of Hell and my back is in knots from balancing on the ladder, but I'm beyond tickled by the result. With fresh paint and new, updated colors, CAMP WILD LAKE shines.

"Done!" I proclaim. Sticking my brush between my teeth, I grab the messy palette and slowly make my way down. By the time I reach the ground, my legs are shaking. I drop the brush into a water-filled bucket Lucas fetched earlier. "I'm never doing that again."

Lucas grins. "I rather enjoyed it."

I grace him with a coy smile as I close the distance between us. His eyes heat, then widen with beautiful, authentic shock as I slap the paint-smeared palette to his bare chest.

"How about now? Still enjoying it?" I casually smear the plastic plate over his pecs and down his stomach.

"Do you and Damien want to come over for dinner?"

I freeze. A greenish-yellow blob drips from his collarbone and splats onto my hand. His expression matches his voice—nervous—and I actually *feel* the blood drain from my face, heavy and viscous as it vacates my brain. A memory floats forward of the time Lucas cracked three large eggs on my head. It feels a bit like that. Only a lot worse.

A wave of dizziness hits, then passes. I wish I could blame it on the paint fumes.

"I, uh..." I clear my throat, awkwardly peeling the palette from his skin. "I was expecting that stunt to go in a different direction."

I can't meet his gaze, which I feel searching my face.

"I know," he says softly. "But I'm not retracting the question. I want to spend time with Damien, and I want him to know how much I care about you."

My stomach, already near my knees, bottoms out around my ankles. Panic scraps like sandpaper against the back of my neck. In my armpits. Inside my throat.

Turning, I find our designated mess bag and put the palette inside, then grab a rag for my hands. Not that it does much. Thoughts ping inside the vacuum of my head.

I'll need acetone to get the paint off my hands. Do I have any nail polish remover at home? It's probably expired. Does acetone expire? When was the last time I even painted my nails?

"Celeste."

"I need a minute," I say in a harsh whisper. The trees off the side of the road blur, then snap back into focus.

"That's just the thing," he says, his voice coming closer. "With everything going on with my mom, your parents, the camp… I realized that I've been so terrified of you rejecting me, I've lost sight of the fact that a minute isn't guaranteed."

"Lucas," I say piteously. "Stop."

He doesn't.

"I love you, Celeste, and I already love Damien. I know I can never replace Jeremy. I don't think either of us wants me to try. But I can be yours—and Damien's. I want to be yours." His voice is now right behind me. "Do you want me to be?"

YES!

Maybe?

I don't know.

Because my brain hates me, it chooses that moment to show me a visual of Jeremy when he proposed. His dark eyes bright with hope, his hand shaking on the little ring box.

His face forever young.

"It's not that simple," I say, spinning to face Lucas, forcing myself to stare into his eyes. "What happened to taking things one day at a time? We've been having sex for a week. Now you want to jump into a full-blown relationship?"

His jaw tenses and releases. "We've basically been in a relationship for twenty-five years."

My laugh is maniacal. "Come on! We were kids, and we were best friends. That's it. We've been strangers for the last twelve years."

"Not buying it. We know each other better than anyone. We always have and always will."

I throw my hands up. "For fuck's sake, Lucas! Why now? We had a rocky reunion, but things have been getting better, right? We're working together. We're friends again, with benefits we both enjoy. Aren't things complicated enough? The last thing I need right now is more chaos."

Hurt flares in his eyes. "That's what you think we are? Chaos?"

"You're my Peapod. The place I feel safe."

The memory—and all the others like it—vibrates between us. To my everlasting horror, my eyes begin to sting.

"I care about you, Lucas. Of course I do. But my priorities are Damien and getting this camp up and running, not starting a new relationship. If what we have going isn't enough for you, then let's stop this. I don't want this drama. I don't need it on top of everything else."

The words, *I quit*, are on the tip of my tongue, but I can't make them pass my lips. I need Camp Wild Lake. I need it in a way I don't truly understand, with a soul-scorching conviction I've never felt before. And somewhere deep inside me, past all the layers of hurt and memories and grief and longing, is another facet of the truth.

I need Lucas, too.

But I'm not brave enough to admit it. And right now, I'm too overwhelmed to acknowledge how scared I am that he will, in fact, want to stop.

Lucas scrubs fingers through his hair, sending the strands into orbit. His eyes are frantic in a way I recognize—the same helplessness and panic that I saw so often when we were kids. That he only showed me in my backyard at night.

The ground shifts under my feet, a precursor to a free fall.

"Please, Lucas," I whisper. "Just... give me some time. I'm not saying no. I'm saying I'm not ready. It's been a week."

"A week," he echoes, nodding. Some of the wildness leaves his eyes, but to my dismay, what replaces it is a blankness I also recognize, one that means he's retreating into himself. "That makes sense. You're absolutely right."

"Lucas—"

The smile he gives me is so fake my hand itches to slap it off his face. "I completely understand. I pressured you and I shouldn't have."

"You're under a lot of stress," I say weakly. "It's okay."

He glances at his watch. "I just remembered I have a meeting with our marketing guy in twenty. Can you do me a huge favor and run the paints and supplies up to the Art Barn?"

"Sure, no problem."

Another forced smile. "Great. Thanks, Celeste. And the sign looks amazing."

Nothing about this feels right, but I'm powerless to find the words to change it. All I can do is watch him walk to his car, unload the bags from the trunk, then get inside and start the engine. With a brief wave in my direction, he flips a U-turn and disappears.

38

Lucas

MICHELLE BLOWS on her steaming coffee, too smart to take a sip even though she's jonesing for it after her early flight. Joan's behind the counter of Anne's Pie Shoppe this morning, and we both know she sets the heat on the coffee machine to nuclear. Burned tongues are a rite of passage at Anne's, but we learned our lessons young.

I fish an ice cube out of my water glass and drop it in my own coffee, ignoring the sniff of affront from my sister. She considers watered-down coffee a travesty.

"Her point is valid," she says, finally giving up on the caffeine and taking a sip of her own water. "I mean, you basically backed her into a corner. We're talking about Celeste, dude. She's almost as stubborn as you. Or she was."

"She still is," I grumble.

"Have you talked to her since Wednesday?"

"Just a few phone calls. Work related. I'm trying to keep things professional, like she wants."

What I don't say is how hard it's been to keep away from her for the last two days. I'm almost grateful for the massive distraction of the intervention today.

Almost.

"You're an idiot."

Michelle stares me down, her eyes laser focused despite being bloodshot—eyes the same eerie, pale hazel as our father's. Whereas I take after our mom in coloring, she takes after him. But it's never bothered me. She's his opposite in every way.

Before I can ask my oh-so-wise little sister why I'm an idiot, Joan approaches our table with two plates. Mine is a basic egg and veggie scramble, while Michelle's plate is piled high with pancakes, sausage, hash browns, and eggs smothered with cheese.

"Joan, you're a saint," she gushes.

"Don't I know it." She slides a few napkins and the bill onto the table. "You sticking around too, kiddo?"

"Just for a few days," Michelle says around a bite of sausage. "I missed my big brother."

"Huh. Here I thought it was a family reunion. Saw your aunts and uncle at the grocery store last night."

Michelle chokes. Joan pounds her back until she waves her off. "Jesus, Joan. Been lifting weights?"

"You caught us," I tell Joan with forced levity. "If you see my mom, don't tell her anything. It's a surprise reunion."

Joan gives me a look that's too perceptive for my liking but nods and meanders away.

"Fucking Sun River," Michelle mumbles. "And what the hell were they thinking? I thought you said they promised to lay low until this afternoon."

I shovel a forkful of eggs into my mouth, chewing and swallowing without tasting them. "Hell if I know. When I left them at the hotel, they had everything they needed. Maybe one of them got diarrhea or something."

Michelle makes a face. "Seriously, Lucy? Also, does Joan have a photographic memory or something? How did she —" She stops as she realizes it's only been five years since they were here last, and Joan must have spent time with them then.

At our father's funeral that neither of us attended.

I take a few more bites. Automatic chewing. Automatic swallowing. After the fourth bite, I give up and push my plate away, instead cradling my now-drinkable coffee. I sip as I watch Michelle go through the same cycle I did: forcing herself to take a few bites. She eventually pushes her plate away, too, and gulps her coffee down.

"By the way, we're not done talking about Celeste. I'm personally invested now because when I was a kid, I had high hopes of being a bridesmaid in your wedding."

I grimace. "Way to make it about you."

Michelle grins, unrepentant. "Anyway, let's put it on hold until tomorrow. Run me through the plan for this afternoon again, then we'll head to the hotel and loop in the aunties and uncle. Deal?"

I can't help smiling. Even bone-tired after a late night working on a time-sensitive project and her flight this morning, Michelle is—as she's always been—a force to be reckoned with.

"Deal."

The next hours pass too fast, the majority of them spent reviewing our homework from the interventionist. On a Zoom call earlier this week, she asked us each to write down a list of five to ten times when Mom's drinking negatively affected us or caused concern, being as specific as possible.

Michelle and I wrote ours over the phone together, which only slightly alleviated the shittiness of having to pick the top ten out of close to fifty. I wish I could say the process was cathartic, but it was just depressing.

When the interventionist meets us at the hotel to run through her strategy and likely scenarios, my nerves start to sing at a fever pitch. I see the same tension reflected on the faces around me, even as the interventionist does her best to calm us down. She repeatedly tells us that we're not responsible for Mom's decision at the end of this. That we have to let go of the result.

Logically, I get it. Mentally, I'm prepared.

Emotionally, I'm a dumpster fire.

Ten minutes before it's time to leave, I step outside with my phone. I'm powerless over my fingers as I unlock the screen and open my contacts to dial Celeste. I'm not expecting her to pick up, so when she answers, I'm struck mute.

"Lucas? Hello?" There's a long pause. "Are you okay?"

My heart rate immediately drops ten or fifteen bpm, and I take my first deep breath of the day. Maybe I'm chaos to her, but she'll always represent peace to me.

I clear the hesitation from my throat. "Yeah, yeah. I'm okay. We're almost ready to leave for Mom's house." I take another breath. "Celeste, I'm sorry. I know I've been distant the last couple days—"

"Don't," she interrupts. "No apology necessary. I know you're going through it. No matter what's going on with us, I want you to know that I'm here for you."

The words take the air from my lungs. "I don't deserve you," I whisper.

"Shut your mouth on that nonsense. Everyone deserves a best friend."

A smile tugs my mouth. "Best friends, huh?"

She makes a small, humored sound. "Like you said, no one knows us as well as we do. But enough about that. Do you remember what you did before every swim meet? I want you to do it now."

A laugh tumbles out of me. "No way."

"Lucas," she growls. "Put the phone on speaker and do it."

I glance at the hotel to see my aunts, uncle, sister, and the interventionist leaving the elevator and crossing the lobby.

"Uhh…"

"Now!" snaps Celeste.

"Fine, fine!" I put the phone on speaker and drop it onto a patch of grass to my left.

Without giving myself another second to think, I do three jumping jacks, four burpees, five chest slaps, and seven rapid claps—all while reciting our ridiculous pregame chant.

"From city to city, we show no pity.
From state to state, we dominate.
When we swim, we lead the pack.
When we swim, we don't look back."

When I finish, Celeste's cheering through the phone is almost as loud as Michelle's hollering and clapping from five feet away. My aunts and uncles are grinning, and even the interventionist has a wide smile on her face.

I feel like an absolute fool. And I also feel better.

Retrieving my phone, I take it off speaker and tell Celeste, "Thank you. It's time to go."

"You're welcome. Now go kick ass, little fish."

I groan at the familiar moniker that annoyed me to no end in high school.

"Call me after if you can?" she asks.

"I will."

"Good luck. And, Lucas?"

"Yes, Peapod?"

"Don't poop in the pool."

39

Celeste

LUCAS DIDN'T CALL last night, so I have no idea how the intervention went. I'm trying not to think about it. About what he must be feeling if it didn't go well—or how he's handling things if his mom did, in fact, agree to inpatient treatment.

I don't call him, either. I'm self-aware enough to admit it's because I'm chickenshit. After what happened Wednesday and the limited contact since, the warring halves of me are stalemated.

The part of my heart not atrophied by the past wants to throw caution to the wind and take him up on his offer. An official relationship. Together, as that same part of me has always believed we should be. But the rest of me can't seem to wrap my head around the idea. I can't let go of my safety net—for I know now that's what it is. My perpetual singleness. My aloneness. The way I've filled my life with my son, my family, hobbies, my various careers.

That net was woven by capital F fear. Nylon rope and watertight.

After I lost Jeremy, at the encouragement of friends, I joined some Facebook groups for young, widowed mothers. And thank God I did because otherwise I would have felt like I'd fallen asleep and woken up on a different planet. Those groups and the raw, heartbreaking posts in them, are the only way I know right now that I'm not crazy. That the abstract, crippling fear I feel at the prospect of opening my heart again is normal.

Normal or not, the acknowledgment doesn't alleviate the problem. The question. The crux of it all—

What if Lucas dies, too?

I told a therapist my fears once about being in another relationship and she asked me, "What if they *don't* die suddenly and tragically, Celeste? What if your partner lives to a ripe old age? What if you pass before them? We can't know the future. Do you want to live in a prison of fear your entire life?"

Although I barely remember that woman's face, I remember what she said.

But no matter how much time has passed, I'm still not sure the risk is worth the reward.

DAMIEN and I spend Saturday morning at my parents' house. I broke the news of their imminent departure a few days ago; he took it far better than I did.

Ah, the resilience of youth.

I do find out—with some not-so-subtle questioning—that my parents haven't seen Mrs. Adler since yesterday. They weren't home when the intervention took place, but they report that they didn't see any lights on inside the house last night. I'm really hoping that detail means she went to treatment.

After cleaning up breakfast, the four of us load up my dad's ancient station wagon and drive to Wild Lake to prep for the Art Barn painting party. Close to twenty families signed their kids up to help revamp the mural, which I spent six hours yesterday re-taping with the new design. Still an eagle—but not our eagle.

As we drive slowly into the camp, I scan our surroundings for Lucas's car. But we're the first ones here.

"You feeling okay about this?" asks my dad as we unload his giant cooler from the trunk and walk it to the side of the barn.

"Of course. Why wouldn't I be?"

"Well, you put your heart and soul into the original mural. It meant a lot to you kids. Change is hard."

"Change can be good, too."

He grunts, knowing as well as I do that change and I aren't friends. Avoiding his stare, I flip the cooler lid and start packing in sodas. Damien drops a bag of ice beside me.

"Thanks, kiddo."

My almost-teenager issues an intelligible grunt and heads back to the car. I smirk to myself, thinking about the text from Zoey this morning informing they had a last-minute change of plans and will, in fact, be bringing Daphne to the event. I forgot to tell Damien, but I'm secretly glad I did. It'll be fun watching how swiftly his mood changes.

"Things are really shaping up out here," notes my dad.

Thankful for the shift in topic, I sit back on my heels and follow his gaze around the camp. Billy has done absolutely incredible work at superhuman speeds. I can hardly believe it's only been a week since his team started. The volleyball and basketball courts are finished. The additional bathrooms are framed. The dining hall porch is done, the roof issues repaired, and the foundation for the new music cabin is laid.

"It's surreal," I say, unable to help the grin that spreads on my face.

"What is?" asks a voice that sends a powerful shiver down my spine and causes my heart to skip a beat. I glance over my shoulder, my brain absorbing details faster than my eyes. Messy dark blond hair. Unshaven face. Worn jeans. Navy blue T-shirt with a faded band logo on it. He looks tired, his smile more polite than genuine.

"Hey, there, son," says my dad, breaking the awkward silence to give Lucas a back-pounding hug. "How's your mom?"

Leave it to my dad to pull off the proverbial Band-Aid.

"Safely ensconced in the best private treatment center in Boise."

"Glad to hear it," my dad says gently.

My chest deflates with relief. Standing, I take an uncertain step toward Lucas. "Good. That's so good. Are you—how are you?"

Lucas nods, his eyes briefly meeting mine. "I'm okay. Can I talk to you for a minute in private?"

"Sure."

"I've got the cooler," says my dad.

"Thanks." Lucas smiles; still not the regular wattage, but better. "I won't keep her long." He meets my probing stare. "Lake?"

I nod, and we walk side by side toward the glittering blue expanse. As the silence stretches, I start to have a queer, tingling feeling of dread. The feeling grows and grows until my palms start sweating.

When we're standing side by side on the shore, not far from the pile of decaying wood that used to be the dock, Lucas clears his throat.

"I think you were right."

My dread intensifies. "Right about what?"

"About us." He takes a deep breath, and I feel like he's sucking the oxygen straight from my lungs. "I know I agreed with you on Wednesday, but it was disingenuous. I hadn't really processed what you said to me."

"What did I say to you?" I whisper.

He gives me a wry look. "You remember."

I straighten my spine, gathering courage around me like a tattered cloak. "I think I said that I wasn't ready to be in a relationship with you, but that I care about you a lot. I also said I didn't think things had to change."

He nods. "You did say that. The part I'm agreeing with, though, is the first bit. I hear you. As much as it goes against every instinct I have, I'm not going to pressure you into being with me."

"You didn't—"

He barks an insincere laugh. "I one hundred percent did, and you know it." His voice falls to a near-whisper. "I basically guilt-tripped you. I told you I loved you."

"It wasn't the first time," I say before I can stop myself. There's a hint of desperation in my voice that I can't hide, fueled by the bitter realization of what happened, what he's revealing.

I broke his heart.

He grimaces. "Yeah." His tired gaze meets mine. "I've loved you most of my life, and I'm not sure that will ever change. But…" He trails off, eyes turning to the water. Eventually, he sighs. "Even though it's hard—really fucking hard—to accept, apparently, loving someone who doesn't love me back in the same way has closed me off to finding something good with someone else."

My heart drops. My cheeks go numb.

Clearly, he had some deep conversations with Michelle yesterday and today. The powerful, soul-searching, revelatory kind. And I don't disagree with what he's saying. In a twisted way, I've never been prouder of Lucas than in this moment. Even if my own heart is caught in the crossfire of his growth.

"I understand," I murmur.

"Thank you for letting me clear the air." He sticks a hand toward me. "Partners and friends?"

In my mind, the Titanic is sinking. I'm holding on to a deck chair as it slides toward oblivion.

My cold fingers grasp his warm ones. "Partners and friends."

His hand relaxes. Releases. And I wonder if I'll ever touch him again.

"I can't undo the choices I've made in the past, Celeste," he says softly, "but I want you to know that if I could, I'd only change one thing."

"What's that?" I choke out.

"I wouldn't have stepped aside."

He walks past me toward the camp where, in a few hours, the past will be painted over.

40

Celeste

I MAKE it through the day.

Through welcoming the families at Lucas's side, overseeing the painting of the mural, and chatting with parents about our expected program offerings and our timeline.

I hand out the pre-registration flyers Lucas's magical marketing guy whipped together, with a QR code that links to our website where they can be put into our new database for early-bird offers. I distribute snacks and sodas and waters, offer sunscreen and give at least ten mini tours of the site.

I make it through Damien gluing himself to Lucas for the first hour. Following him around, laughing, talking, more animated than I've seen him in some time. I'm relieved when Daphne shows up and my son immediately abandons Lucas. Then I feel guilty for being relieved.

That night at home, Damien and I order a pizza. Instead

of disappearing into his room after eating, he puts on a movie and sits next to me. I stare at the screen, not really seeing it, until he mutes the volume and pivots toward me.

"What's going on with you and Lucas?"

I jerk in place. "What do you mean?"

"Don't play dumb, Mom."

My mouth opens and closes. I can barely meet my son's stare, a fact that fills me with shame. "I think..." I stop, swallow, and start again, "I think what happened was old friends reconnecting and mistakenly... uh..."

"Hooking up?"

I've never wanted to be a turtle before, but here we are. If only I could tuck my head into a shell on command.

"It's over now. I'm sorry."

His brows draw together. "What are you sorry for?" He sighs, picking at nonexistent threads on his pants. "It was nice seeing you happy for a minute. But the last few days you've been different. Today especially. You had this crazy smile on your face all day, but your eyes were all weird and sad."

Jesus.

"Damien." I reach for his hand and squeeze, surprised and almost moved to tears when he doesn't immediately release me but grips me tight. "It's complicated—Lucas and me."

"I like him," he says, low and with a thread of defiance. "He's nice, and cool, and pretty funny for an old guy. I don't get why you don't want to see if..." He sighs, releasing my hand. "Forget it. It's your life."

"Oh, honey."

I'm too late. The hormonal tides have turned against me, and he rockets off the couch and stalks to his bedroom. At least his door doesn't slam, but a minute later, I hear aggressive metal music turn on.

My head flops back onto the couch.

"Fuck."

I MAKE it through the next day.

And the day after that.

Without actually agreeing to it, over the course of the week, Lucas and I fall into a habit of communicating solely via email and text. He's bogged down with the business and construction side of things. Working out bugs in the website. More marketing. Training handbooks. Insurance. Permits. The list seems endless, and I'm very glad I'm not responsible for any of it.

I have my own laundry list of tasks to complete, including fine-tuning the different programs for different age groups—day camps for littles, overnights for grades eight and up. I also mock up daily and weekly schedules for each camp and spend hours making inventory spreadsheets, researching, and ordering supplies: everything from mattresses for the bunks to tools, art supplies, kilns, and forks and knives for the kitchen.

We have just over a month until our dozen newly hired and rehired staff arrive for orientations, six weeks until final inspections, and eight weeks until the first trial-run camp.

My anxiety simmers like a pot of water on eternal verge of boiling.

But I've never felt more alive.

I somehow carve out time to plan Damien's birthday party coming up on Saturday, and on Wednesday we celebrate his actual birthday with our tradition of a low-key dinner at my parents.

I smile. I rejoice.

I tear up when he blows out the candles on his cake.

Thirteen.

After dinner and opening of presents—I got him a new skateboard he's had his eye on, and his grandparents got him a new helmet and a video game he's been wanting—I join my dad in the kitchen.

I try not to think about time moving, slipping darkly through an hourglass. *How many more times will I find him making his decaf coffee before they leave for their new adventures?*

"Hey, Dad."

There must be something in my voice because he wipes his hands on a dishtowel and opens his arms. "Come here."

I walk into his hug. He squeezes me tight, then kisses me on the head. "There's something I've been meaning to give you, and I think it's time."

Chuckling weakly, I step back. "Not my birthday, Dad."

He chucks me under the chin. "Come on. It's upstairs."

I follow him down the hallway lined with pictures,

pointedly not looking at the one where a young boy and girl grin on the shore of a lake.

I linger on the threshold of my parents' bedroom as my dad rummages in the bottom drawer of his dresser.

"Really, Dad, I don't—"

"Ah, here we are." He stands and turns, proffering a short stack of envelopes wrapped in a thick red rubber band.

"What are those?"

I don't like the sympathy in his eyes. Not one bit. It makes me take a step back.

"At the time, your mom and I made the decision to keep these to ourselves. It's been so long we honestly forgot about them. And for that, we owe you an apology."

He scratches his cheek, a nervous affectation that only elevates my need to rewind time and escape this moment.

"What. Are. Those."

He crosses the bedroom and offers me the bundle. I don't move, staring at the oldest envelopes, slightly yellowed, their corners curling. Then I see what my mind is already rejecting—the handwriting on the front. My name in a familiar scrawl. The return address in Seattle.

"Whatever they are, I don't want them."

My dad merely lifts my numb hand and wraps my fingers around the envelopes. There must be fifteen of them. Some of them are thin, some thick.

"You don't have to read them tonight. Or ever. Hell, you can burn them unread if you want. But they're yours,

Celeste. We got the first one a few months before you married Jer."

My thumb swipes across the rubber band. "Why, Dad?" I whisper. "Why didn't you give them to me?"

His expression falls into lines of remorse. For the first time in my memory, I have the thought that my dad looks old.

"I had a feeling. A father's intuition, I guess. You were so happy, and I knew these had the potential to change that. Then you lost Jeremy, and they kept coming, and... Honey, all I can really say is that I'm sorry. I understand if you're angry—you have every right to be. So does he."

When I shake my head, it feels like my brain sloshes around. Unmoored from reality. "I don't understand."

But I do.

My dad's default mode is protective Papa Bear, which only increased when Jeremy died. He sensed a threat to me and acted accordingly.

But understanding that instinct—and loving him for it —apparently doesn't negate the betrayal that begins as a burn at the base of my skull and travels through my body like rippling currents of electricity.

"Thank you," I say stiffly, tucking the envelopes under my arm and walking quickly downstairs. I grab my purse and walk into the living room. "Damien, we're leaving."

He looks up from the Uno cards in his hand. "But I—" He registers my expression, and his eyes widen with alarm. "O-okay. Raincheck, Grams?"

My mom's gaze scans my face, then drops to the

envelopes. I look away before her expression morphs into what I know will be there: guilt.

"Of course, Damien," she says, her voice thready.

Ten minutes later, as we walk into our loft, Damien asks softly, "Mom? Are you okay?"

The undercurrent of fear in his voice breaks through the chaos of my thoughts, clearing it away like a stiff breeze. "Yes—God, I'm sorry. That was a really shitty way to end your birthday dinner."

His dark eyes scan mine. "Grams was beating me at Uno anyway." He pauses. "I've never seen you so mad, though. What happened?"

I think of the envelopes tucked into my purse. I want to hide in my closet with a flashlight and read them—I also want to start a fire with them.

Instead, I take a deep breath and remember that being a good mom means navigating the thin line between honesty and tact. I don't want to lie to my son, but the whole truth isn't something I can burden him with, either.

"You asked me a few days ago why I don't want to be with Lucas. He—well, he was my best friend. Even before we met your dad, we were best friends."

Damien nods. "I know that."

I nod back, then power through the rest. "I felt really betrayed when he wasn't there to support me after your dad died. We fought, and... hurtful things were said. We didn't speak for a long time. So it was kind of a shock when he came back to town."

"He's trying to make things right," says my suddenly-idealistic son.

"Yeah," I say weakly.

"What does this have to do with what happened tonight?"

I chew my lip in thought, then say, "Let me ask you this: if you found out some information that you knew would hurt me—or maybe hurt Daphne—would you tell us or keep it to yourself?"

He frowns. "I don't know. I guess it would depend on what it was. Like if it was something you needed to know or not."

My heart melting, I stroke the hair back from his brow. "Exactly. It's a super hard question. Long story short—I have a sore spot where Lucas is concerned, and apparently… well, apparently, he wrote me a lot of letters many years ago. Gramps and Grams hid them from me because they were scared they would hurt me."

His eyes widen. "No way. No wonder you're mad."

"I'm not mad anymore," I say gently. "I know they were trying to protect me. I was really shocked in the moment, though, and—"

"Surprises are hard for you because of Dad."

Tears prick my eyes. "Pretty much."

"Sorry, but here's another surprise."

My teenager—officially taller than me—wraps me in a hug. Not a two-second one, either. It lasts for a solid minute.

A minute I'll hold onto for a lifetime.

41

Celeste

I READ the last letter first. It's not thick—a single page dated six years ago, a week before Damien's seventh birthday.

> Dear Celeste,
>
> I almost took the painting down today—the one you made me. It's been hanging over my bed ever since. But I couldn't do it. Even if we never speak again, that painting makes me feel close to you.
>
> I don't know why I'm even writing this. By this point, I know you're not reading these letters.
>
> I'm actually kind of glad you aren't. For

the record, I'm not mad at your parents. They did the right thing. Nothing good would have come from you reading those first ones, that's for sure.

I'm sorry for everything, Peapod. I miss you. I'll always miss you. I wish I could have been worthy of you. My only remaining hope is that you're loved and happy.

Lucas

Feeling numb inside and out, I tuck the paper back into its envelope, then shuffle through to the first one. Another thin envelope. Adrenaline courses through me as I see the date. My dad was right, it was two and a half months before I married Jeremy.

My heart pounds a staccato rhythm in my ears as I rip it open and pull out the sheet.

Peapod,

You blocked my number, didn't you? We both know why. I don't blame you. But I'm still going to say what you don't want to hear. What you know is true.

Don't do it.

Don't marry him.

It's me.

It's always been me.

I know I don't deserve you, but I want you anyway. I'm a shit person for doing this. I love Jeremy, but I'm in love with you. It feels like I've been in love with you my whole life.

I know you love him, but you love me, too. I know it. I felt it. And it's different for us. We're meant to be. Can't you feel it?

Call me. I'll come get you. Live with me in Seattle while I finish school. Or fuck it—we can go anywhere you want. I have some money saved up.

Anywhere in the world, Peapod. Please.

Love,

Lucas

"Shit," I whisper, my vision blurring as tears well. One drops, hitting his name and smearing the ink.

Even though I'd had a suspicion of what I'd read, seeing the words in black and white brings a new dimension to the ache in my chest.

What would I have done if I'd read this back then?

What would I have done?

The answer comes easily but doesn't bring me any peace.

I would have stayed with Jeremy. Because I did love him, because he was sunshine and the idea of hurting him like that brings me physical pain even now.

But I can't admit that truth without admitting the other: Lucas was right. He's still right.

It's always been him.

Leaving the rest of the letters sealed, I slide off my bed and wipe the tears from my face. I can hear Damien's music in the room next door, but here, in my bubble of revelations and paradoxes, I'm insulated. There's a low buzz in my ears as I open my closet and reach for the tattered shoe box on the top shelf.

My fingers tingle as I grip it, pull it down, cradle it in my arms. I don't bother sitting down to go through it, just toss the lid to the floor and dig inside, past familiar memorabilia. I don't really see what's there, but I feel each item: photos, two wedding rings, the curled edges of an ultrasound printout, a wedding invitation…

At the very bottom is an envelope I've spent thirteen years pretending doesn't exist.

I told Damien I wasn't mad at my parents anymore for keeping Lucas's letters from me, that I knew they were trying to protect me. But this is the real reason why.

Staying angry would be the definition of hypocrisy.

Putting the shoebox on the ground, I walk the few feet

to my bed and sit, then stare at the letter on my knees. There's no address, just a name in Jeremy's familiar scrawl.

Lucas.

Before Jeremy left for deployment, he'd sat me down and given me three letters. *"Just in case,"* he'd said. One was for his parents, one was for me, and the last was this one. My first reaction had been horror, obviously. Followed by denial, then hysteria fueled by pregnancy hormones. In the end, he'd taken them back and tucked them in a kitchen drawer, where they'd stayed until my mom found them a year later.

Unlike my parents, I didn't withhold this vital piece of history from Lucas for the sake of protecting him. I withheld it because I was angry and resentful, and the young, widowed me didn't want him to have any closure at all.

I wanted him to hurt like I did.

Sighing, I trace my thumb over his name. Over the pen strokes made by Jeremy's hand. Over the past, and the pain, and the regret and emptiness of coming to terms with my choices.

Then I put the letter in my purse.

42

Lucas

"HEY."

Celeste's voice travels down the new dock to where I stand at the end. My heart kicks against my ribs at the sound of it.

I haven't seen her face to face since the mural painting last Saturday. Obviously, I can't avoid her forever, but I don't feel strong like Michelle said I would after some physical distance. I feel fucking bereft.

For a second, I consider diving into the lake and swimming to the other side.

"Lucas?" Her voice is right behind me and sends a shudder down my spine.

Bracing myself, I turn around. As I suspected, she's only grown more lovely since I saw her last. Since I've been avoiding this exact scenario. Since our "talk" where I threw out some bullshit about learning to let go.

I'll never let go.

She's wearing cutoff shorts and an oversized T-shirt. Her tanned legs momentarily blind me. Or maybe it's her hair, braided into messy pigtails that dangle over her chest. Her face, makeup-free and scrunched into a frown. Beat-up Converse on her feet. Just… everything about her blinds me. She's the epitome of perfect.

"I dig the pigtails." I clear my throat when my voice nearly cracks on the last word. "I can say that, right?"

Not touching her—not loving her—feels like a sin.

She smiles, big and familiar, and my breath catches. "Sure. Thanks." Her eyes travel the length of the dock as she stomps her feet against the thick, new boards. "This is amazing. These kids won't even know how lucky they are to avoid the splinters we had to deal with daily."

I force myself to chuckle. "Yeah."

"It was nice of you to give Billy and the crew the day off."

I nod, still contemplating a quick escape into the water.

She tucks a piece of flyaway hair behind her ear. "Are you, uh, coming to Damien's party tomorrow?"

I think of the emailed invite I received yesterday, the complex feelings it evoked, and can't help asking, "Do you really want me to?"

Her suddenly serious eyes lift to mine. "Yes, I do."

"Then I'll come. I hope Damien's okay with an envelope full of money."

She laughs. "I can guarantee he'll be thrilled."

I swallow. Clear my throat. Shift my feet like a nervous

teen. "Celeste—did you really drive up here to ask me about the party? You could have texted me."

Her shoulders sag. "No. I drove by your house, but your car wasn't there, so I came here. I need to give you something I should have given you thirteen years ago. I'm sorry. I hope you can forgive me one day. I want..." She trails off, shaking her head, and reaches into her purse.

An envelope extends my way. Frowning, I take it. When I see my name—and the handwriting—on the front, I'm so shocked I barely register her fingers grazing mine.

"What is this?" I ask, my voice barely there as I turn the envelope over. It's never been opened.

"I'll understand if you change your mind about coming tomorrow," she says in a rush. "It's from Jer, obviously. He... well, he wrote it before he deployed. I'm sorry. So incredibly sorry. Lucas, I—"

"Stop," I plead. "Just stop a second."

A cyclone of emotions whips through me, too many to name, most of them conflicting. I look into her eyes, glassy with tears, and I know one thing for certain: she doesn't deserve the regret she feels.

"It's okay, Peapod. I understand why you didn't give it to me."

She blinks and a tear rolls down her cheek. My hand itches to brush it away, to hold her, comfort her, but despite my words—which are true—my heart is an ice block in my chest. My fingers spasm, crunching the edge of the envelope.

"I'm sorry," she whispers again before turning and jogging down the dock.

I watch her disappear through the line of trees, then obey the directive of my weak knees and sit. My legs swing over the edge of the dock, my bare feet grazing the cool water.

I open the letter. It takes three tries for me to read past the first words.

Hey man,

If you're reading this, I'm either dead or we're old as hell and laughing about me being dramatic. I hope it's the second, but in case it's not, I need you to know some things.

First, thank you. Thank you for giving me the chance to love her. I know you broke her heart for me. I know about the kiss (she told me after we were married). If you hadn't left town, I honestly don't know if she would have stayed with me in the long run. So thanks for being a dickhead and bailing.

I can hear you in my head right now telling me what an idiot I am, that she loves me, blah blah. I know she does. I'm a lucky sonofabitch. But it doesn't change the fact she loved you first. I'm just grateful her heart was big enough for me, too.

Anyway, if you thought that was rough, buckle up.

You know what I want from you. What I'm going to ask. It fucking sucks to even write this, but I figure if the worst does happen, I don't want to gamble on you pulling your head out of your ass without help. So here's your help.

Love her, Lucas.

She's going to fight it, probably. (Selfishly, I hope she does.) But you'll wear her down. You'll find that piece of her heart that's still yours and give it some oxygen. Just leave a little room for me to stay, yeah?

She needs you. If I'm honest, she's always needed you. But right now, she's going to need everything you've got. Love her like I know you've always wanted to.

It's gonna be hard on both of you. Mainly because I'm awesome and you're both going to miss the hell out of me. But do it anyway.

Oh, and another thing. Don't raise my kid to be an asshole like you, okay?

Kidding, kidding.

Final order—Don't waste time with the whiney, guilty bullshit, either. Your dead best friend is giving you everything you ever wanted (just like you once gave him), and you're going to take it with a smile and a "Thank you, Jeremy, you absolute stud."

Got it?

All right, that's about all I can handle. I want to throw up just thinking about all this.

I love you, you prick.

Jer

I read it again.

Then again and again, until the words blur and the past and future melt.

And finally, I fall apart like I should have over thirteen years ago.

43

Celeste

I COULDN'T BRING myself to leave the camp, so I'm sitting on the steps outside the Lodge when Lucas's cry ricochets through the air. A desperate and gut-wrenching roar, chockful of anguish. And so loud that a flock of birds lifts from a nearby tree.

Jolting to my feet, I run back down the path just in time to hear a splash. It makes me run faster, my feet kicking up sand and fine rocks across the beach before pounding down the dock. I skid to a stop beside his discarded T-shirt and watch, the latter pinning down the opened letter. Curiosity flares, then dies.

I scan the water until I find him. Those smooth, strong strokes taking him not toward the buoy but toward the dark center of the lake.

"Lucas!" I holler.

He doesn't pause.

It takes zero thoughts and five seconds to toe off my

shoes and strip off my shirt and shorts. Another to dive into the cold embrace of Wild Lake.

I'm a decent swimmer, but it's been years since I went all-out, and I'm panting by the time I grab the buoy's fraying rope. I scan the lake, but everywhere I look, the surface is smooth.

Panic grabs me in its dark claws.

"Lucas!" I scream, over and over, until his name is choked by sobs.

The water ripples a few feet away and suddenly he's right in front of me, his face dripping water and set in lines of shock.

"Celeste, what the fuck!" He grips the rope, his other arm wrapping around my waist to support me.

Sobbing—now with abject relief—I grab his face. "Why'd you do that? You idiot. Where'd you go? You disappeared!"

His eyes widen, bloodshot and wet with tears and lake water. "You didn't leave?"

"Of course I didn't leave, you jackass. I love you. I love you so fucking much and you screamed and then jumped into the fucking lake. I thought I was in a horror movie or a bad teen drama—"

His mouth smashes against mine, swallowing the rest of my babbling. I throw my arms around his shoulders, almost submerging us before he pulls us tighter to the buoy.

Against my lips, he mumbles, "You love me?"

"Yes," I whisper, tasting his tears and mine as they

mingle between our mouths. "I've loved you since I was nine. I've been in love with you since I was fourteen. I know it makes no sense, but loving Jeremy didn't mean I stopped loving you. I'll always love you, Lucas. Please don't leave me. Don't ever leave me."

The words rip something open inside me, allowing a new facet of grief to surge forward. Turns out acceptance is loss, too, as the lies I've wrapped around myself to avoid pain are stripped away.

This grief is a slow wave, bright instead of the usual dark. As it filters through me, fills me up, it feels like being put together again after decades of being half-whole.

Maybe it will never make sense—that my heart loves two men—but I'm no longer able to deny the truth: I belonged with Jeremy then, and I belong with Lucas now.

He kisses the tears from beneath my eyes. "I won't leave you. I promise. I'll even let you die before me—many, many years from now."

I laugh, which mutates into sobs again. They're softer, though. Spring rain instead of a winter storm. "You're my Peapod, too," I tell him.

He laughs. I laugh, too. And then we cry and laugh and hold each other in the cold water until we hear the familiar rhythmic splashing of oars.

A canoe manned by two fishermen glides close. They give us wide-eyed stares. One of them asks, "You two all right?"

Lucas looks at me. "Yeah, thanks."

"Actually," I say, smiling brightly at the men, "my friend

here isn't a very strong swimmer. I came out to rescue him, but I'm not sure I can support his weight all the way in. Can we get a haul to shore?"

Lucas sighs.

The men smirk and throw us a rope.

WE SIT shoulder to shoulder on the end of the dock, the sun slowly drying our wet skin. The fishermen are long gone, and the air is still, the lake a mirror reflecting wispy clouds and distant mountains that sit like a hat atop the tree line.

Our fingers are linked tight, braced on the warm wood between our knees.

"Do you want to read the letter?" he asks.

I shake my head. "That's okay. I think I already know what it said. He wanted you to come back and take care of me, right?"

He nods, his eyes tearing. Mine are leaking too.

There have been times in the past when I was convinced I had no more tears left in my body, that the necessary function itself was broken from gross overuse. But if I've learned anything, it's that there will always be more tears. Always more joy, more sadness. More to feel.

More life.

"I wouldn't change anything," I tell him, surprised when I find the words honest.

"I wouldn't, either," he says, then he chuckles. "I think

he was wrong, anyway. You never would have accepted me back then. I even tried, remember?"

I do—though I've spent years forcing myself to forget the conversation we had leading up to our fight.

"I'll move home."

I lift my empty gaze from the dirt. "Why?"

"For you, Peapod."

"No," I whisper. "Go back to Seattle, Lucas. I'm fine. I have support."

"But—"

"No. Sun River isn't your home anymore."

A light drizzle mists the air around us, slowly progressing into a steady rainfall. I watch the freshly churned dirt grow darker.

Beneath the numbness, all I feel is rage. Everything is wrong.

Wrong. Wrong.

"I want to do the right thing," he murmurs. "Be there for you and… and the baby."

Somewhere inside my brain, I register his words. Their brokenness. Their pain. But nothing compares to the brokenness inside me.

"I don't want you here," I snap. "Go home."

Now, I tell him, "I read your letters. My dad finally gave them to me."

He's quiet for a beat, processing. Then he winces. "I kinda wish he'd burned them."

I squeeze his fingers, meeting his searching gaze. "I don't.

They made me realize something important—that even when we were apart, we were together. All those years you felt far away, you were still right next to me. If that makes sense."

He lifts our hands and kisses my knuckles. "It does. And it's true."

I shift a little closer to him and lower my head to his shoulder. "Do you believe everything happens for a reason?"

Lucas shrugs. "We can't ever know for sure. But I like to think that life tries to balance itself out."

"Like karma?"

"Maybe. All I know is that this is where I'm supposed to be. I'm not exactly proud of how long it took to get here, but I can't begrudge the journey. It wasn't our time back then."

"Mmm. It's our time now, huh?"

"Sure is. More specifically, it's time to christen Camp Wild Lake's new dock."

A laugh bursts out of me. Lifting my head, I shake it vehemently. "No way. Anyone could show up. The fishermen could come back. I'm not an exhibitionist, Adler."

His arm snakes around my side, warm palm flattening over my stomach. Awareness skates down my spine, lighting up my nerve endings, as blue eyes full of heat and tenderness roam my face.

God, I love him so damn much.

Lowering his mouth to mine, he whispers, "You have

thirty seconds to find a private spot, then, because when I find you, I'm taking you."

I waste five seconds sputtering, until the look in his eyes shifts from mischievous to downright carnal.

Then I jump to my feet and run.

Twenty-five seconds is not long at all.

Definitely not long enough for me to reach one of the cabins or the Art Barn. When I realize that, I change course and sprint north toward the old caretaker's house. I'm not going to make it, but at least the terrain is more heavily forested and therefore more private.

I don't even make it as far as I think I will, mainly because running while trying not to hysterically laugh is a challenge I'm not ready for. Plus: bare feet and pinecones.

He catches me—tackles me, really—when I'm about fifteen yards from the lake house. I don't fall, though. He spins me and lifts me up, slowing our momentum until my back comes to rest gently against a tree trunk.

I keep laughing until he kisses the ability away. Until the sensation of his arms around me, of his warm chest against mine, of him pressing hard and hot between my legs blots everything else out.

Except one thing.

"Lucas?"

He nips my earlobe. Kisses my neck. "Yes, my love?"

Warmth fizzes through me, bright and golden. No more darkness.

"Reverse your vasectomy."

He stills and lifts his head to show me wide eyes. "What?"

Despite the flutter of nervousness in my chest, I double down and go with my instinct. I know him better than anyone.

"We're having kids, so make an appointment. Not an 'army of misfits,' though. One. Maybe two."

He blinks. His lips do a funny little dance before shaping words. "Do I get to marry you first?"

I pretend to think about it. "I guess. If you want."

His hips thrust against mine, making me simultaneously melt and tense in anticipation.

"If I want?" he growls. "Yes, I want. But right now, I want this."

His fingers delve beneath my underwear, shifting them to the side. He curses at how wet I am; I moan piteously as he frees himself and uses my arousal as lubricant.

"Answer me first!" I yelp as he lines himself up.

"Kids, yes. Marry you, yes. All of it, yes."

He sinks inside me in a slow, smooth thrust. There's a single moment when we stare at each other, every emotion shared and reflected back, before all hell breaks loose.

Sex in a forest isn't pretty. It's definitely not graceful. A few times, it's actually painful. I end up with bark scratches on my back. Lucas cuts his foot on a rock.

All in all, we still give it an 8/10.

44

Lucas

ON MY WAY TO help Celeste set up for Damien's birthday party, I make a stop I've been avoiding since I came back to Sun River. The decision is pure impulse—I flip an illegal U-turn and get honked at—which is how I know the timing is right.

Nestled in the hills outside town, from the outside Sun River Cemetery looks more like a nature park than anything else. I pull into the visitor's lot and get out, heading down the main path. From conversations with my mom five years ago, I know where I'm headed.

Giant cedar and spruce shade the path. Sunlight dapples the surfaces of headstones, some flush with the grass, some upright. Many are decorated with flowers, flags, and other memorabilia. To my left and down a slight hill, a funeral is underway. The mournful sound of a violin carries to my ears on a soft breeze.

I take a breath, expanding past the tightness that wants

to choke me, and turn right at the next fork. The air feels progressively more hushed and heavy as I make my way toward a black marble headstone that bears my father's name with the inscription, BELOVED SON, HUSBAND, AND FATHER.

Sourness fills my throat.

There are no flowers at his grave, though the grass is well-tended and the area clean. The boy inside me wants to howl and kick the headstone over. Good thing the man inside me knows I'd probably break my foot.

I don't speak, having said everything I needed to him when I left Sun River the first time. Nothing has changed since then except one thing: I don't hate him anymore.

The realization makes my next breath deeper, fuller, as a weight I've carried around my whole life cracks free from its foundation and melts away.

He doesn't mean anything to me now. He can't hurt me. Hurt Michelle. Hurt my mother. Hurt *anyone*.

And I'm nothing like him.

"Fuck you, Dad," I tell him, "and rest in peace."

"Amen," says a woman behind me.

I jolt and spin around to find Angela Torres standing a few feet away, a bouquet of flowers in her hands. She smiles softly and tilts her head toward the path behind her.

"Care to join me?"

My voice nowhere to be found, I nod. As we walk farther into the cemetery, the trees get bigger and older. When the familiar grave comes into view, surrounded by other, older markers bearing the Torres name, Angela stops and faces me.

Her dark eyes smile up at me. "You're coming this afternoon, right?"

I nod. "I was actually on my way to help Celeste set everything up."

"Wonderful." She pauses, her eyes softening as they scan mine. "And how's our girl doing?"

"She's good," I say weakly, aware that my face and neck are in the process of heating to about a thousand degrees. "I mean, she's okay. I don't, uh..." I trail off, utterly mortified.

My God, I'm twelve again.

Angela chuckles. "I hope that means you two have admitted what the rest of us knew the second you landed back in Sun River."

I stare at her. "W-what's that?"

Transferring the flowers to one hand, she pats my arm with the other. "Jeremy was her first chapter, Lucas. They were darling together and loved each other very much. But that chapter ended, and her next is long overdue." Her eyes mist with tears. "What I mean to say is, I want you to know how happy we all were when you came back. There's no one else I'd rather see with her than you. So—are we there yet?"

I think of yesterday and all the tomorrows Celeste and I promised each other and choke back tears.

"Yes, Mrs. T. I think we are."

Angela sniffs and gives me a wobbly smile. "That's very

good news." Then she laughs, a bright sound that reminds me of summer dinners and running around her backyard with popsicles. "Especially since you just won me two hundred bucks!"

My eyes widen. "I did?"

Her smile turns into an embarrassed grimace. "There might be a pool going as to whether or not you two make it official."

I groan. "Seriously?"

She shrugs. "It's Sun River," she says, like that explains it.

Honestly, it does.

"For the record, Lucas, I know Jeremy—wherever my boy is now—is happy for you both."

The words hit me like a mallet to the heart. My chest convulses and I bend over, hands on my knees. A rough sob escapes me, then another, while Angela's small hand rubs circles on my back.

"I know," she whispers. "It's okay. He loves you, Lucas. He loves you both."

Minutes pass before I can pull myself together, before Angela and I resume our walk to Jeremy's grave.

There, we change out the wilting flowers for fresh ones, and we stand side by side in silence, in remembrance, as a breeze—no longer heavy, no longer hushed—dries our tears.

EPILOGUE

Celeste

I TAKE my tea onto the porch of the lake house and settle on a chaise to wait for Lucas. The afternoon air is warm and still, the lake glassy except for the wake left by his strokes.

He's on his way back to me.

My favorite part of this ritual begins less than a minute later: watching my husband climb the ladder at the end of our dock, his beautiful, lithe body delivered in increments to my greedy eyes.

He pretends he doesn't notice me, but I know he does because he takes an extra moment to sluice the water off his broad chest.

"Tease!" I call out.

His laughing eyes meet mine and he strides toward me. I suspect what's coming, but I don't move as he clears the steps to the porch in a leap and bends over my chair to shake his head like a dog.

"That's rude," I comment as I take a sip of tea. The water actually feels nice on my flushed skin.

His smile grows sharp right before my mug is snatched from my fingers. Grabbing my hands, he pulls me to my feet. "Nice try, Peapod. I know what it means when you wait for me to come in from a swim."

I arch an eyebrow. "Oh, you do?"

He nods solemnly, though his eyes dance. "It means you want to shower with me."

I sniff. "I already showered today, and we have to be at the Lodge for this year's first welcome in"—I glance at my watch—"an hour. I thought we could rehearse."

He chuckles. "Rehearse a speech we've been giving for eleven years?"

I somehow manage not to smile. "It's the first time the twins are here for overnight camp, and I'm nervous. Did they settle in okay this morning? Do they like their counselors? Are they making friends? What if I'm distracted looking for them and mess up my lines?"

"Celeste," he says softly, eyes full of compassion. "Jack and Ava basically grew up at Wild Lake. They've been waiting for this day since they could talk. And Daphne and Damien are both there, remember?"

I nod as I move casually toward the door. "I'm really grateful they came back this summer to work for us. I feel better knowing they'll keep an eye on the twins."

"Me, too. Especially since they're menaces like their mother."

"Pfft." I pause and glance back, glad to see he's still standing by the chaise. Poor, clueless man. "Okay."

His lips quirk. "Okay, what?"

I open the door and edge inside. "First one in the shower gets to say the line!"

Surprise widens his eyes—even after all these years.

By the time he gets his wits back, I'm at the base of the stairs and running full tilt. I take them two at a time, squealing when I hear his heavier tread on the wood below me.

"I can't believe I fell for that shit!"

I laugh manically and book it down the short hallway and into our bedroom. Three more strides and my hand touches the frame of the bathroom door.

That's as far as I get.

An arm around my waist hauls me into the air. The breath leaves my lungs with an undignified, "Oomph," as my back hits our bed. Lucas crouches over me on all fours, looking annoyingly triumphant. Above our heads is the painting I made all those years ago.

"I won," I pant. "I totally won. I touched the door."

I'm still in competition mode, braced to octopus myself around him if he tries for the bathroom, so I'm unprepared when his lips seize mine in a searing kiss.

"Fine," he says, punctuating the word with a gentle bite to my bottom lip. "You win."

I jerk my head back as far as the mattress will allow and grin. "Really?"

He laughs. "Yes, really. I'm the real winner, anyway."

Before I can ask what he means, his body lowers onto mine and I forget all about winning. He was right, after all: this is what I really wanted when I watched him come back from his swim.

The skin of his waist is taut and warm under my fingers. He makes a little, satisfied grunt when I tug his swim trunks over his hips and grab his bare ass. Thanks to his daily swims—lake in spring and summer, private pools in winter—he's just as fit as he was at thirty-four. The touch of gray at his temples, the smile lines around his eyes… they're just the icing on the cake. I'm even more attracted to him now than I was when I was young.

Squirming commences as he helps me remove my shorts and T-shirt. I didn't bother with underwear or a bra.

"Hallelujah," he whispers, eyes alight as they take me in.

Even though time and two more kids have left their marks on my body, Lucas never seems to notice.

He still loves my breasts most of all.

I smack his head when he bites around my nipple hard enough to leave a mark. "Easy, tiger."

"Just claiming my territory," he says, smirking as he shifts forward, as my legs lift naturally around his hips.

He sinks inside me slowly, watching me accept him with an avidness that time hasn't dented. Quite the opposite, in fact. Our obsession with each other has only grown as years have passed, as we've weathered every storm. Withstood heartaches and embraced joys.

Marrying him on the Wild Lake dock in front of our

family and friends. Buying our first house together. Pregnancy and the birth of the twins (and his second vasectomy shortly thereafter). The hectic newborn months. The horrendous toddler era. Picture days and sick days. Tantrums and cuddles and a thousand small, perfect moments.

Damien's high school years. His first girlfriend, first breakup. Varsity soccer and two fender benders. Watching him grow into a funny, confident man. His long-distance friendship with Daphne blossoming into love when they attended the same college. Birthdays and anniversaries and holidays. Monthly potlucks with the Torres family.

The loss of Lucas's mother when, after almost three years sober, she started drinking again and eventually died of complications due to alcoholism. The near-loss of my dad after a massive heart attack two years ago. He's doing well now. My parents still live in the house I grew up in. A new family lives next door.

So much life, all on top of running Camp Wild Lake, which has brought both incredible stress and unimaginable contentment. We are officially one of the most well-known and coveted summer programs in the Western United States.

All of it, everything, we've done together.

I gasp as he begins to rock against me, creating perfect friction inside and out.

"I love you, Lucas," I whisper into his mouth.

He shudders, his forehead dropping to mine. "Never gets old. I love you, too. Always and forever."

He shows me the truth of his words in how well he knows what I need, the exact rhythm and motion that makes me fall apart, the deep, consuming kisses that melt my heart. I clutch him tightly, riding out the waves of bliss as he groans and finds his own release.

We lie in a sweaty heap until our heart rates return to normal. Then he leaps from the bed. Laughing like an evil villain, he sprints into the bathroom and cranks on the shower.

"I'm the winner!"

Instantly irate, I scramble off the bed and stalk into the bathroom. "No way! You conceded!"

He grins at me from beneath a shower spray that can't possibly be hot yet. "You said 'first one *in* the shower wins.' Therefore, I've won. Plus, I had my fingers crossed earlier."

"You…" I sputter, then sigh. "Dammit."

"How about we both say it?" He holds out his pinkie finger, eyebrows raised expectantly.

I bite my lip, then give in to the urge to smile. Linking my pinkie with his, I step into the shower.

"Deal."

AN HOUR LATER, standing on the stage in the Lodge in front of a hundred and twenty kids, counselors, and staff, Lucas and I step forward and say the words that mean more to us than anyone here knows.

"Welcome to Camp Wild Lake!"

L.M. HALLORAN

. . .

THE END

★ Stay Connected ★

- Want to be notified of special offers and new releases from L.M. Halloran… and read a FREE novella? Sign up for the newsletter by visiting www.lmhalloran.com

- Curious about the inspirations for characters and settings from *Time for Us?* Here are my Pinterest Character Board and Spotify Playlist.

www.lmhalloran.com
lmhalloranauthor@gmail.com

I hope you enjoyed Celeste and Lucas's second chance love story! If you have a minute, please consider leaving a brief review.

xo,

L

AUTHOR'S NOTE + ACKNOWLEDGMENTS

There are pieces of me in every book I write, but I can honestly say I never fully understood the adage "Turn pain into art" until I wrote **Time for Us.**

While I lost my own husband in a vastly different way than Celeste did, and while my own journey back to love couldn't be more different, the core of our journey is the same.

Four years, twelve years, twenty-five years… it doesn't matter. Grief never wavers, never lessens. We just grow bigger around it—*life* gets bigger around it—as we keep moving forward one hard step at a time.

> *"Every moment in which we experience the fullness, the brightness, of deep love, we simultaneously experience the future loss of it."* (Chapter 35)

These are the truest words I've ever written in any book. I don't know if you can relate (honestly, I hope you can't), but if you can, I see you. I hear you.

I'm giving you the biggest hug.

We can do this.

We *are* doing this.

I'd like to give a shout out to the incredible ladies who read this book first, most of whom have been with me (as beta readers or ARC team members) for years: Dawn, MJ, Rebecca, Rachel, Amanda, Jennifer, and Jaime. Each one of you made your mark on this book. Thank you.

Special thanks to you, the reader. Whether you're brand new to me or have been around since 2016, I can't tell you how stunned and grateful I am to know you're here.

Since I was ten years old, I dreamed of writing books. I never really thought anyone would read them.

You made my dream come true.

More thanks go to the usual suspects. The moon in my sky, my daughter, Stella Grace. And to Lacee, Lauren, Jessica, Molly, and my mom.

And finally, thank you to Dave. My surprise twist. My lighthouse in the dark. Not my "chapter two" as widow's call it, but the hero in a whole new book.

Until the next one.

xo,
Laura

ALSO BY L.M. HALLORAN

FORBIDDEN ROMANCE

The Dark Before Light

The Fall Before Flight

The Muse

ROCKSTAR ROMANCE

Breaking Giants

Breaking Silence

SMALL TOWN

Room for Us

Time for Us

DARK ROMANTIC SUSPENSE

Double Vision

Perfect Vision

The Golden Hour

Art of Sin *(Illusions Duet #1)*

Sin of Love *(Illusions Duet #2)*

BILLIONAIRE ROMANCE

The Reluctant Socialite

The Reluctant Heiress

• • •

URBAN FANTASY / PNR
AS LAURA HALL

THE WHITE ORDER

Wellspring

Scroll of Secrets

THE ASCENSION SERIES

Ascension

Reckoning

Unraveling

Rebirth

Tribulation

Revelation

ABOUT THE AUTHOR

When not writing or reading, the author can be found chasing her daughter. Some of her favorite things are puzzles, podcasts, and small dogs that resemble Ewoks.

Home is the Pacific Northwest.

lmhalloran.com

facebook.com/lmhalloran
instagram.com/lm.halloran
bookbub.com/authors/l-m-halloran
goodreads.com/lmhalloran
amazon.com/author/lmhalloran
pinterest.com/lmhalloranauthor

Made in the USA
Monee, IL
21 February 2025